AMERICAN YAKUZA II
The Lies that Bind

AMERICAN YAKUZA II
The Lies that Bind

ISABELLA

SAPPHIRE BOOKS

SALINAS, CALIFORNIA

American Yakuza II - The Lies that Bind
Copyright © 2013 by **Isabella** All rights reserved.

ISBN -978-1-939062-20-8

Cover Design by Christine Svendsen
Editor - Lisa Boeving

Sapphire Books
Salinas, CA 93912
www.sapphirebooks.com

Printed in the United States of America
First edition – June 2013

Dedication

To the inspiration behind American Yakuza - Schileen.
My heart, my love, my dreams are yours until I take my
last breath!

To my sons.
Forever in my heart.

Acknowledgements

To the readers!
You've been generous with your time, your comments, and your love, thank you for being here every step of the way.

To my editor and my friend, Lisa Boeving. Thanks is never enough, buddy!

To the authors who've decided to join me on this writing journey - Linda Kay, Kim, Lynette, Beth and Linda - you ladies are awesome.

Peggy - thank you for joining the team.

Sandy and Lee Ann - thanks for being such great friends.

Chapter One

Luce slowly lowered the lid of the casket. Her haggard appearance reflected in the highly polished black lacquer as it finally rested closed. Tears threatened and she squeezed her eyes shut. She couldn't let them fall, not in front of her *family*. She wanted to be the last person to see the Oyabun. It was selfish of her but she didn't care, he was her only family and now she would bury him today. Luce gasped, finally releasing the breath she had been holding. Her heart seized and she clutched her chest, imagining her grandfather on the other side of the lid. So close and yet gone to her forever.

His last moments would forever be etched in her soul. As she bowed and kissed the casket, she remembered his last words to her.

"Come, sit next to me while I share my last moments on this earth with my favorite granddaughter," *he said, weakly patting the bed.*

Wiping at the tears streaming down her face, Luce replied as she always did when he said that. "I'm you're only granddaughter, Grandfather."

"Awe, but you're still my favorite." He brushed her tears away with a thumb. "Why are you crying Kaida? This day was preordained."

"I'm just being selfish. I don't want you to leave me. I have so much to learn still. Please Grandfather, please," she whispered, rubbing the back of his hand

against her wet face. "I'm sorry."

"Kaida, don't be sorry. I'm the one being selfish. Your grandmother has been waiting for me for two decades and I miss her." He pulled her hand to his frail lips and kissed the gold dragon pinkie ring he had given her last Christmas. "No one is promised tomorrow. It is a gift, and as such, we must cherish what we have been given. I have received many gifts for which I am thankful, and the most precious is you."

Pursing her lips, she tried to stop them from quivering, but could only shake her head. The lump in her throat stopped her from answering.

"Kaida, let me give you a few last words of wisdom from an old man." Tamiko licked his dry, cracked lips and swallowed hard. He labored to breath as he continued, "Kaida, as a tree struggles to find purchase in a granite rock it grows without assistance. It finds life where none should exist in the cracks of the hard rock, determined to grow, even when it should be impossible. Brooke is the tree to your rock. She gives you shade, grows with you when others would perish, and finds nourishment in your soul."

"She's a wonderful woman, grandfather."

"Then marry her. You are in a place now that will cause those around you to test you. You will find out when I die who is an ally and who is an enemy. Just as Frank betrayed us, others will, too. They will tell lies and make you doubt the truth when you are faced with it." Gently, he patted her hand in reassurance. "Brooke is your strongest supporter. Don't let her go, Kaida. She's wonderful for you. Good for your soul. I can see she softens your rough edges."

Luce smiled at the inference. She had definitely seen the world through different eyes since being with

Brooke. *Her life felt complete and settled, not off kilter and skittering out of control as it had in the past.*

"Promise me."

Nodding she whispered, "I promise."

"Good. Now, one last thing, Frank—"

"He's a dead man when I find him," she growled. "I promise you that, too, Grandfather. He won't live out the year."

"He's not just an enemy, he's one of the worst kinds. He betrayed his own family and there's no place for a man like that today. Remember, your word is your bond. It is the only thing, other than your name, that you can give freely. Do not take it lightly when you give it."

"I remember, Grandfather. I haven't forgotten our tea lessons." Luce's favorite time with her grandfather had also been those times when he would gently remind her of her duty in the world. "Take little and give much. Better to make ten friends than one enemy who could make one hundred enemies for you," he would say.

"I understand, Grandfather."

"Good. I'm tired, Kaida. I think I'd like to sleep now. Go and kiss Brooke for me." He swished his hand about, as if is he was shooing her away. "I love you, my little Kaida." He closed his eyes and let out a long deep sigh.

"I know, Grandfather," Luce said, clutching his hand as if it would keep him with her longer. "I love you, too."

A blaring alarm broke the silence Luce had created in her mind when she spoke with her grandfather. A nurse ran in to assess the situation. She turned the heart machine off, patted Luce's slumped shoulders and whispered, "Take as long as you need, Ms. Potter."

Luce could only shake her head. Tears dripped from her chin as she stared at her grandfather, committing his face to memory for the last time.

Chapter Two

*B*rooke watched from outside the hospital room *as the love of her life wept so hard it broke her heart. She and Luce had been on a long awaited vacation when the phone call came late on their first night in Hawaii. Forty-five minutes later, they were on a flight to Mercy Hospital. Luce hadn't left her grandfather's side since.*

Brooke walked in and ran her palm across Luce's broad shoulders, Brooke bent down and whispered, "Luce, Honey. What can I do to help?"

Luce sat with her arms crossed and rocked back and forth. Brooke pulled the shivering Luce against her, and started threading her fingers though the unruly, thick black locks. Suddenly, Luce grabbed Brooke around the waist and buried her head against Brooke, weeping like a child. Moments like this were few and far between for them, so Brooke hugged her tightly, murmuring words of sympathy.

"Marry me."

"What?"

Brooke's chest tightened as she searched Luce's puffy, wet eyes. "That's not how I envisioned my first marriage proposal."

"You've never been asked before?"

"No and I don't think yours constitutes one right now either, honey."

"I don't want to lose you, too." Brooke sensed Luce

was panicking.

"I'm not going anywhere, sweetheart. It's time to grieve and when it's our time we'll know it."

Luce looked down at her grandfather and stroked his hand lovingly. "I promised my grandfather that I would marry you, so—"

"When you've had time to grieve and time to think rationally, ask me then."

Luce nodded and buried her head against Brooke, clinging to her, and clutching her grandfather's hand. Sobs wracked Luce, but Brooke could hold her lover tighter, wishing she could take this burden from her.

Squatting down, she held Luce's face and kissed her gently, reassuringly. "We'll make it through this, Luce. I promise."

❧❧❧❧

Luce stood anchored against the side of the casket. She wasn't sure she could leave her grandfather, but she knew she needed to be strong for those sitting behind her.

"Luce, honey, are you all right?" Brooke touched her back softly, rubbing small circles.

Luce nodded back at Brooke and tried to give her a calming smile. It barely broke, but it was there. "I'm okay."

Luce faced the crowded temple. She looked out over the somber faces that filled the room to capacity, searching for one she knew best, Auntie. Auntie sat stoically in the front row dabbing at her eyes. She had seen as much death as Luce and was always the one sitting next to her at times like this. Auntie was the last one of her *family*. She was surprised to learn that her grandfather had owned the Korean restaurant she enjoyed weekly, and in his will he had left it to Auntie. Smiling at her Aunt, Luce nodded and winked, then addressed the crowded room. "Thank you everyone for coming. My grandfather would have been humbled by all the kind words and memories each of you have shared with us." Her voice cracked as she held back tears that threatened to fall. Her swollen eyes welled up with endless tears. "We've planned a dinner at his favorite restaurant and hope you'll join us there to celebrate his life and share more of your stories. Thank you for coming."

With that, the ceremony was over. Luce waited, shaking the hand or accepting hugs of condolences from everyone who streamed past the casket. She heard Brooke as each member of the *family* filed past and treated her with the honor reserved for a wife— Luce's wife.

"Sammy, can you bring the car around?" Brooke whispered as he approached.

"Of course, Ms. Erickson," he offered with a low bow. "Oyabun, my deepest sympathies. He was like a father to me. I'm—so—sorry."

Luce clasped his hand between hers and pulled him close. "Be strong, brother. He was proud of you. So am I."

Sammy bowed and without another word excused himself. The line before Luce stretched out and around the temple. It would take time to greet everyone, but her duty was such that she would be honored to hear the small stories of how the Oyabun had helped someone, friended them, or simply made them feel more secure in the neighborhood. Clearly, her grandfather was loved, and she now had to share his final moments above ground with those who cared about him, too.

"Are you okay, my love?" Brooke whispered. She rubbed Luce's back again, but smiled at a stoic face.

"I'll be okay."

"I'll send them away and we can leave if you're too tired to do this."

"They loved him as much as I did. No, I'll stay and honor his memory."

The line moved slowly, but finally they had shaken the last hand. The temple was empty save for the long, black lacquered casket, Luce and Brooke. Luce melted into the front pew and buried her hands in her face to shield herself. She wanted to let her tears fall and knew she couldn't stop once they started, even if she tried. The memories of her mother's funeral came flooding back as she thought about all the tough things in her life her grandfather had seen her through. This time she would have to do it alone. In fact, this was the new normal for the rest of her life.

Brooke's warm embrace pulled Luce closer and she rested her head on Luce's. She wasn't alone. Not really, she had Brooke.

One night after a fight with Brooke, she had sought her grandfather's counsel. *"Don't let pride be another person in your relationship, Kaida. It will add nothing and only cause you misery. "Let yourself lean on Brooke. She is strong. Be weak with her, she'll understand."*

Luce wrapped her arms around Brooke's waist and nuzzled her wet nose into Brooke's neck.

"Kaida, will you be okay?" an old, knowing voice caressed her ear.

She looked up and gave her Aunt a weak smile.

"I'll be fine, Auntie. Will you join us at the mausoleum?"

"No, I've seen the inside of that thing one to many times. Besides, this is a family moment. The old man and I fought like a couple of junk yard dogs." Auntie patted Luce's back. "I'll see you at the restaurant."

"No matter what you say, I know you two cared for each other. He left you the restaurant. That isn't the action of an enemy, Auntie."

"No." Auntie dabbed at the corner of her wrinkled eyes. "He could be one of the most generous men, Kaida. Never forget that, no matter what?"

Luce frowned at the cryptic remark, but let it pass. She loved her grandfather beyond measure and knew how generous he could be. *Hell,* she was the biggest benefactor of his mentoring and time.

"I'll remember that, Auntie. Thank you for coming. I'll see you at the restaurant, then."

Kissing her Aunt on each cheek, she accepted the warm embrace in return and sighed. She hoped she wouldn't be attending her funeral anytime soon. She shook her head, shamed at letting that thought have wings.

"Ready to go?"

"I want to wait and walk him to the hearse."

"Okay."

"I love you," Luce whispered then sucked in a breath.

"Here, sweetheart." Brooke offered another tissue.

"Thanks. What would I do without you?"

"You would manage, I'm sure of it."

"I wouldn't. You've turned my world upside down and I wouldn't know how to right it without you."

"We're ready, Ms. Potter." A stately looking man

said. Luce was sure his sincere expression had been practiced many times.

Brooke grasped her arm to help her up, but the gesture only made her feel more helpless. Luce shook off the assistance and stood ramrod straight. She'd had her moment of grief, now it was time to accept her responsibilities and make her grandfather proud. Yet, with her emotions so raw, she knew just a wrongly spoken word would be her undoing.

"Let's take your grandfather home, honey."

"He loved you so much." Luce patted Brooke's hand firmly clasped in hers. "You were one of the last things we spoke of before he died."

"He was a wonderful man, Luce. You were lucky to have him and he was lucky to have you. I think the admiration was mutual."

Luce followed the casket to the hearse, watching as her grandfather was loaded into the cavernous mouth for the journey to his final resting place. The Yoshida family crypt was the destination for all Yoshidas, including herself. Some day she would lie next to her mother and hopefully, when that day came, she would face it with the same dignity as her grandfather had.

The slamming door almost made Luce's knees buckle as she searched through the window for one last glimpse.

"Shall we, Ms. Potter?" The same man pointed to the limo behind the hearse.

"Thank you, but I have my own car and driver."

Sammy stood waiting to open the door to Luce's car, where six men and women from Luce's inner circle waited.

"They'll escort my grandfather into the crypt."

"As you wish, Ms. Potter."

Luce motioned for Sammy and the others followed, each face sullen. A few wiped tears from their eyes as they climbed into the limo.

"We're so sorry, Oyabun," Lynn said, bowing.

"Thanks. I'll see you at the cemetery. Ready, Sammy?"

Sammy had been by her side since Frank had dishonored her family by switching sides to become a player in the Russian mafia. He was the reason Sammy had lost his pinkie, and Luce carried that guilt as a constant reminder every time she looked at Sammy. He had proven indispensable when he helped locate her father. Sammy watched as she killed JP Potter, wanting to do the deed himself, but understanding Luce's need to exact revenge for her mother's death and her father's betrayal.

"Yes, ma'am."

Luce gently tugged on Brooke's hand and waited for her to climb in before speaking to Joey. "Any news on Frank's whereabouts?"

"Not yet, Oyabun."

Luce patted Sammy's shoulder and looked away. "How's the finger?"

"All healed."

"Good. Let's get going. I'm ready for this day to be over."

"Yes, Oyabun."

Luce slid next to Brooke and intertwined their fingers. Brooke scrubbed her cold hand and then blew warm breath on it. Luce's heart felt as cold as her hands. She wished something could reach in and warm her soul.

"Where are your gloves, my love?"

"I don't know. Probably sitting on my dresser at

home." Luce gave a thin smile as Brooke continued to work on her cold hands.

"Sammy, can you turn on the heat for the Oyabun?"

Luce jerked her head in Brooke's direction and stared at her. She had never used that term before and Luce wasn't sure how she felt about it. The title was honorific for the men and women who worked for her, but for her most intimate lover to call her Oyabun seemed strange.

"Why did you call me that?"

"What?"

"Oyabun, why did you call me that?"

"I'm sorry, I didn't mean to offend you. I just thought—"

Luce pressed her finger against Brooke's lips to stop her. "It's fine, but we share something much more intimate. Oyabun is reserved for those who work for me, not for you. You're special and I don't want to blur those lines, ever."

"I'm sorry."

Luce's nerves were raw, exposed, and ready to snap any moment. It took every ounce of control to restrain her anger. *But why am I angry?* she wondered. She wasn't angry at Brooke; she had been nothing but supportive. The Russians were at bay, so they weren't a factor. She would find Frank and exact the debt that he owed her family, although it was just her, now. Her grandfather had left her an orphan. He had chosen to release his grasp on life and leave her here alone. She'd been left behind to sort out the rest of her life by herself.

Luce gasped and then swallowed hard. She was angry with her grandfather for dying.

Chapter Three

A re you all right?" Brooke's voice echoed the worry she felt in her heart. She had never seen Luce so despondent, so dark, so not in control of her emotions. It broke her heart to see how deep Luce had fallen into the depths of despair. Yet, all she could do was offer a kind word, a shoulder to cry on, and a warm heart to extend to her lover.

"I'm fine. I just realized why I'm angry."

"You're angry? Why?"

"Because my grandfather left me." Luce turned and watched the gray clouds roll by, mirroring her own mood. "I know I'm being completely selfish, but I still feel like I need him."

"Luce, the cancer was more advanced than the doctors even knew."

"I know. But he..." She held her breath and focused on the emerald eyes of the dragon pinkie ring she twisted around her finger. She hated herself for what she was about to give voice to. "He didn't even fight it. He surrendered and gave up. That's not the man I knew."

"Oh, Luce. Don't judge him too harshly. He lived without the love of his life for almost twenty years. He's watched as his family died, his friends betrayed him, and his granddaughter made a successful entry into the family business." Brooke turned Luce's face towards hers. "He believed in you and knew you could handle anything, otherwise he would still be here with us."

New tears etched their way down Luce's face as Brooke continued, "Your grandfather placed everything in your hands for a reason. He told you on more than one occasion that he trusted no one but you."

"You're my voice of reason. You make me see things in ways I might not have otherwise."

"You would have eventually seen it, my love. Right now, your heart is wounded and can only react. In time it will see reason again, but for now it's time to grieve."

The trip to the cemetery was short, leaving little time to discuss the future. They pulled in front of the marble mausoleum. The Yoshida name splashed across the top in big, bold letters. She pulled out her gloves and handed them to Luce. "Here, it's freezing outside and I don't want you catching a cold."

"I'm fine."

"Luce."

"Thank you. It is chilly out," Luce conceded. She pinched Brooke's cheeks, and kissed her. "What would I do without you?"

"You'd—"

"I know, I know, *manage.*"

Brooke took Sammy's hand and slipped out of the limo, waiting for Luce to join her. The cold seeped through her heavy coat and assaulted her bare legs. She should have opted for slacks, but she had come straight from her office to meet Luce at the temple. She was glad she could be there with Luce when her grandfather died. No one should be alone when they pass, or be alone to witness a loved one take that leap to the other side.

Brooke grabbed Luce's hand to pull her close. She landed a quick kiss on Luce's cheek just as the pallbearers unloaded Tamiko's casket. They moved quietly in slow precision to the massive mausoleum. Inside, golden light reflected off the white and grey marble, giving Brooke an artificial sense of warmth. Brooke gazed down the small hallway where an altar had been prepared with a beautifully framed picture of Tamiko, his wife, and Luce's mother. A prayer bench sat in front of it, waiting, as if calling to Brooke to pay her respects. She'd knelt on enough prayer benches in the Catholic Church to recognize the scent of burning incense and candles. It had been years since her last appearance at church, but not so long that she'd forgotten the symbolism, the smells, and the traditions attending mass had ingrained in her.

Brooke grabbed Luce's upper arm and tightened the grip on her hand. She leaned closer, hoping Luce would absorb some of her strength. The casket slid into the wall. Luce sucked in a breath and held it. The pallbearers retreated out to the limo, leaving Luce and Brooke alone as the marble front was set in place. The room was eerily quiet. They stood there staring at the marble slab inscribed with Tamiko's name, his birth and his death dates neatly chiseled, black on the gray marble.

"Luce?"

"Hmm?"

"It's cold, honey. We should go," Brooke whispered. "When you're ready of course."

Luce pulled Brooke into a tight embrace. She leaned down and laid her forehead on Brooke's shoulder. Her soft sobs echoed off the cold walls of the room.

Brooked rocked her, squeezing Luce tightly. "It'll be all right, sweetheart. Trust me, we can make it through this. I promise."

"I know. I just want to get it all out before leaving this room. Once I'm out that door, I won't cry again," she said, swallowing hard.

If it had been anyone else, Brooke would doubt her resolve, but Luce was another story. She hadn't shed a tear after killing her father—if that is what you could call JP Potter. She had strength beyond measure, so if she said it, it would happen. Brooke, on the other hand, knew she would cry like a baby for weeks if anything happened to her parents or grandmother. That was just the way she was built. Brooke had cried for weeks when her photographer, Mike, had been killed on a mission in Europe. They had worked together for almost three years. Losing him the way she did was the whole reason she'd gotten out of investigative journalism. She and Luce were two different women who viewed life and death from diverse spectrums.

"I'm ready."

"Are you sure?"

"Yeah, I'm sure. I love you."

"I love you, too."

"We have guests at the restaurant. Let's go listen to stories about my grandfather."

≈≈≈≈

Through the long lens of the camera, she could almost make out the couple holding each other in the mausoleum. The glare off the door made it impossible to get a clear photo. Sliding back out of the car window, she started snapping when they walked out holding hands.

"Awe fuck, tell me that isn't Brooke Erickson."

"Why, do you know her?"

"You could say that. *Shit.*"

"Didn't you notice her at the funeral?" The man sitting next to her in the front seat asked.

"Nope, couldn't get a clear shot of her, just the back of her head. Shit!"

"I heard someone saying that they were going to some Japanese restaurant for the wake."

"Good, we can get shots of all the Yakuza members there. There'll be Yakuza from all over the US showing up to pay their respects to the new Oyabun." She adjusted the lens and snapped off a few more shots before laying the high-powered camera in her lap. "Brookie, Brookie, Brookie, since when did you get mixed up with a crime family like the Yoshidas?"

She pulled a pad from her blazer and scribbled something down. She handed it to the man with instructions. "Have someone pull the file on this name and tell them to get me everything they have on her."

"You got it."

"Damn, this is gonna get messy."

❧❧❧❧

The reflection of the camera lens caught Luce's attention. Rolling her gaze towards the blue sedan, she could make out two occupants, but that was all. She'd expected undercover police to hover outside her grandfather's funeral. It irritated her that they would follow her to the cemetery. If she could, she would have closed it down to only her party, but the attendant informed her that was impossible. *Plan for every possibility and you won't be surprised*, her grandfather had once said.

"Sammy." She motioned for him to come close and continued in a whisper, "The blue sedan over there, have Lynn and the others drive past it and get a visual on the two people inside. Also, find out anything you can on the plates."

Sammy bowed deeply. He gave a nod and went to pass on her instruction.

"Everything okay?" Brooke asked.

"Everything's fine. I just remembered that I needed Lynn to do something for me before they go to the wake." Luce rubbed Brooke's hand reassuringly again and steered her to the waiting limo. "Let's get out of here, it's cold." Luce hesitated and stared at the blue sedan for a moment, willing the driver to pop his head out of the window. She just wanted to catch a glimpse.

"Sammy?"

Sammy nodded his head and ran to shut her door. "All done, Oyabun."

"Good, let's get to the restaurant and get this day over."

"Yes, Oyabun."

Chapter Four

I have that information you requested, Agent Water." Agent Scarr held up a folder and waived it in front of Colby Water's face trying to get her attention. Scarr had been a pain in her ass since she'd been promoted over him. He hadn't taken it well and pushed her buttons every chance he got. *Spiteful, prick.*

"Great, just toss it on the desk," Colby said, teeth clenched around a number two pencil.

She had left the funeral procession this morning and raced back to her office, hoping to locate more information on Brooke Erickson. Seeing Brooke on the arm of one of the most notorious Yakuza leaders still left her shell-shocked. Colby didn't want to be accidently spotted at the restaurant where the wake was being held, so she stationed a few agents to watch the comings and goings. She hoped a few dignitaries of the underworld would show up, but she doubted it. Luce Potter tried to keep her life as low-key as possible. Attending the funeral was enough to show their respect.

"What'd that keyboard do to you?"

"What?"

"What's got you so fired up, Colby?"

Pulling the pencil from her mouth, she flexed her jaw, then tossed the pencil on the desk and turned towards the man. "Agent Scarr, is there something I can do for you?" Now he had her full attention.

"Nope, just wonder if they're going to issue you a new keyboard when you pound your fingers through it." He spun on his heels and chuckled all the way down the hall.

"Very funny, Scarr. Very funny," she said, picking up the file and thumbing through it. "Fucking prick," she muttered to herself.

Laying the open file on her desk, she slowly turned each page at the corner as if it had a contagious disease. The slim findings gave her little information on Brooke Erickson. She had uncovered more when she'd Googled Brooke's name. The shooting in Europe, the exposé she did on Luce Potter, and a few articles Brooke had written in the past few years.

From what she'd pieced together, Brooke had been with a top-notch magazine before giving it all up and taking a position with the *Financial Times*. While the *Financial Times* was a respected magazine in the financial sector, it wasn't on par with her former career. Clearly, Brooke had changed.

To say Colby was shocked to see Brooke holding hands with the head of one of the up and coming Yakuza organizations was an understatement. It was true that it hadn't gone well the last time they had seen each other, but that was four years ago. Hopefully, there had been enough water under the bridge to wash away any bad feelings. Somehow, she doubted it, but eventually she would get to question Brooke.

After making a few notes, she returned to the report she had started on the white slavery trade and gunrunning tied to the Russian mafia in recent years. The money trail from Europe vanished the minute it reached the United States. The Russians were good at playing hide-and-seek with their cash, divesting into legitimate businesses, real estate, and trade goods. Those commodities went back offshore and would translate into munitions. The turmoil in Northern Africa made it ripe for the picking of any venture capitalist who traded in guns, shoulder-fired missiles and death. She suspected the Russians were partly behind the nuclear proliferation on the Arabian Peninsula and gunrunning in Africa, but she couldn't prove it yet.

"Agent Water, Deputy Chapel wants to see you." An effeminate young male's voice cracked through the phone intercom. Colby was sure her assistant was gay, but she wasn't going to ask him. While don't ask-don't tell was finally an afterthought in the military, it was firmly entrenched in the Treasury Department. The security clearance she coveted kept her personal life at arm's length and probably explained why she had a hard time finding a woman who could live in the closet. It was just as well. Her little binder of women would make men envious and it kept her as satisfied as womanly possible. Standing, she pulled at the seam of her slacks and grabbed her jacket off the back of her faux leather chair. After a quick trip to the restroom to freshen-up she would make her weekly mandatory meeting with the deputy.

Exiting out of the stall, she practically walked into the back of a woman primping in the mirror.

"Oh, sorry. I didn't see you standing there." Colby ran her hands around the waist of the woman who still had her fingers straightening out her hair, nuzzling the back of her exposed neck. "Hmm, you smell good, Nicki."

"I never thought I was going to get a moment alone with you today, tiger. Lucky for me I saw you come in here."

"Grrr," Colby growled into the woman's ear. "I never thought I was going to get a free moment either, baby."

Colby let her hands glide slowly over the tight body wiggling into her lap. Stilling the hips in front of her, she rubbed herself against the firm ass. "By any chance did you lock the door?"

"Of course, now—"

"Shh. We don't have much time before the lunch rush hits," Colby said, pushing Nicki over and sliding the tight skirt up her ass. Cupping the firm cheeks, Colby slid down and bit the ripe apple in front of her face.

"Oh, so that's how you want to play today?" Nicki grabbed Colby's hands and slid them up under her blouse, to her breasts and rubbed them over her taut nipples. "God, I've missed you. How long are you going to be on this new case, Colby?"

Pulling down silk panties, Colby tongued the cleavage and moved down lower on Nicki. "Hmm, don't know," she said between licks. Turning Nicki around, she flattened her tongue and swiped it across the slim patch of hair between Nicki's legs. "Spread," Colby commanded before thumbing the new cleavage in front of her tongue. Nicki did as she was ordered and spread her legs, leaning back against the counter.

"Oh God, Colby."

"Shh, we don't want to get caught do we?"

"Oh, if you keep this up we're going to get caught red-handed," Nicki said, looking down at the blonde head of hair bobbing on her clit.

Colby pointed her tongue and slid between the slick lips, spearing the hard clit. Flicking it with her tongue, she elicited the desired response from her partner in crime. Reaching around, she pulled Nicki's hips tight against her mouth, her other hand sliding up to demanded entrance to her wet pussy. Nicki's fingers laced in her hair and held her tight.

"Oh shit!"

Moving harder against the tight opening, Colby added another finger and pushed up to her palm and back out again until she felt muscles tightening around her fingers. Nicki's impending orgasm made it tougher for Colby to hold on, but she did her best to stroke Nicki's clit faster as Nicki's hands pushed her head harder against her trembling pussy.

"Faster, Col. Come on baby, faster."

Carefully, Colby gave Nicki more fingers as she shuddered out an orgasm against Colby's hand.

"Fuck, Colby. I could spend all day with you and your magic fingers." Nicki tried to right herself, but her knees wobbled a bit a Colby pulled her body firmly against hers.

"Hmm, that sounds like a proposition. I'll have to take a rain check." Colby licked her fingers and smacked her lips as she pushed the towel dispenser. "I hate to eat and run, but I have a meeting with the deputy, so scooch," she said, bumping her hips against Nicki's.

"When do I get to return the favor?" Nicki pouted.

Soaping her hands and face, Colby could only smile and whisper, "Soon."

࿔࿔࿔࿔

Deputy Director Jane Chapel was, for lack of a

better couple of words, a 'battle axe' that had survived the end of the cold war and the push for more women into higher ranks at the Treasury Department. Now nearing retirement, she wanted to go out on top. Colby hated working with someone whose time was terminal. It affected their decision making process, how they approached the job and who they moved— no pushed—up the ranks. As a special agent in charge of watching the money flow to and from organized crime, Colby had it better than some agents. Her job could keep her out in the field if she wanted, or it could keep her sitting behind a computer, searching for a thread to unravel the neatly constructed webs spun by the cartels, mafias and gangs to protect their criminal activities. Once she had the start of a string, she moved rapidly into a field operation, trying to infiltrate the complex structures of the gangs.

Deputy Chapel's door was open and Colby could hear the one-sided conversation she was having. She stepped back, hoping she hadn't been seen. No such luck. Chapel addressed her and motioned her in, dashing any hope of exclusion from a clearly heated conversation.

"Agent Water, step in please. I'll call you later, Mike. I think I'd better take a rain check on golf. Please give your wife my best."

"Deputy Chapel. Good to see you, ma'am." Colby shook her hand firmly and then sat across from the deputy.

"Agent Water." The deputy grabbed her reading glasses and peered at the open file on her desk. I see you're working the Russian angle on the white slavery trade. Any news?"

"Nothing new to report, ma'am."

"I hear you're looking into the Yakuza, too."

Fucking Scarr, she thought, trying to figure out what one had to do with the other. "Yes, ma'am."

"And?"

"I've been investigating Luce Potter and her business dealings, trying to determine how her second in command, Frank Yeow, figures into the Russian picture."

"I don't understand."

"Frank Yeow changed sides just before the old man, Yoshida, died. He's with the Russians now and I'm trying to figure out why. Is he a plant or did he switch sides for a reason?"

"I see there's another piece to this puzzle as well," she said, pulling the glasses back to the edge of her nose. "A Brooke Erickson. Seems her cameraman was shot and killed by someone associated with Kolenka Petrov. Is that right?"

"I just got the report before I walked in here, ma'am, so I'm not quite up to speed on that yet." Colby felt a cold sweat break out and her face flush. Hopefully, that was the only information the deputy had on Brooke.

"I have it on good authority that Petrov is going to make a move on Potter's territory. So maybe this Frank fellow is speeding up that process?"

"Could be. He was pretty high up and I'm sure he knows where all the bodies are buried. I've got Agent Uvenko looking for him." Colby crossed her leg and rubbed the leather of her Dr. Martens. She hated when those higher-up started digging into her cases. Her weekly reports obviously weren't enough for Chapel, hence the reason for the meeting. Twisting her shoelace, she thought about what information she should divulge and what she should keep close. "Frank disappeared, just after JP Potter was killed. Word on the street was Luce Potter killed her own father. Seems she thinks he was responsible for her mother's death. How Frank figures into this, I don't know yet, but the Yakuza are a patriarchal set-up. I figure he couldn't handle taking orders from a woman once the Oyabun retired."

"Agent Water, I don't have to tell you how big this could be if you get the trifecta of organized crime: Russian, Japanese and the drug cartel all in one felled swoop."

"The drug cartel isn't involved in what I'm seeing, Deputy."

"Look closer, Water. Dig deeper and you'll find it. They're always around prostitution, bars and money laundering. So don't stop digging till you hit water." Deputy Chapel giggled at the half-assed joke at her expense. *Like I haven't heard that before.*

"Hmm."

Looking down at her watch, Deputy Chapel stood and extended her hand. "Okay, so keep me in the loop on this one, Water. It looks like it could mushroom into a big deal, making both of us look very good in the director's eyes. If you know what I mean."

"Gotcha," was all Colby could say as she shook the now limp hand.

She was being played, but she hadn't figured out how just yet. She hadn't seen any link between the Yakuza and the drug cartel, but it didn't necessarily mean it wasn't there. It was more likely that the Russians and the cartel were in bed together, but why would Deputy Chapel send her on a wild goose chase? Maybe she just hadn't seen a connection yet, but she doubted it. She didn't miss much when it came to her job. This was serious shit if Chapel was right, but it just didn't pass the smell test.

Stomping to her desk, she stuffed the files into her briefcase and grabbed her overcoat. Colby was in for a long weekend, and an early start would help her stay ahead of the looming trifecta.

Chapter Five

Luce moved from group to group, feeling less like the Oyabun of a major Yakuza organization and more like a child who had lost her best friend. She had promised herself at the crypt she would be the strong, powerful woman everyone saw her as, but inside it felt as if someone had their hand around her heart and squeezing. The loss coursed through her. A pounding headache and swollen eyes were her only companions at the moment. Brooke's warm hand stroked her back reassuringly, but beyond that Luce had emotionally shut down.

Slamming her whiskey neat, she ordered another and tried to offer Brooke a reassuring smile.

"You okay, honey?" Brooke said softly.

Patting Brooke's hand, she smiled meagerly and nodded.

"I'm fine, it's been a long day."

"Your grandfather had quite a few friends," Brooke said, scanning the crowded restaurant.

"Yeah, and maybe a few wanted a free meal," Luce said cynically.

"Honey..."

"I'm sorry. I'm—" She stopped when she spied Dr. Maggie Williams talking to someone in the corner. Luce said, "There's Dr. Williams, I'm going to thank her for coming. I'll be right back."

Without another word, she shook a few hands,

and worked her way through the crowd, but not before someone had tried to commandeer the good doctor towards the front of the restaurant. Maggie Williams was a good-looking woman for her age and Luce might have considered dating her if not for their professional relationship. Maggie's reputation often preceded her and made her a hot topic of discussion in some circles who knew of her bondage expertise. As a part owner of the Dungeon, it was obvious she wasn't a practitioner of the art of bondage; she was an expert on the subject.

"Dr. Williams, thank you for coming."

"Ms. Potter, I just wanted to express my sincere condolences for your loss."

"Thank you, Dr. Williams." Luce accepted the offered hug, then stepped out of the embrace. She and Brooke hadn't spoken about Maggie and her services, but then Luce hadn't needed them lately. Finding Brooke open to new sexual experiences had quenched Luce's appetite for rope play beyond her bedroom.

"It's been a while, Luce. You haven't come around the club lately."

"I've been busy with grandfather and work." Luce sounded almost apologetic.

"And Ms. Erickson?" Maggie said, nodding in Brooke's direction.

"Yes, she's been a good diversion, but I think I might need to come by the Dungeon. I feel like I need...something."

"I understand. When we find ourselves faced with these types of situations, we need something to make us feel alive."

Luce searched Maggie's face for understanding. It wasn't that Brooke didn't understand what she was going through. In fact, she had been more than supportive. Luce was in a dark place—a place she hadn't been in a long time. It was like a seed had taken root in her soul and she felt it growing. She had managed to keep it tamped down, control it before it took over, but it had returned and Luce was worried. Maybe giving voice to it might rein it back in before it was too late.

Maybe.

Luce felt the need to let someone else take over control of something, at least metaphorically. Brooke wasn't ready for that kind of responsibility yet. Not the kind of 'taking control' Luce needed. She required an adept hand, an experienced touch that would help her go someplace else. The expertise would allow her to embrace her inner darkness, and if she couldn't harness it's power of hate then she would release it back into the universe.

"When would you like to schedule an appointment, Luce?"

"Soon," Luce looked over at Brooke, who glanced in their direction and then looked away. "Maybe tomorrow? I'm not sure. I have an appointment with my grandfather's attorney, so either way I…"

"I'll clear my schedule and you may come in when you're ready, Ms. Potter." Maggie nodded at Brooke who had walked up during the conversation.

"Dr. Williams, it's nice to see you again. It's been a while."

"It has, hasn't it," Maggie said, directing her comment towards Luce. "I'm always here if you need someone to talk to." Maggie looked at Brooke and added, "Professionally of course."

"I appreciate that, thank you."

Suddenly the moment became awkward when no one spoke. Luce cleared her throat, took a sip of her newly acquired whiskey.

"I'll let you get back to your guests. Take care, Ms. Erickson."

"Dr. Williams."

Luce smiled at the wink Maggie threw her way, instantly regretting the action when Brooke cast a stern glance at her.

"Dr. Williams looks," Luce watched Brooke follow the swaying ass to the door and then turn towards her. "Healthy."

Luce studied Brooke trying to figure out if she was jealous or curious about the good doctor. "What would you like to know, Brooke?"

"What do you mean?"

"You know what Maggie does. You know how I know her. In fact, I think you've seen her in action if I'm not mistaken." Luce knew she was baiting Brooke, but she couldn't help it. A fight would solve her problems and give her an excuse to go to the Dungeon without an explanation. It was devious, but right now she didn't care.

"Yes, it would seem that I *have* seen her work," Brooke said, looking at Luce's breast and then blushing. "Have you seen her since then?"

"Brooke?"

"Luce?"

"I don't think this is the place or time to discuss my proclivities for whips and bondage do you?"

"You don't have to be crass, Luce."

"I'm not trying to be classless, Brooke. I'm simply stating the obvious."

"Is that what you ladies were talking about? Another visit?" Brooke raised her hand dismissing Luce before she could respond. "Don't answer that.

I'm sure it's privileged information."

Suddenly the room exploded in commotion.

"Comrades, I see you're having party and I wasn't invited. Seriously, Luce, I'm shocked at your bad manners." Kolenka Petrov tried to push his way through the group of men and women surrounding Luce and Brooke. Petrov was a pain in Luce's ass that wouldn't go away. She had made it clear that if he didn't take his skin pedaling business and other illegal ventures out of her town she would make sure his heirs had their inheritance early.

"Luce, funny we should be at same restaurant at same time. I didn't know you liked sushi." He laughed around the squat cigar that protruded from his pudgy lips.

"You're clearly drunk, Petrov. It's the only excuse you could have for interrupting my grandfather's wake."

"What? Old man is dead? No shit? I thought fucker would live forever. I should tell Frankie, he'll be saddened by the news. You remember Frankie, *da*?"

Cursing Petrov, Luce was suddenly consumed with anger, giving her dark side license to freely roam. Luce pushed through her bodyguards, reached through the line and grabbed Petrov by the lapels. Pulling his face within inches of her own, she snarled, "Look you fat, disgusting bastard. Give Frank a message for me. He can hide behind your fat ass, but eventually I'll find him. When I do, I'll personally cut every digit from his right hand and then I'll break every finger in his left so he won't be able to wipe his own ass."

"Wow, you're still really pissed?"

"You have no idea, but let me show you," she said, reaching down and grabbing his crotch and squeezing.

With her other hand she pulled her stiletto and flicked at the buttons of his shirt, scattering them on the floor. Another flick of her wrist and she carved a quick line up his sloppy gut, deep enough to let a little blood drip. What she really wanted to do was plunge it into his squealing hide and gut him like the pig he was. Before she could push the stiletto in further someone grabbed her wrist.

"Sammy!"

"Oyabun."

Everyone around Luce spread slightly and looked down at the dancing Russian, still screaming as she held his pants. He looked down to see a line of blood down his stomach and slid his fat hand across the scratch.

"You fucking bitch. I kill you, trust me. You will meet your grandfather soon."

"Get his ass out of here, Sammy," Luce said, quickly pushing the button that would sheath the chrome vengeance back into its protective home. "Sasha, take Brooke home and make sure no one follows you." Turning towards the stunned crowd, Luce continued, "I want to thank everyone for their wonderful stories about my grandfather, but the party is over. Thank you for coming."

"Luce?"

"Brooke, go home and I'll call you later."

"But—"

"Go home, Brooke," Luce commanded. "Lynn, you're with me."

"Yes, Oyabun," Lynn said, bowing.

Walking out of the restaurant, Luce watched as Brooke was escorted to a car and driven off. Running her fingers through her wild hair, she threw an elbow at the window of her car as she got close. Particles of glass scattered everywhere as if scrambling to get out of Luce's way.

"Take me home, Lynn."

"Yes, Oyabun."

"I don't want visitors," Luce said, pulling the door shut. The implication was simple. Plan on staying and making sure that she wasn't disturbed.

"Ms. Erickson?" Lynn said, through the intercom.

"No one."

Luce punched the com off, pulled her stiletto out and flicked it open. Without a second thought she pushed the blade across her skin opening a slight cut, blood oozing out and down her arm. She embraced the pain, letting it be her guide into the darkness. It was that easy.

❧❧❧❧

Brooke listened as her call went to voice mail again, for the third time in as many hours. She had never seen the side of Luce that she put on display for everyone earlier. She knew Luce hated Petrov, but to threaten him in front of everyone and then assault him in front of witnesses wasn't Luce's style. The normally reserved head of the Yakuza family was always, always in control of her emotions and Brooke was worried for Luce.

"Sammy?"

"Yes, ma'am?"

"Can you please call the Oyabun for me?"

"Yes, ma'am."

Brooke pulled on her necklace, nervously gliding the diamond back and forth across the chain. Luce had given her the expensive token on their first anniversary. Call her superstitious, but once Luce had placed it around her neck, Brooke never took it off, for fear she would jinx their relationship. If it was removed, Luce would be the one to do it, officially ending their connection. She couldn't put her finger on why she felt that way, but she did. She had tried to explain it to Luce when she questioned why Brooke didn't wear her other necklaces anymore, but it had only sounded silly. Somehow, it seemed like a pact that little girls would make between their best friends.

"I'm sorry, Ms. Erickson, the Oyabun isn't answering her phone," Sammy said.

"Can you try her car?"

"Yes, ma'am."

Now she was worried. She suspected Luce was avoiding her, but why?

"I'm sorry, but she isn't answering."

"Thank you, Sammy. I'll try her when I get home."

"Yes, ma'am."

Now she was really worried.

Chapter Six

The smell of whiskey, incense and sweat saturated the dark room. Tossing the two fingers of whiskey back, Luce pulled the bottle off the coffee table, almost dropping it on its way to refilling the crystal tumbler. A generous pour lightened the load slightly as she fumbled to reset it on the glass table. She grabbed a piece of paper off the table, attempting to focus on the writing and reread what only minutes ago felt like entering a nightmare. Betrayed again, this time by her own grandfather. How could it be? How could he? Searching her mind, she tried to remember exactly what the lawyer had said. He had been waiting for her in her study when she got home tonight, telling her it was critical he speak with her immediately.

What could be so important that it couldn't wait until tomorrow when she was a day further from the death of her grandfather? she wondered.

"Tom asked me to personally deliver the news of part of his bequest."

"Tom?"

"Oh, that's how I knew your grandfather, as Tom Yoshida."

"I don't understand," Luce said, *a headache starting at the back of her head and traveling forward. Twisting her head, she hoped she could relieve it with a few strategic rotations, but it wasn't to be.*

"Well…" The lawyer's discomfort was obvious,

but Luce wasn't in a compassionate mood.

"Yes?" Luce closed her eyes and rubbed her temples, wishing the sweaty little man would disappear quickly.

"Ms. Potter, how much did you know about your grandfather?"

"You need to quit talking in riddles and get to the point, before I set you out on your ass. Sammy?"

Silently, Sammy appeared behind the man and bowed. "Yes, Oyabun."

"This man was leaving, please see that he is escorted off the property," Luce said, turning to leave.

"Ms. Potter please, this could affect your inheritance. A moment is all I need. Please," he implored.

Luce nodded and Sammy exited as unobtrusively as he had arrived.

"You have three minutes," Luce said. She checked her watch.

"Ms. Potter your grandfather has left a sizeable amount to someone. He is clear about how this is to transpire and when."

"Continue." Luce waved her hand impatiently.

"Tom is leaving an apartment he had in the city and a monthly allowance that is to be dispersed on the first of the month, to a Ms. Amanda Linwood."

"What?"

"If you contest the will, it will automatically send it into a conservatorship and you will be sent a monthly allowance as well."

"I don't understand. We transferred most of the businesses into my name years ago. How…what's going on? I don't understand." Luce searched the man's face trying to grasp what he was saying. A woman? What woman? "Okay, you have me at quite a disadvantage.

What woman are we talking about?"

"I had urged Tom to tell you about Amanda. He said he would, but I guess things happened so quickly, he—"

"Wait. Stop. What the fuck are you talking about?"

"Your grandfather had a wife, sort of a wife."

"What?" Luce felt herself sway and then the lawyer was by her side helping her sit on the sofa. "You mean my grandmother?"

"I'm afraid not."

"What the fuck are you talking about? My grandfather had another wife, or sort of a wife?"

"I'm sorry to be the one to tell you all of this, especially so soon after his death. I would have hoped he would have shared all of this with you, but—"

"But he didn't, so you get the honor." Luce stood and grabbed the man by the throat. "I'm clearly not in the mood for bullshit, so get to the point before I lose my temper even more."

"Ms. Potter. I have a letter he asked me to give you. I think it will explain everything. I need your signature to finalize the requirements of the will."

"No wait, I'm not signing anything until I've read everything." Her head was spinning so fast she couldn't focus long enough to comprehend what she was being told. How could her grandfather be married, or sort of married, and she hadn't known about it? Why hadn't he told her? Who was this woman? Was she a gold digger? So many questions, or were they lies? She needed a moment—hell she needed hours to digest what she was being told.

Pulling the letter from his trembling fingers, she tore it open and unfolded it. "Sit."

Her mind blanked as she recognized the

handwriting. Each sentence barely registered as she bounced from word to word, finally finishing the letter. Her grandfather's life had been a cleverly veiled lie. At least that's how she was reading the letter. A woman had taken up residence in his life and he had conveniently forgotten to tell her. Where was she while her grandfather lay dying in the hospital? Why hadn't she come to the funeral?

"How much money are we talking here?"

"Excuse me?"

"Her allowance? How much are we talking about here? Where does the money come from?"

"Tom had investments put away just for this instance."

"Tom." Luce couldn't wrap her mind around the name let alone the fact that her grandfather had a mistress. She couldn't accept that he had a wife—no she was an interloper— an intruder on Luce's nicely packaged life, or former life.

"So if I fight this what happens?"

"Part of the money is to go to you in five years, but if you fight his wishes, he cuts you out and leaves everything to her."

Luce was wealthy enough for her tastes, so the money wasn't an issue. Another woman was the issue. "How much could we be talking about? I have all the business assets, so it can't be that much?"

"The holdings alone are worth two million, the monthly payments are worth about one hundred thousand. She gets an allowance."

"How much?"

"I'm sorry, Tom asked me to keep that confidential, but what's left is put into an account and in five years you get the bulk of that account."

"I can't believe what I'm hearing. My grandfather, Tom as you like to call him, had a mistress—"

"Wife."

"Whatever, and all you need is my signature so she gets her money."

"No, actually I need your signature agreeing to everything, otherwise she gets everything and you get nothing if you fight it."

"Fuck. I can't believe what I'm hearing."

"Ms. Potter, the letter explains things, but I can only say I wish your grandfather had told you about Amanda. She's a wonderful woman who made your grandfather very happy."

Jealousy reared its ugly head as Luce stared at the man trying to plead her grandfather's case on his behalf. She thought she had made her grandfather happy, but clearly, it wasn't enough. How could he have lied to her? How could he have hidden something like this from her? They were close, but obviously not that close. Lies, their life together had been full of lies, or at least half-truths and now she was left alone to deal with what was left behind. Hell, now she was sounding like a jealous wife herself.

"How long?"

"I'm sorry?"

"How long were they together?"

"They knew each other for years."

"How long?"

"Almost ten years."

"What? I don't..." Luce's voice trailed off as she tried to think about the timeline and where she was during all that time. "That's about the time I was starting to take control of parts of the..."

"Yes, once you started to run things it freed up his

time more and well, things sort of happened. Ms. Potter, your grandfather was finally happy for the last few years of his life. He was thrilled you were doing so well with the organization and the businesses were running like a finely tuned watch. He was very, very proud of you."

"Is there anything else you need?"

"No, I know this is a surprise—"

"You have no fucking idea. Now where do I need to sign?" *Luce pulled a pen from her blazer and waved the papers over.*

"Ms. Potter—"

"Don't. Don't say another word. Just leave."

"If you have any questions." *He pulled a business card from his pocket.* "Don't hesitate to call me."

Luce slammed the whiskey and poured another, pitching the letter to the floor. Finishing her whiskey, she poured a full glass. Why sip it when what she wanted was relief from her memories, or were they lies? She was confused, pissed, and trying to sort the facts from the lies of the last ten years.

"Oyabun?"

Luce sat silent as the knocking continued.

"Oyabun? It's me, Sammy."

No shit, she smiled at the obvious and then gulped her drink down. The welcome burn added to her already heightening pain. Her head lobbed back against the tall back of the chair. She closed her eyes trying to stop her world from pitching, but it was no use. Her mind wandered back and forth over the past decade, searching for any signs that she might have overlooked. She felt like a wife that had been cheated on. She was rarely sympathetic when she heard about women who complained that they never suspected a cheating spouse. *They only saw what they wanted to see, overlooking obvious cheating behavior because they couldn't handle the truth.* Now she was trying to search for signs she might have missed with her grandfather. Had she been so caught-up in her own life that she had completely missed his need for companionship? Now she was sure sounding like a wife and not a granddaughter. *Shit,* her world no longer resembled the one she'd woken up in this morning. It had taken a sudden shift and was careening out of her control.

"Oyabun?"

"I'm fine, Sammy. Go home." Luce rubbed her aching chest.

"Why don't you let me call Ms. Erickson?"

"No. I'm fine," Luce yelled. "If you value your job, go home, Sammy."

"Oyabun—"

"Sammy. Go. In fact, send everyone home."

"But, Oyabun—"

"Sammy..."

"Yes, Oyabun."

"You and everyone else are fired. Now get the fuck out of my house. Do you hear me?"

"Yes, Oyabun."

Luce stopped and waited until she heard the front door shut. Standing, she swayed almost going ass over as she tried to walk. She hurled her empty glass against the wall, barely missing a high-dollar piece of art. Next, she tossed over the coffee table, breaking the thick glass top.

"Fucking bastard. How could you? How could you forget my grandmother like that?"

Luce stumbled around in the dark room, practically falling over the couch, landing dead center of it instead. Arms flailing, she punched the thick cushions. The coarse fabric rubbed her knuckles raw as she assaulted the defenseless object.

"Fuck."

The cut on Luce's arm throbbed and reopened as she continued her assault. Rubbing it, she could feel warm blood smear across her hand, but it wasn't enough. Luce righted herself on the couch and slowly, calmly pulled her stiletto and flicked it open. The smell of blood drove her deeper into her pain and provided a path to manage her anger.

Chapter Seven

D amn it Luce, answer." Brooke let the phone ring until it went to voice mail again before slamming it shut.

It wasn't like Luce not to answer her phone. She *always* answered her phone in case something happened within the organization. As the head of a crime family, she needed to be there when quick decisions were necessary. At least that's how she explained it to Brooke when her phone went off in the middle of the night. Luce had sent her away just as her mother did when she didn't want Brooke seeing her cry. She wasn't a child anymore and Brooke was damn sure she wasn't going to let Luce send her away because she couldn't handle her grief.

Maybe Luce was with Maggie, being entertained. Luce hadn't seen Maggie in months. Did seeing her at the Oyabun's funeral trigger some unspoken need in Luce? Or maybe Maggie had taken advantage of Luce's grief and offered her *services*?

Brooke's mind scattered in all directions trying to rationalize why Luce had disappeared and now she wasn't answering her phone. She hit a button and called the one person she knew would understand her, John Chambers, her editor. He was dialed in to the inner workings of human emotion; he was a gay man, not to mention the closest thing Brooke had to a girlfriend. The only thing missing was his ability to share her clothes and make-up, but what he lacked in *girl style*, he made up in *gay style*.

"Okay, this has to be bad if you're calling me at midnight," John said.

"You weren't sleeping yet were you?"

"Honey, are you serious? I'm going over the articles before publication. I never get to bed before two on night like this. Besides I'm glued to the news channel covering that situation over in Europe. If they don't get their shit together, the markets are going to tank over here and I want to shed some financial weight before it hits hard. What's up?"

"Ever the optimist, John. I'm surprised Carl hasn't turned you around and set you straight on the way the world works."

"Is that a straight joke, Brooke? I'm surprised at you."

"Freudian slip maybe," Brooke laughed. "Look, I need to talk to someone, so if you're busy, I'll catch you at the office."

"Naw, spill it, princess."

Brooke did just that, explaining what had happened at the funeral and the altercation at the restaurant with Petrov. She had never seen Luce so dark and foreboding. She had pulled her knife and practically sliced him wide open. She threatened to kill Petrov in a room full of people. People who probably would turn their backs on whatever happened between Luce and the Russian, but nevertheless she had gone rogue and it scared Brooke.

"I can't get hold of Luce. She isn't answering her phone and I'm not sure what to do."

"When was the last time you talked to her?"

"About three hours ago."

"Oh, my goodness," John feigned a shriek. "Did you call the police?"

"You think I should?"

"No, of course I don't think you should. Geez, you spoke to her three hours ago. She'll be home any minute and you cats can have crazy kitty sex."

"I'm at my house, John."

"You mean your house, *house*?"

"John, have you been drinking tonight?"

"No, why?

"Because you keep repeating everything I say and it's damn aggravating."

"Oh sorry, but I think you're blowing this way out of proportion. She lost her grandfather and I think it's pretty normal that she would need some time to herself. Don't you?"

"I suppose so." Brooke grudgingly agreed.

"You want me to come over and we could have a pajama party, just us girls?"

"Aren't you a little old for a sleep over? Besides, what about Carl?"

"Oh he's sleeping already; he had an early day at the shop."

Brooke was still amazed that someone like John dated a mechanic. He always seemed to like his men rough and tough. Grease under the nails kind of guys that were roguish to his feminine. People who didn't know John's home side only saw the polished professional in the well-fitting suit and spit-shined shoes.

"I appreciate that but I think I'll pass. Besides, we would just sit around sipping wine, painting each other's toenails and gossip about all the bitches at work. If my boss found out he would kill me." She giggled, shaking her head.

"Well, I have it on good authority your boss is a sweetheart. So there. Look, don't worry, give Luce some space and time to adjust to her new normal. She's been through a lot: the cancer, the long process of watching her grandfather dying, and now life without him. I can't imagine all the stuff she is going through mentally right now."

"I guess you're right."

"Of course I am, now listen to your fairy godmother slash boss and take a hot bath, have a glass of wine and try and enjoy your weekend. If this financial crap keeps up, I can see a few long weeks of reporting with no breaks for us until it's over."

"You're right, she needs her space."

"Brooke?"

"Yes?"

"Don't call her when you hang up with me. Let her be."

"I'm not going to call her."

"Yes you are, so don't. I know you. Give her time. You want her to need you, and one of the ways that happens is when you let someone realize you're gone. Not permanently or anything, but when she looks around her place and she can't find you, she'll call begging you to come over and save her from herself. Trust me, honey, it works every time with Carl."

"Hmm, maybe."

"Call me tomorrow, but not too early. I'm sleeping in before the big crash."

"All right, John. Thanks for the advice."

"Anytime, honey. Talk to you later. Kiss, kiss."

"Kiss, kiss."

Brooke tossed the phone on the counter and

frowned at it. She wasn't convinced John was right, but Luce had said she needed her space and would call Brooke. They had been inseparable for the last year, now she looked around her apartment and realized she was glad she hadn't gotten rid of it. Where would she have gone if she had moved in with Luce when she had suggested it? Something in the back of her mind always made her keep some roots away from the main plant in case something happened. Even though she lived in the shadow of Luce, who provided her with everything, it was still nice to know she had a place of her own, just in case.

Tapping out a nervous tempo with her manicured nails, anxiety crawled through her body. Something was wrong, she could feel it. The question was, what would she do about it. Luce was a rock, things that would topple the average person bounced off her, and yet she persevered. Frank's betrayal had played more havoc with her than the death of her father. Somehow, Luce had taken his sudden death in stride, almost too easily. When Brooke had asked her how she felt, she barely shrugged it off. Now, her grandfather's death, while not sudden, had thrown Luce for a loop. The fact that she wasn't returning Brooke's call was making all the alarm bells go off. Call it a woman's intuition, but she could feel something was out of place in Luce's world. She never, ever dodged Brooke, not even when they fought. Luce was more of a go in and get things handled personality. She wasn't an avoid and hope the problem went away kind of gal. Honestly, that was more Brooke's style. Confrontation with her lover left her anxious. She wasn't afraid Luce would leave her if they fought, she didn't want one of them saying something they would have to live with later. Words were her profession and she knew how badly they could hurt if used carelessly and in anger.

She flipped her phone open and dialed Sammy again. "Sammy? How is Luce?"

"Ms. Erickson, I can assure you she made it home safe and sound."

Something didn't feel right with Sammy's answer. He wasn't usually so formal with her and it made her feeler go up again. "What aren't you telling me?"

"Ms. Erickson?"

"Don't Ms. Erickson, me. We've known each other long enough now to be on a first name basis. Are you at the house now?"

"No ma'am."

Again with the formal. It was starting to irritate Brooke. "Thank you, Sammy. I'll just stop by Luce's and find out for myself how she's doing."

"I wouldn't do that, Ms. Erickson."

"Why not?"

"She needs sometime to herself. Just give her some space. She'll call you when she's ready."

"I don't need relationship advice, Sammy. I want to know how Luce is."

"Yes ma'am," Sammy said sternly.

"I'm sorry, Sammy. That wasn't very nice. I'm worried about Luce."

"Yes, ma'am." Another terse response then silence.

Shit. Sammy was an honorable man. Brooke was asking him to divulge information about his boss and then insulting him when he didn't give her what she wanted.

"Thank you for checking to make sure Luce got home. I'm sure you're right, she'll give me a call when she's ready."

"Yes, ma'am."

Brooke dropped her head in her palm and sighed. "I'll speak to you tomorrow, Sammy. Good night."

Brooke closed the phone and began her nervous staccato on the counter again. She could sit here and wait for Luce's call, or she could check on Luce herself. She would have to gauge how pissed Luce would be if she just showed up. It wasn't as if they were merely friends with benefits, they were practically living together. So what was the problem?

Without giving it another thought—in case she tried to talk herself out of it—she grabbed a jacket, her purse, and keys. A quick trip across town to check on Luce would provide her with all the proof she needed to ease her anxiety.

Chapter Eight

D o not answer that, Agent Water," the sultry voice commanded.

Colby pulled her head from underneath the covers, wiped her mouth and reached for her phone as she was being pulled back.

"I said, don't answer that."

"Oh, you sure are bossy, kitten."

"Well, it's so rare that I get you all to myself."

Colby pulled her bed companion closer as she grabbed the phone. "This better be good."

"The subject you wanted me to watch is on the move."

Colby looked over at her clock. "Okay, it's late, but not noteworthy, Agent Scarr."

"No, but the two cars following her are."

"Two cars?"

"Yeah they pulled out behind her. Not very stealth if you asked me. If she's the least bit observant she'll make 'em."

"Well, her driver will see them and report it to their boss."

"She's driving herself."

"Okay, are you following the train?"

"Yep, I'm the caboose on this meandering line."

"Okay, call me if things get hinky."

"Is that a technical term?"

"Call me if anything happens."

"You got it."

Colby dropped the phone to the floor and muttered, "Asshole." She wondered why Brooke would be out at this time of night. More importantly, she worried who would be tailing her. One could be her protection detail, which she was sure Luce had on her twenty-four-seven, but the other car was the wild card. If she were a guessing woman, she suspected it was the Russians. They had tried once to kill Brooke and Colby doubted they would stop just because she was now dating one of the most powerful women in the country. Agent Scarr would keep things under control. At least she *knew* he took his job serious.

"Okay, where were we?"

The body next to her stiffened as she touched her back. "Awe, come on. Don't be like that, Cheryl. I had to take the call. Good news is I don't have to go out."

Cheryl turned and cuddled into Colby.

"Ouch," Colby screamed, grabbing her nipples. "Whadya do that for?"

"Oh, I thought you liked it rough. You said you were checking out The Dungeon, so I thought maybe you were looking for some spice."

Rubbing her palms against her aching nipples, she frowned. "I was following a lead on a case."

"Uh huh."

"Seriously, I've got this case and I needed to check out a lead. Why? You wanna try something new?" Colby reached down and cupped Cheryl between her legs and rubbed her palm against the still wet clit.

"Maybe."

"Oh now this sounds promising." Colby let her lips linger on Cheryl's neck, then slid down to a nipple. She gently bit it.

"Ouch. What did you do that for?"

"I saw it done at The Dungeon and the woman begged for more, so I thought...."

Colby smoothed the rough tip with her tongue and then moved over to the other as she slipped her finger between wet lips. Cheryl thrust her hips up and Colby slowly eased her finger out and added another before sliding in again.

"More," came the gentle command.

If Colby was anything, she was accommodating when it came to her dates. Sliding another finger inside, she slowly sped up the rhythm.

"Down," the insistent voice ordered.

Colby worked her mouth down over Cheryl's sweaty stomach, lazily playing with her belly button, dipping her tongue down into the circle.

"Colby." Her command came again in a breathless plea.

The slow torture worked both ways, and Colby could feel her body tighten in anticipation. Her skin tingled as her date's heady aroma permeated the warm air under the covers. The salty, musky smell was like an aphrodisiac to Colby and she was ready to make short work of the task ahead. Sliding down to the hard clit waiting for her, she practically inhaled it, pulling it into her mouth and sucking.

"Oh shit, that's it." Her hips bucked up as Colby tried to push them down and part legs to gain easier access to what she really wanted. Replacing her fingers, she dipped her tongue lower into the wet hole, spearing it with her hard tongue. Flicking it back and forth she moved closer, flattened her tongue and swiped it up across the hard clit and then began the process over again until Cheryl thighs tightened and pushed up signaling her impending orgasm.

"Oh fuck, oh fuck, baby!"

Colby didn't stop until she felt Cheryl push her head.

"Oh god, stop! I don't think I can take anymore."

"Oh I think you can." Colby slipped a finger deeper and then turned her hand upwards hitting the elusive G-spot. Cheryl's muscles tightened instantly around Colby's fingers, her hips grinding against them and suddenly Cheryl was moaning and spasming as another orgasm peaked across her body. Goosebumps and hard nipples, Colby's reward for a job well done.

"Phew, that's never happened before." Cheryl rolled on top of Colby, resting her chin on her fists. "You're really good and now it's my turn."

Colby wrapped her arms around Cheryl, stopping her from moving. "Uh huh, I'm good."

"What?" Cheryl frowned. Clearly, she wasn't used to a partner who didn't need her to reciprocate. "But—"

Colby put a finger against her lips. "Agent Turner, how would you like to work undercover?" Colby smiled and then planted a kiss on the frown.

Chapter Nine

Brooke watched the headlights in her rearview mirror turn behind her for the third time. She expected to see Sammy or one of the other members of Luce's inner circle following behind her in his black sedan, as per her usual protection detail. Since Petrov had threatened to kill anyone Luce loved, protection wasn't an option, it was mandatory. However, this wasn't Sammy's car following her. In fact, she didn't recognize the long Cadillac with blacked out windows and no front license plate.

Instead of heading straight for Luce's house she meandered through the city hoping to lose the tail. She blew through a few red lights and veered off her usual route. This only put a little distance between them. The car was back on her rear as quick as she thought she'd lost it. She dug out her phone again to dial Luce, hoping this time she would pick-up. *Why didn't she go straight to Luce's?* The answer was easy. Luce's place was off the beaten path. The long, dark road to her estate would give the person tailing her the opportunity to overtake her and force her off the road. Now she wished she *had* called Sammy and asked him to take her to Luce's, but what was done, was done. She couldn't go back home, to John's, or anyone else's house. It would put them in danger and she had learned from Luce that you didn't put other people at risk.

She got Luce's answering machine again. *Damn*

it, Luce, answer. She tossed the phone on the seat next to her and tried to think of some way to lose her tail. Without a second thought, she sped up and quickly slammed on the brakes putting her Mercedes Roadster into a sideways slide. That driving course she had taken at Laguna Seca when she'd bought her Mercedes was about to pay off. Not exactly in the way she had anticipated, but definitely paying off. Yanking the wheel to the left, she turned the car around and pushed the gas, sending her speeding past her tail. Hoping to catch a glimpse of the driver, she slowed slightly but hit the gas again when the blacked out window offered her nothing. The light nighttime traffic gave her a clear path through the city as she weaved through its dark streets.

Brooke bolted down a side street and noticed a city garage. Another quick turn and she spun into it, barely clearing the cement barriers meant to keep the traffic to one lane. She flipped her lights off and drove to the back. The crawl up the garage's steep incline put her on the third floor in a matter of seconds. She stopped, watching for movement in her rearview mirror. Out of the corner of her eye she caught site of an empty stall between a truck and a wall. Thankful for an opportunity to hide, she backed into the space. Brooke slid down in the seat and waited, letting her car idle in case she had to make a quick exit. Assuming she didn't get blocked in, of course. If that ended up being the case, she would take her chances and ram the idiot following her. Sacrificing her car would mean nothing if it saved her life.

Her heart hammered in her chest. Her fight or flight response was engaged and she was ready. Rummaging through her purse, she looked for something to defend herself. Luce had presented her with a small revolver one day, but Brooke had insisted that she didn't need, nor want something that had the potential to kill. Remembering Mike had made her pass on the protection, but now she wished she had accepted it. At least with it she had a chance. Brooke practically jumped out of her skin when her phone rang. She rushed to open it, worried that if someone was close they'd hear it ring.

"Brooke?"

"Sammy?"

"Where are you?"

"What?"

"Where are you?"

Brooke barely peered over the dash of her car hoping not to see the black Cadillac coming towards her. Her strategic location blocked her view of everything except what was immediately in front of her car. *Shit.*

"Brooke?"

"I don't know." Brooke suddenly realized that she hadn't been paying attention to the streets while getting as far away as she could from Petrov's man. Now she was in a garage, scared out of her wits, hoping she was alone.

"What do you mean you don't know? I lost you when you pulled that pit maneuver back on Cambridge."

"That was you in that black Caddy?"

"No, I was the second car, right behind the Caddy."

"Well who was in the Caddy?" Brooke sighed, she should have known she wouldn't be all alone out there, but fear had gotten the best of her. "Don't answer that,

I'm sure we both know who was following me."

"Petrov."

"Probably one of his goons. That would be my guess."

"Then who was in the car behind me?"

"What?" Two cars following Brooke, but why? And who was in the third car? "Are they still following you?" she asked.

"No, I lost one back when you pulled a *Mario Andretti*. They're both out here trying to find you. So tell me where you are. I'll come and get you and take you home."

"I'm afraid to get out of the car. I'm in a public garage on the third floor. I'm not getting out to see if—"

"Brooke, I'm following the black Caddy. I'll peel off and come back around to get you. Stay where you are and don't move. If any car comes in the garage, call 911. There are only two public garages in this area. I'll call you when I think I'm close."

"Okay, but hurry. I'm scared, Sammy."

"Gotcha."

Hearing the phone go dead only added to Brooke's anxiety. She hadn't even given it a second thought when she decided to go to Luce's and now she was paying for her carelessness. Trying to look around the front of the truck, Brooke squinted in the sparse light. If something or someone was out there she couldn't see or hear anything. She briefly thought about tossing her jacket over her head to conceal herself, but that would prevent her from seeing anything coming at her, too. *Fuck, fuck, fuck what should I do?* What she wouldn't give to talk to Luce right now.

❧❧❧❧❧

"What do you mean you lost her?" Colby fumed.

"She pulled some quick maneuver and jetted past me and whoever was following her, too."

"So let me get this straight, you lost a civilian in a bright red Mercedes?"

"Look Water, she handled that car like a pro, so don't give me that shit about her being a civilian. She's—"

"So you're telling me that you're in over your head. Maybe you'd rather be driving a desk. I'm sure it's safer and you won't get lost as easily."

"Fuck you, Water."

"Get your ass back to her house and wait. If you've lost her, you've lost her. Geez, Scarr."

"Yes, *ma'am*," he said in that patronizing way she hated.

"Scarr, what about the other cars following her, what happened to them?"

"They got lost, too."

"Are you sure?"

"Yea, we're all out here running around like the three blind mice."

Colby smiled, Brooke was surprising her at every turn. First, dating the head of a Yakuza organization, then the bondage revelation, and now the ability to lose an agent trained in defensive driving tactics. She was full of surprises.

"Okay, well get back to her house and wait. She's bound to go home, eventually. Make yourself scarce."

"I'll let you know when she gets home."

"I'll send you a replacement soon. By the way, did you happen to get the license plates of the cars following her? I wanna see who's interested in the Yakuza's girlfriend, too."

Colby had thought the way to get to Luce was through Brooke, but it was starting to look like she wasn't the only one trying to get to Luce using Brooke.

"Yep, sent it in already. I figure it will be on your desk when you get to the office in the am."

"Good job, now maybe we can see who all the players are in this little street opera."

"Later."

"Later."

Colby chewed on the inside of her lip, as she tried to figure out who, or what was behind all the tails on Brooke. Was it blow-back for being with one of the most powerful women in organized crime? Of course it was, you didn't date a woman like Luce and not pick up her enemies, too. What was that saying, the enemies of my enemies...no that wasn't it. Oh hell, it didn't matter. Brooke knew what she was getting into when she decided to become involved with Luce. *However, this was Brookie,* and it twisted her that Brooke could be in danger. Unless Colby took up Brooke's tail, there would be little she could do to make sure Brooke stayed safe. Thinking about all the possibilities, though, Colby knew she would do it if she had to. Let's hope Luce was into Brooke enough that she made her safety her primary concern. A woman like Brooke didn't come along that often and maybe Luce needed to be reminded of that.

Chapter Ten

The lid of the humidor squeaked as it was tossed back without a care. The fragrant aroma of the cigarillos mixed with the sweaty, bloody aromas circling the room. Snipping one end of the small cigar, Luce brought it up to pursed lips. The light from the matched flared as it lit the end. Taking a deep pull on the roll of tobacco, the end flamed. Holding her breath, she could taste the brandy used to soak the petite cigar.

Sloshing the whiskey around in the crystal tumbler, she finally raised it to her lips and swallowed it in one gulp. Luce knew she was beyond drunk, but she was beyond caring, so it worked out. Daylight had faded hours ago, but she refused to turn the lights on. She wanted, no needed, to shroud herself in darkness. Her mood wouldn't permit anything else.

Closing her eyes and puffing on the petite cigar, she thought about why all the men in her life were liars. Her father, JP - his lies had cost him his life. He had killed her mother and Luce had thought it only fair that she return the favor to her father. What had made JP's crime worse, was joining Petrov's crime organization. Flaunting his membership around her clubs as if he was untouchable, just because he was her father. Wrong answer. Frank had betrayed the family when he defected to Petrov. *Let's not forget how he had served up an unsuspecting Sammy's as part of his betrayal.* She was going to find him and make him pay with his life, but not before she tortured the bastard. Oh, she was going to take her time making him suffer. Luce owed it to her grandfather.

Her grandfather - the biggest...what? Disappointment? Liar? What was he? A wife or mistress of ten years that she knew nothing about. It took work to hide something like that. It took time and effort to keep something like a wife concealed from friends and family. *Why would he do it? Why didn't he trust her enough to share something like that with her? Why lie? Why hide? Why?*

Pissed, she staggered to her desk and picked up her personal line. Punching the numbers in, she flung herself against her leather chair and almost slid out of it completely. Luckily, her knees banged against the desk and stopped her from rolling onto the floor. *Yep, I've had had too much to drink, but who the hell cares?*

"Auntie, you knew didn't you?"

"Kaida?"

"Yes, Auntie."

"Kaida have you been drinking?"

"How long did you know, Auntie?"

"Kaida."

"Answer me!" she screamed into the receiver. "How long did you fucking know?"

Without asking what Luce was talking about she answered Luce's question.

"A year, maybe two," Auntie whispered.

"Why?" Luce's thoughts bounced around in her head. "The restaurant was payoff for your silence wasn't it? That's why he left it to you, isn't it?"

"Kaida." Luce heard the steely resolve seep through the phone. "I didn't know your grandfather owned the restaurant until he died. I was just as surprised that he would leave it to me, Kaida."

Luce stumbled to the overturned table, searching for the whiskey bottle. Tipping it upright, she poured the last of the whiskey into her glass and tossed the empty bottle against the wall. It only bounced off and landed at her feet. Her aunt had to have known what the old man was up to, even if they didn't see each other on a regular basis.

"Have you met her?" Luce continued her interrogation.

"I saw her once or twice, but it was maybe over a year ago."

"Why didn't you tell me?"

"He was the Oyabun, Kaida."

"Did he threaten you?"

"He didn't have to. I knew what the rules were."

"So, you being my auntie meant nothing? Being my mother's best friend didn't make you want to say something?"

"There are rules, Kaida. You know that. You may not like it, but you know that. While your grandfather might have been an old fool, he was loyal to your grandmother's memory. He waited a very long time before he finally found someone who made him happy."

"Why didn't he tell me?" Luce gulped her drink down while she waited for an answer.

"I don't know. I honestly don't know, Kaida."

"Ten years, he was with her ten years, Auntie."

"That long, huh?"

"Yep, that long. All that time he hid it from me. All that time he lived a lie. He saw me almost every day and never, ever said a thing to me."

"I'm sorry Kaida, I truly am. I don't know why he

wouldn't say anything. I wish I knew why, but I don't."
The pain in her aunt's voice was evident as she tried to
console Luce. "Is Brooke there with you?"

"No, I told her I needed time to myself."

"Sammy?"

"I fired him tonight. He wouldn't leave me alone,
so I fired him and the rest of the staff."

"Before or after you started drinking?"

"What does it matter? They work for me and I
can fire them whenever the fuck I want."

"I'll come over and —"

"No, no, I don't need anyone to take care of me.
I assure you I can take care of myself. No problem. So
don't worry, Auntie. I'm good."

"Luce, where's your stiletto?

Chapter Eleven

The eerie silence in the garage was starting to freak Brooke out. Sammy had called to tell her he was on his way but that had been almost twenty minutes ago. *Where was he? God, why did she have to go out in search of Luce tonight? Why didn't she sit nicely in her house and wait by the phone like every other girlfriend did when their significant other pushed them away? Who uses the term "significant other" anyway? What kind of term is that for the love of your life? It's so impersonal, so...so...distant.* Her thoughts raced through her fragile mind, as she tried to peek around the truck for the hundredth time tonight. No one had driven past her in over half an hour and she was ready to jump through her skin.

She scrunched further down in the seat thinking it would shield her voice when she dialed Sammy's number again. Her mind was beyond reason and she knew it, but until she was out of danger and looking at Luce, it would focus like a crazed lunatic. Sporadically.

"Ms. Erickson."

"Sammy, where are you?" Brooke pleaded.

"I'm trying to find the garage."

"I'm sorry, maybe I should drive out to the street and wait?"

"No, no. I'll find you. Do you remember anything near the garage? A sign, a car, anything that would help me find you?"

"Umm," Brooke closed her eyes and tried to remember something that would help Sammy. Scratching her head she groaned. "No...wait...there was a one of those small tiny cars. You know those little cars that are popular now?"

"Mini-Coopers?"

"No, those tiny cars. They look like a giant snail. You know?" Brooke knew her description was vague, but for the life of her she couldn't remember the name of the new cars.

"You mean those big two-seaters? Those energy cars?" Sammy wasn't helping.

"Yes. Yes the ones that are super small, but sit higher up?"

"I think I know which one you talking about. Okay, that's a start. Color?"

"Hmm, white I think. Oh, oh, and the garage has one of the entrance lanes blocked off with a huge cement barrier and I think there was some graffiti on it."

"I passed that one. Okay, I'll backtrack and be there in about two minutes."

"Oh thank god, Sammy. I'm so sorry. Please stay on the phone with me until you find me."

"No problem, Ms. Erickson."

"Were you able to lose the people tailing you—I mean me?"

"Yes, ma'am."

Brooke sighed, relieved that help was finally on its way.

"I'm pulling into the garage now, Ms. Erickson."

"I'm on the third floor. You'll see a blue pickup. I'm right next to the wall."

"I see it. Let me go up and turn around. When

I come back down the passenger door will be right in front of your car. Jump in."

"Thank god."

Brooke saw Sammy's sedan pass in front of her. The squeal of his tires signaled his return as his headlights reflected off the car opposite of hers. Grabbing her bag, she bolted from her car and practically bounced into the passenger seat of Sammy's car.

"Thank you, thank you, thank you, Sammy. I was so scared. I didn't know what to do." Brooke felt like crying now that she was finally safe.

"The slick move you pulled back there on the street was pretty good, Ms. Erickson. You lost all of us."

"Sorry."

"No, no, I'm impressed."

Sammy slowed down and inched closer to the garage exit. He eased the nose of the car out of the garage, studied the street on both sides, and moved out farther.

"Do you think they followed you? I mean you lost them, right?"

"Better safe than surprised." Sammy motioned his hand down. "Why don't you duck down, just in case."

"Seriously?"

The look he gave Brooke conveyed his seriousness. His boyish face, while offsetting to some when they found out he was Yakuza, belied his emotion. He was dead serious.

"Fine." Brooke leaned down and waited until she had the all clear from Sammy.

"Take me to the Oyabun's house," she

commanded.

"I don't think that's a good idea."

Sitting straight up, she returned Sammy's no-shit attitude. "If you don't take me I'll call a cab and go over there. So, either you take me, or you'll be following a cab and don't you want to go home to your wife and daughter?"

"Ms. Erickson. I don't think the Oyabun is in the mood for company."

"Sammy."

Throwing his hands up, he acquiesced. "Fine, but I warned you."

"What aren't you telling me?"

"It isn't my place to say, Ms. Erickson."

"Sammy."

Shaking his head, he continued to the Oyabun's house in silence.

"Sammy, did something happen tonight?"

He still didn't look at Brooke and it was starting to piss her off. The Yakuza were loyal beyond measure. To the point that they would self-mutilate to prove their loyalty. Sammy's missing pinky was proof he wouldn't divulge any secrets, not even to her.

"Fine. I'll find out when I get there." Brooke crossed her arms and steamed.

Within minutes Luce's stately home with the carved dragons on the doors looked down at Brooke. It stood dark and ominous with only a few lights outside directing the way to the ornate doors.

"Where is everyone?" Brooke asked.

"She fired everyone earlier, so I told everyone to leave."

"You what?"

"She's the boss, we don't question her orders. I

figured when she came to her senses we would all get called back."

"What am I walking into, Sammy? Tell me that at least." Brooke's pleading question sat between them unanswered. "Fine, I'll find out myself."

Brooke tried to open the door, but it was locked. Turning to Sammy she raised her hands in question and motioned to the door. A minute passed before she frowned at him in disgust.

"Open the door or I'll break a window or something. This is fucking ridiculous." When Sammy hesitated, Brooke reached down and picked up a decorative rock, ready to toss it at the closest window.

"Fine."

Sammy opened the door and swept his hands wide.

"Thank you. You can leave. I'm sure I'll be fine."

"I'm not going anywhere."

"Suit yourself." Brooke pushed past him and into the darkened room. Silence, nothing but darkness and silence. Luce might be in bed. After the day she'd had, Brooke wouldn't blame her. Hell, she would have crawled into bed, pulled the covers over her head and stayed for a week. Tossing her purse on the small table in the foyer, she started for Luce's bedroom. Sammy followed right on her heels. He would be smart enough to give them privacy once she was in the bedroom, otherwise he would face the wrath of his boss. Luce might have said she fired them all, but in reality, Luce was speaking out of grief and not logic.

"Luce?" she said, peeking past the door. "Luce, honey." The blackened room was empty. Luce wasn't sleeping. No one was around. "Hmm."

She moved quickly past Sammy down the long

hallway to Luce's office. The same office where she had interviewed Luce when she was working on the article for the *Financial Times*. That seemed so long ago now. The memory of how Luce had pinned her to the couch during the interview made Brooke blush. *Those were the days.* She smiled.

The door didn't budge when she pushed on it, so she tried the handle. Locked. Frowning, she looked over at Sammy leaning against the wall. All he could do was shrug and offer a repentant smile.

"Luce?" she said softly. "Luce, honey, are you all right?"

Silence. Looking around the frame of the sturdy door, her options were limited: kick the door in, or try and pick the lock. Suddenly she realized she couldn't do either. "Luce, baby. Open the door."

"Sammy," came Luce's stern voice from the other side.

"Yes, Oyabun."

"I told you, you were fired. What the fuck are you doing here?"

"Oyabun, Ms. Erickson said she was coming one way or the other, so I decided to make sure she got here safely."

"Do not tell Luce about what happened tonight. She has enough to worry about. I don't want to add to it," Brooke whispered.

"Sammy, didn't you tell her that I was busy?"

"No, ma'am."

"Why?"

"I didn't want to lie, Oyabun."

Brooke's head swiveled around and clipped him with a glare. "Lie about what?"

Sammy shook his head, he wasn't about to

disclose information that should come from his boss.

"Luce, I know you're taking your grandfather's death hard, baby. Let me help."

Maniacal laughter echoed in the room and seeped out, shocking Brooke. Her gut was right, something was definitely wrong.

"You have no idea, Brooke. You have no idea." Luce slurred her words as her voice rose.

"Open the door Luce or I'll break it down." Brooke hoped she sounded threatening, but she knew she couldn't pull it off.

"Right...Sammy get her ass out of here."

Before Sammy could move, Brooke put her hand on his chest. "Don't touch me, or I'll call the police and have you arrest for assault and we both know that wouldn't go well." Brooke knew she could pay for the veiled threat, but Luce was her priority. The police were always looking for a reason to break open the Yakuza organization and a phone call would do just that.

"Luce, open the door now, or I'll break it down."

More silence.

"Luce."

Nothing.

"God damn it, Luce."

Without thinking, Brooke launched herself against the door and bounced off. Picking herself up off the ground she tried again. This time bringing her foot up she kicked at the door, close to the knob. Nothing. Looking over at Sammy, she raised her eyebrows and tossed a nod at the door.

"Do you mind?"

Before she could say anything, Sammy sighed and whispered, "This is going to cost me my job," he said. He busted through the door, splintering it off its hinges.

Nothing in the room moved. The darkness enveloped what lay inside, struggling to keep the secrets hidden.

ᘯᘯᘯᘯ

Luce was beyond caring as wood fragments flew around her. She puffed on her petite cigar, staring at one of the shadows moving into the room.

"I wouldn't do that if I were you, Brooke." she advised, and then puffed again, blowing smoke rings into the air. At least she hoped she hadn't lost her touch for smoke rings. *Funny the things you think about when you've been drinking.* Just a minute ago she was craving a thick steak. Another whiskey cured that craving.

"Luce, it stinks in here. Let me open a window."

Before she could warn Brooke again, the sound of crunching glass and curses echoed in the room.

"What the fuck happened in here?"

"The coffee table broke." Luce took another puff, pursed her lips and pushed the smoke. "I told you not to come in here. Now get your ass out of here before something happens that we're both going to regret."

The sound of the light switch made Luce shield her eyes from the blinding glare of the overhead lights.

"What the fuck happened in here. Sammy?"

"Get out Brooke," Luce said, trying to stand, but having little luck. She swayed back on to the sofa.

Luce followed Brooke's face as she looked around the room. She had to admit that it resembled more of a disaster area than her pristine office. The coffee table was now chucks of glass. The whiskey bottle had left a hole in the wall where she tossed it and the layer of smoke that hovered over her didn't help.

"What the fuck happened?" Brooke rushed over to Luce and grabbed her arm. "Sammy get me a wash cloth and towel." Brooke picked up Luce's bloodied left forearm. A smattering of blood dotted her slacks and soaked into her white shirt.

Luce yanked her arm back. She stung Brooke with a stare that froze her in her place. "Get. The. Fuck. Out. Brooke. Do you hear me?"

"What have you done to yourself? Did you cut yourself when the table broke? You need medical attention, Luce. This looks bad." Brooke tried to grab Luce's arm again.

"You have no idea."

"What do you mean? Are you hurt somewhere else, Luce?" Brooke scooted closer and tried to touch Luce. Worry replaced the anger she had thrown around when she came in. "Luce what happened, honey?"

Luce felt a warm hand slide down her arm. She wanted to lean into the touch, but couldn't. Part of her wanted to be wrapped in those loving arms. Brooke was always her island when she needed to beach herself mentally. Now though, she wasn't risking a connection that could hurt her. Brooke wasn't her enemy and neither was her grandfather. But knowing he had kept something so important as a wife from her—she couldn't trust anyone at the moment. It wasn't logical, she knew that, but it was how she was built. Learn from life's lessons and you aren't likely to repeat them.

"Get out, Brooke."

"No."

"Get the fuck out, Brooke."

"No. I don't know what's going on, but you don't want to kick me out, Luce. We're…" Tears started to fall. "We're lovers...more than lovers...we're..."

"I don't need you to remind me of what we are. I know."

"Luce, don't shut me out. Let me help. Please." Brooke pleaded as she reached for Luce's hand. Pulling it from Brooke's grasp, Luce looked anywhere but at her crying girlfriend.

"You want to help me, Brooke?"

"Of course, tell me what you need, baby."

"Have you lied to me before, Brooke?"

"What?"

"Have...you...lied...to...me?" Luce reached for her tumbler with a sip of whiskey left in it. "Got any skeleton's in your closet you want to tell me about?"

Chapter Twelve

B rooke's head tried negotiating with her heart. Lies? What was Luce talking about? What had happened in the few hours since she had last seen Luce. She was a hot mess, the likes of which Brooke had never seen before. The cigar smoke was choking, the heat of the room stifling, and the office looked like it had been tossed by a pro.

"What happened tonight, Luce?"

Brooke's girlfriend was more of a stranger right now that the woman she had loved for the past year. She took in the sight of Luce in total, finally landing on the bloody line on her arm. She squirmed a little, seeing the open cut still oozing droplets of blood.

"Why are you avoiding my question, Brooke?" Luce slurred.

"What was the question, my love?" Brooke tried to defuse what was starting to feel like a potential argument. Was Luce purposely trying to pick a fight? Was it the alcohol, or was this the product of something else that happened tonight?

"Hmm, yes you are my love aren't you?"

"I am, so let's talk, baby."

"About?"

"How about what's gotten you so upset." Brooke slid closer to Luce and reached for her hand again, but Luce pulled away. Trying to look Luce in the eyes, she reached up and pulled Luce's chin towards her. "Luce?

What happened?"

A smirk was her answer.

"Luce, what happened?" Brooke tried again, more softly this time.

Pursing her lips together, Luce shook her head, her eyes barely slits. She let out a long sigh, and Brooke thought her resolve was beginning to crumble.

Luce crossed her arms and pierced Brooke with a glare that would wither someone who didn't know her. When Luce didn't flinch or break off the stare, Brooke looked down at her folded hands, clearing her throat. She had buckled ever so slightly under the pressure. Even when Luce was drunk, she was imposing, perhaps even more so. Alcohol seemed to lessen her restraint. She wasn't a mean drunk, she simply lost her logic skills that kept her on an even keel. Emotion ruled her head when she was drunk.

"Sammy you can leave, I'm staying with Luce tonight."

"Sammy you can take Brooke home."

"I'm staying." Brooke said defiantly.

"Sammy..."

Brooke felt sorry for the ping ponging, Sammy. He didn't know which way to turn as each woman gave him orders. Finally, he stood ramrod straight and scowled at Brooke, then Luce.

"Oyabun. You've fired me, so I'm sorry, but I'm going home. Ms. Erickson, I'm sure you know how to call a cab and get home." Bowing at Luce, he continued. "Oyabun, call me when you need me." With that he disappeared down the long hall. A door shutting in the distance signaled his departure.

"Well, this is awkward." Luce slurred.

"Are you going to tell me what happened

tonight?"

"You need to leave."

"I told you, I'm not leaving."

"Brooke, trust me when I say you need to leave, now." Luce stood, suddenly lucid and menacing.

"You don't scare me, Luce." Brooke lied. Luce's sudden demeanor change always signified something bad was about to happen to whoever failed to follow her orders. Luce had never directed that kind of anger towards her, until now. "Let me in, Luce. I want to help, please."

"I've fired everyone tonight, Brooke. You should know when to step off."

Whiskey breath patted the side of her face as Luce stepped closer.

She could barely handle the sight of her own blood, so the coppery smell of someone else's blood made Brooke start to gag. This was like a bad nightmare. No matter how hard Brooke tried, she couldn't figure out what had happened in the last few hours to turn her lover into a monster. Wanting to get to the bottom of whatever was eating at Luce, she threw herself down on the sofa with a plop.

"Since I'm not an employee, you can't fire me, so I guess you'll have to throw me out."

Suddenly, Luce had positioned herself over Brooke. Strong arms bracketed her petite frame and Luce's chest forced her against the couch. "I'm not in the mood for fucking games tonight." Luce said, through grinding teeth. "Now get your happy ass off my sofa, and get the fuck out of my house, or you'll force me to do something we'll both regret."

Brooke felt the start of tears welling up in the face of the ominous threat. Without thinking she reached up and ran her hands along the arms that usually cradled her to sleep at night. Tonight those arms were somehow different.

Luce jerked back from the light caresses and pulled Brooke up from the couch. In one quick movement she was crushed against Luce's chest, her mouth assaulted by the warm taste of whiskey, and a tongue darting in to lay claim to what was Luce's. Holding on for dear life, Brooke pushed herself willingly against the power that buffeted her body. Luce was like an animal trying to devour a meal. Her hands wandered over Brooke's body, scorching every inch she touched. Pulling Brooke's hair, she latched on to Brooke's neck. Her teeth grazing the porcelain column in their haste to find the spot Luce knew would put Brooke on her knees.

Brooke jerked as lips suckled at the pulse hammering beneath them. Threading her fingers into the unruly dark locks of hair, Brooke pushed harder. Her mind stepped out of the way and let her body take control. Reacting on instinct, she slid her hands up underneath Luce's shirt and glided up under Luce's bra. Slipping the bra up and over the generous breasts, she thumbed the already hard nipples and pinched the rough contours of pebbled areolas. Like clockwork, Luce moaned against Brooke's neck.

The familiar rhythm of their bodies acting and reacting took over. Luce slid her hands down Brooke's back and grabbed her ass, pulling her closer to Luce's hard body. Brooke worked her hands down and into Luce's pants. Unbuckling the front with one hand, she slipped the other between Luce's legs suddenly spread wider, and wet lips desperate to be touched. Brooke's finger slipped past slick hair and dipped into the wet confines of Luce's pussy. She added another finger as contractions signaled the impending orgasm Brooke so often recognized when she made love to Luce. It was always quick when Luce was troubled, which wasn't often, but it seemed to be happening with regularity lately.

"Fuck me hard, I've been bad." Luce whispered, her words once again slurred.

Nothing registered in Brooke's brain, the words floated above her as she pushed harder against Luce.

"That's it, baby," Luce whispered.

The rocking of Luce's pussy against her hand anchored her to Luce and Brooke pressed on, harder, faster. Synchronized in their actions, she felt Luce stumble and then arch. A hard spasm rolled off her and Brooke welcomed the intimacy. Her tie to Luce strengthened in a weird sort of sexual dance she had come to recognize was Luce's way of abandoning herself with Brooke.

Falling to the couch, she cradled Luce tightly in her arms, their bond tenuous.

Silence.

She was afraid to say anything, to ask the why, or who had come between them tonight. What had kept Luce from sharing what happened earlier, still kept her at arm's length even now as they lay entwined together on the couch. The tension between them now was worse—even palpable—not like the serene moments they usually shared after making love.

"Luce?"

"Don't. Just go." Luce sat up and straightened her clothing. "I'll call you when I'm ready."

Within an instant, Brooke was sitting on the sofa by herself, suddenly scared Luce might not call.

Chapter Thirteen

She slammed the door, rocking the photographs hanging on the wall of her bedroom. Luce cursed her momentary weakness when it came to Brooke. She should have sent her away and yet she allowed her to see her drunk, bleeding and worse, out of control.

Wiping the steam from the mirror, she barely recognized the reflection that stared back at her. Her eyes had taken on a hard, coldness. Her mind dissected the emotions running through her, and settled on one, betrayal. It was easy enough to figure out, but harder to accept. She ran her fingers over the edge of the dragon tattoo on her left shoulder and breast. Perhaps she needed another tat? *The pain and ink to cover-up the emotional and physical scars of betrayal,* she thought running her finger over the razor sharp cuts on her forearm that barely bled now. She wasn't a cutter, but the sudden release seemed to briefly liberate her demon, *briefly.* But that wasn't something she was willing to do for release every time she had an issue. She had scared herself with the ease she had flicked the stiletto across her skin. The alcohol had been numbing. The loss of inhibition shook her and she realized that maybe deep down inside she was teetering on the edge of evil. Maybe Brooke coming over had been a blessing in disguise. Who knew how much further she would have gone, left to a little more alcohol and time.

Pulling gauze and tape from her cabinet, she bandaged her cut and set about getting dressed for a night out. She needed to release this torment or she would do something more drastic, more impetuous. Sorting through her clothes, she picked out a few black items and threw them on the settee in her walk-in closet. The leather and color reflected her mood. Now if she could get it all back under control.

⚜ ⚜ ⚜ ⚜

Luce felt as if she were being consumed in the overstuffed leather chair. She rolled the crystal tumbler between her hands before she sipped the amber liquid, letting the smoky taste of the whiskey roll around in her mouth before swallowing it. She had consumed more alcohol than usual hoping it would numb her pain. Now she was sitting in Maggie's office waiting for something that would do exactly the opposite and bring her pain into sharp contrast. Instead, she hoped that she could release it by adding more to the equation and excise it from her soul.

Hypnotized by the burning fire, she watched as the flames licked at the logs like a lover licking her conquest into submission. The flames continued their assault on the log and opened the crack wider, exposing the burning embers inside before being devoured by the consuming heat. Her body ached for the same treatment. It had been over a year since she'd been to the Dungeon and suddenly she felt the need for the kind of release Brooke couldn't give her. It wasn't that she didn't trust Brooke to provide the relief she needed, but Luce was always in the dominant position with Brooke. She doubted that she could be flipped and bottom to Brooke's top, assuming Brooke felt comfortable topping her. The dynamics in bondage were hard to negotiate when someone was new to the scene. Luce knew instantly what Brooke wanted and how to give her what she needed, but flip the equation and Brooke...it didn't matter, Luce wasn't ready for that scenario yet. It was a conversation they would have, but not right now, not when Luce was in this frame of mind. She needed a trained professional to fill her needs.

"Luce, sorry I'm late. I got delayed with a client." Maggie leaned down and air kissed each of Luce's cheeks.

"No problem. I was sitting here watching the fire, relaxing."

"So," Maggie said, leaning against her desk. "The usual?"

"Hmm, yes and no." Luce stood and placed her glass on the side table. "I don't know how to say this, Maggie. You've always taken care of me, but I want to respect what Brooke and I have, so I think I should have someone else top me tonight."

For a fraction of a second Maggie couldn't hide her surprise, but she quickly recovered, returning to the cool, clinical Maggie that Luce was used to seeing.

"Well, I'm surprised." Maggie shuffled a few things on her desk.

"It's nothing personal, Maggie. When I see Brooke again, I don't want to have to lie to her when she asks me how it went tonight. She'll be polite and understanding, but I don't want her to think—"

"What, that you see another woman to fulfill something in you that she can't fulfill?" The hint of jealousy in Maggie's voice couldn't be denied.

"No, that there is something going on between you and me," Luce corrected.

"Really, Luce. We've been friends for a long time. I'm surprised that you would let a woman control you like that."

"Really?"

"Well, I mean emotionally." Maggie tried to correct her mistake.

"Really, Maggie?"

"You know what I mean."

"I do, and you and I both know that eventually Brooke and I are going to have a discussion about all of this." Luce gestured to the wall of whips, paddles and leather accoutrements prominently displayed behind Maggie's desk. "She's a comfortable bottom and I like to dominate, but at some point she's going to ask me to flip."

"Luce, are you ready for that?"

"Maggie, that's for me to decide, you had to know this that day would come. Besides, you have other clients who need you. I just need to feel release tonight, but not with you."

"Fine, I'm sure I can find someone who meets your standards." Putting her finger to her lips, she thought for a moment. "I know, Sylvia will be a good match. She's strong, firm and knows how much and where to inflict those lovely little welts."

"A new girl?"

"It's that, or me. Everyone else is taken."

"Fine."

✺✺✺✺✺

The slow, rhythmic strokes assaulted Luce's body.

Swick, swick, swick. She could feel her skin heat up as the leather left its mark on her body. Sylvia had been in consultation with Maggie for half an hour before her session began. She was sure Maggie had advised her on how she wanted the session to go. Usually Luce had her session in the privacy of her home, but somehow she felt as if she was cheating on Brooke to have it there. Consequently, the Dungeon would have to do for this session. She let her mind go blank as the pain took over. Her skin started to prick as the leather did its job of taking control. Someone else was in charge, someone else could control her if even for the briefest of moments. Closing her eyes, she imagined herself getting lost in a fog, evaporating and floating with the cool layer of mist that blanketed the ground. Her body covered someone else's, their fingers gently gliding over her body. The start of a tremor eased through her.

"Would you like me to help you?" a soft voice asked.

The bite of leather against her nipple added to her quaking. Then another, and another. The handle of the whip glided against her lips and she opened her mouth to bite it.

"I'm here to help," the voice whispered against her ear.

"No, please continue," Luce said, pulling at the last of the words before her body started its revolt. Slowly, softly she felt the tears wet the blindfold as she remained ramrod straight. "Harder please."

"Is that how you ask?"

"Please may I have it harder, ma'am?"

"That's better."

The leather lay firmly against her ass, the heat flushed through her body. Each heave of her breathing released more tears. Grinding her teeth she struggled between wanting to come and wanting release. The need of each warred within her. The tremor started again as the leather whip was traded out with a small swatch of leather from a crop. The snap of the contact gave rise to another tremor and then another, and without warning Luce's body shivered in a controlled orgasm. Holding it tightly within, her skin betrayed her when goose bumps ran the length of her taut body.

"No one said you could come, my pet," her dominatrix chided.

"No, ma'am."

"So how shall we handle your indiscretion?"

Luce bowed her head in submission, this is what she needed to pay for her earlier anger with her grandfather. Correlating the two acts would release Luce from her shame of blaming him for dying and her need to excise her pain.

"I don't know, ma'am."

"Well, it's a good thing I do, my pet."

Another firm slap echoed through the room as Luce embraced her pain and hung her head in silent resolve. Once she left tonight, she would be the strong Oyabun she needed to be, piss on everything else.

Chapter Fourteen

Colby thanked the young woman, but not before checking her out, as per her usual habit. She enjoyed beautiful women like some enjoyed a fine wine. Savoring every minute with her, taking in her full body, and then smelling the delightful bouquet.

"Seduction," Colby said, offering her hand to the woman.

"Excuse me?"

"You're perfume, Seduction." Colby smiled and gently cupped both of her hands, turning them over and bringing her wrists up so Colby could take a sniff. Women were predicable, they always dabbed perfume at their wrists, their necks and between...she lowered her hooded gaze and smiled...their breasts.

"Why, yes it is. Thank you for noticing," Stella said, smiling.

The Colby charm was working and if she had more time she would've pulled the assistant closer and whispered something seductive in her ear. Colby would wait while she blushed, and then giggled innocently, and accepted her offer or politely rejected it explaining she was straight.

"It would be hard not to notice. I'm here to see Ms. Erickson. Is she available?"

"I'll check." She waived her hand towards a chair in the waiting area of the lobby. "Please have a seat and I'll see about Ms. Erickson."

"Thank you."

"My pleasure."

Oh no, trust me it's all mine. Colby's gaze followed the tight ass going down the hall.

"Ms. Waters?"

"Water."

"My apologies, Ms. Water."

"Yes." She stood and smoothed down her pressed slacks.

"This way please, Ms. Erickson is in her office."

"Thank you."

Moving further down the hallway, Colby observed a buzzing office with TV monitors running the latest stock market numbers. Computer screens were watched intently, as if they would come to life on their very own if the viewer turned away.

"Please let me know if you need anything," Stella said, pushing the door open slightly.

Colby's lopsided grin and wink were her only answer as she passed the assistant and entered the brightly lit room.

"Stella, can you bring us some tea, with…" Looking at Colby, Brooke continued, "You still take cream and sugar?" Colby nodded. "With cream and sugar."

"Yes, Ms. Erickson."

"Thank you, Stella."

"Ms. Erickson?" Colby was being polite for the assistant. Otherwise, she would have been more familiar with Brooke.

"Agent Water, to what do I owe this honor?" Tossing a gaze over her shoulder, Brooke stood from her desk and closed her computer.

"Ms. Erickson, I apologize for intruding on your

day, but I'm here to ask you a few questions about Luce Potter."

"Really? In what capacity?"

"Capacity?" Colby weaved her eyebrows together and cocked her head. "I don't think I understand the question."

"Cut the bullshit, Colby. Why are you here? I haven't seen you in years and suddenly you show up at my office to ask me questions about Luce Potter. Coincidence? I don't think so. So that only leaves two options, you're following me or you're following Luce. Which is it?"

"Can we sit down?"

"Of course, *where are* my manners?" Brooke said, rather acerbically.

Brooke sat first in an armchair opposite the sofa that faced a huge window offering a stunning view of the city. Colby was impressed, if for nothing else than the status having a corner office conveyed.

"So, are you following me, Colby? Or would you prefer, Agent Water? You *are* still with the DOJ aren't you?" Brooke questioned.

"Treasury."

"Ah, Treasury. My mistake. What do you want, Colby?"

"I wanted to ask you a few questions about Luce Potter." Suddenly, Colby wished she had gone with her gut and left Brooke alone, but the temptation to see her overrode her good judgment. *Professional curiosity, purely professional curiosity,* she told herself.

"I don't have anything to say to you about Luce Potter."

"Really? I knew you liked bad girls, but Luce Potter, Brooke? Really?" Colby couldn't hide the sarcasm in her voice.

"Well she isn't a closeted womanizer. Get to the point, Colby." Brooke sparred back.

"Touché, Brooke. Feel better?"

"Not even close, but give me a few minutes and you'll walk out of here with your pride in tatters if that's what you want. Somehow I suspect you're here for something more than a little verbal sparring."

Colby threw up her hands in surrender and smiled at Brooke. "Look, I know we didn't exactly end on the best of terms, but that was a long time ago and a lot of water has passed under the bridge. I'm trying to do my job. When I saw you with Luce Potter, you became part of my investigation. If you don't want to talk about Luce, I get it. Trust me, I get it."

"That would be a first."

"What?"

"That you would walk away from something without getting what you want." Brooke's accusatory tone pricked at Colby. She knew Colby would try to persuade her otherwise. She had history with Colby and she of all people would know if Colby was playing her.

"I see you haven't let go of that anger yet, have you Brooke?"

"Oh, I've let go of it a long time ago, Colby. I don't have time for people who are less than honest with their feelings or the feelings of others."

"Well, if it's any conciliation, I feel awful about how I ended things."

"How you ended things? I don't remember you ending anything. In fact, what I do remember is you leaving and sending me a text message informing me of the 'changes in your life' and how you needed to 'move forward with your career'. You mean that 'ended things'?"

"Yeah, I guess I don't quite remember it that way."

"No. I bet you don't." Brooke's anger made Colby decide that she'd better change the subject.

Colby pulled a note pad from her blazer. Leafing through the pages she went back and forth between two pages before settling on one. Clearing her throat, she locked eyes with Brooke and cleared her throat one more time before starting.

"I'm sorry to hear about the death of your cameraman in Eastern Europe. Can you tell me what you were doing there?" Colby patted her chest searching for a pen. "You wouldn't hap—"

"Here," Brooke said, tossing a pen in Colby's direction.

"Thanks."

"So you want to know about my experience in Eastern Europe, huh?"

"It's a start." Colby scribbled on the pad and gave Brooke a lopsided smile. "Seems it's dry. Do you have another?"

"Why am I not surprised?" Brooke passed another pen.

"What's that supposed to mean?"

"Nothing,"

"So, let's start this again. What were you doing in Eastern Europe?"

"I was an investigative reporter. I was investigating," Brooke said sarcastically.

"No shit. Can you be a bit more specific?"

"What is this about Colby?"

"I'm obviously doing an investigation of my

own, Brooke."

"Let's keep this professional, call me Ms. Erickson."

The room suddenly went into a deep freeze as Brooke stood when Stella knocked on the door. Taking the tray, she placed it on the coffee table and started to fix Colby's tea without thinking. "Did you say you still take creamer with your tea?"

"Yes, thank you."

Brooke didn't have to turn around to know Stella still stood at the door watching them. "Thank you Stella, that will be all."

"Yes, Ms. Erickson." Stella smiled at Colby and winked before leaving.

"Don't even think about it, Colby. I don't know what you said to my office assistant, but she's straight."

"Are you sure about that? She seemed pretty interested earlier."

Brooke rolled her eyes and shook her head. Would Colby's arrogance never surprise her? Probably not.

Studying Colby over the rim of her porcelain cup, it was clear life had been good to Colby. It hadn't lived her as much as she had lived it to the fullest. She wondered why all of a sudden her past would walk in her door. Knowing Colby it was strictly work related, which was fine with her. Maybe.

"So how long have you and Luce Potter been dating?"

"Dating? Or fucking, Colby? Isn't that what you really want to ask?"

"No, if I wanted to know how long you've been *fucking*, I would ask that—"

"But you don't get to ask me that. It's none of

your business."

"Does Ms. Potter know your ex is a fed?"

Brooke casually studied Colby, trying to figure out what Colby's game was this time. She hadn't thought about Colby in almost two years and it didn't cross her mind to mention her to Luce, at least not until now. What would Luce think? Would she think Brooke had deliberately withheld the fact that her ex was a federal agent for the Treasury? What would Luce say if she found out?

"That isn't any of your business, Agent Water."

"I take it that's a no. So when you're in post-coital euphoria you don't talk about your pasts? I find that hard to believe, Brookie," Colby said, stirring her now lukewarm tea.

"Why is it so hard to believe that we haven't talked about you, Colby? Are you so self-absorbed that you think the world revolves around you, that somehow we would spend our nights discussing ex's?"

"Even the truth by omission is a lie, Brooke."

"What the fuck do you want, Agent Water?"

"I told you I'm performing an investigation. So, the sooner you answer my questions the sooner I'm out of your hair." Colby went back to her pad and tried again. "So can you tell me what you were doing in Europe when your cameraman was shot?"

"I was working on a story."

"About?"

"The Russian mafia and their *enterprises*," Brooke said, making air quotes.

"Can you tell me what happened?" Colby's tone had changed from her casual carefree to a more cold matter-of-fact tone. "To the best of your recollection."

Brooke closed her eyes as a cold chill fingered

it's away throughout her body. She had tried her best to forget Mike's death, but the memories raged back easily enough. Her throat tightened and she felt like she was going to be sick any moment. Sipping her tea, she cleared her throat and tried to speak but nothing came out.

"It's okay, take your time," Colby said reassuringly.

"We were meeting an informant who had promised to give us information about one particular crime boss."

"Petrov?"

Brooke furrowed her eyebrows together. How could Colby know whom she was investigating?

"How do you know about Petrov?"

"An educated guess."

"No such thing."

"What kind of lead where you working on?"

"I was following the money. He has business dealing all over Russia and the US, and I was working on a line that was floated to me through an informant."

"Did you get the information from that informant?"

"No."

"What can you tell me about Petrov?"

"I'm sure that you know more than I do."

"Maybe, maybe not," Colby reached for the teapot. "Do you mind?"

"Not at all, please make yourself at home."

Brooke waited as Colby topped off her teacup. She was damned if she would wait on the interloper again. She definitely didn't want to give her ex the wrong idea or let her feel any more comfortable than she clearly was already feeling.

"So, what did you find out in Russia that would cost your cameraman his life, Brooke?"

The stab hit her directly in her heart. She hadn't thought about how her investigation might have cost Mike his life. She had chalked it up to the evil Petrov could rain down on anyone who took too much of an interest in his business. Her eyes welled up thinking about the scared look on Mike's face as he realized he'd been shot. She remembered seeing blood coat his hand as he touched his chest and then looked at her. Then suddenly she was pulled up and pushed towards a train, by what she assumed was her informant.

"I watched the girls he snatched up and brought to the US to work in the skin trade. I followed the money. It all pointed back to him, in a roundabout way."

"How?"

"He has a shipping business, so that makes it easier to bring the girls in. Once here they go to work in a variety of business. They're here without papers, family or money. So they do what they're told. They don't have a choice. He also dabbles in real estate, laundering his money that way." Brooke sipped the cold tea and grimaced. She hated cold tea, but she wasn't about to pour another piping hot cup and give Colby the idea she was settling in for a long discussion. That was her former life and she had successfully moved on, until now.

"Did you know Luce hangs out at a place called the Dungeon?"

The quick U-turn practically gave Brooke whiplash. "Yes."

"Do you know what they do at that place?"

"Yes."

"Interesting, I didn't know you were into that kind of stuff, Brooke?"

"Are we talking about my love life now, or are we still talking about the Dungeon? I thought you were interested in finding out more information on the Russians."

"Are you denying it?"

"Denying what, Colby?"

"Well if Luce is into kink, I find it hard to believe that she doesn't bring that home to your bedroom."

Brooke wasn't about to let Colby's calm demeanor shake her. She knew she was taking a cheap shot, but she didn't care if Colby imagined Brooke taking part in the things she had seen going on at the Dungeon. Even if it made Colby overheat.

"Who said she doesn't?"

Colby face was beet red now and that Brooke all but confirmed her question. She was sure Colby's mind buzzed with all the questions she wanted to ask.

"Is that what you really came here to ask me, Agent Water? To confirm your suspicions about my love life?"

"My job is to investigate. I'm sure you can appreciate my thoroughness. It used to be one of the qualities you liked about me." Colby raised her eyebrows and smiled. "If my memory serves me right."

"Are we done here?"

"Not yet. Give me a few more minutes and I'll be out of your hair."

"Somehow I doubt that."

Colby shrugged and continued. "Why did you stop your investigation? Ms. Potter?"

"Are you suggesting that I dropped my investigation because it led to Luce?"

"Honestly?"

"Uh-huh."

"I think that the trail led to Luce Potter and you two..."

"What, Colby? Are you insinuating that I was less than ethical?"

"Not quite. What I'm saying is that maybe you..." Colby shrugged and held her hands wide. "You became infatuated with Ms. Potter. I hear power is a strong aphrodisiac. Maybe you succumbed to her charms. She is quite easy on the eyes."

"Get out," Brooke stood, yelling. "Now you've gone too far."

Colby shook her head and looked up at the steaming Brooke. "These are questions someone is going to ask, Brooke. It can either be me or another agent. Maybe you'd feel more comfortable if I asked Ms. Potter?"

"Is that a threat?" Brooke stood over Colby, her breath raining down on the agent. "If you think you're going to blackmail me or something, you've got another thing coming Agent Water."

"I'm not threatening. I need to do my job and unfortunately, you find yourself right in the middle of my investigation. I can't help that, Brooke. It isn't my fault."

"No, but if you think that somehow I'm going to crumble because you want to out yourself to my girlfriend, think again." Brooke didn't move. "I'm not that same Brooke you knew the last time you saw me, Colby. I don't take threats lightly anymore."

"Are *you* threatening *me*?"

"Not at all. I'm impressing upon you that you aren't going to coerce me into talking to you. So go out and do your job. Investigate to your heart's content, but we are done here."

Brooke threw open the door and stalked out, leaving Colby alone in the office.

"Stella, please see my guest out," she said, moving down the hall.

❧ ❧ ❧ ❧

Brooke found the first door she could exit from and walked into a puff of smoke. *Great, the smoker's patio.* Trying to swish the smoke away she coughed and turned towards the smoker.

"John, I thought you were quitting?" Brooke said.

"I am. Doesn't it look like it?" He blew a smoke ring, then flicked an ash.

"Can I have a puff?"

"You don't smoke, Brooke."

"I do right now." She reached for the extended cigarette. "Fucking, bitch."

"Oooh, did you have a fight with Luce?" John took the smoldering stump back and pulled a long drag.

"I wish."

"Anything you want to talk about?"

John had offered her a job when she left the newspaper after Mike's death. He had told her that talent like hers needed to get back on the horse and start fresh. His faith in her abilities to write a good story kept her from falling into a deeper depression. In fact, he had put her on the Luce Potter story and she owed him a thank you for it.

Brooke held the smoke tightly and with a quick exhale she forced it and the memories of Mike out of her. Colby had gotten to her on so many levels. Showing up out of the blue, had both unsettled her and pissed her off. Their parting had been rushed, like their relationship. It blazed fast and bright and then like a super-nova, it burned itself out with barely a text message from Colby saying she'd been transferred and had to leave that night for a new assignment. Was it true? Brooke would never know.

"I had a visit from an ex, who just happens to be a federal agent."

"Oh."

"Yeah, oh."

"Does Luce know?"

"About?"

"Your ex being a fed."

Colby had just thrown the biggest monkey wrench in her relationship, intended or not. Now, she had to decide whether to tell Luce about Colby or let it ride and see what happened.

"Fuck," she said. She scrubbed her face with her hands. What *was* she going to do?

"You don't want Luce to find this out on her own, Brooke. She'll think you were hiding it for a reason. You aren't *are* you?"

"No, John, I'm not hiding anything."

"Good, then you don't have any reason not to tell Luce."

"Awe, but I do. Seems Colby is investigating the Russians and Luce. She was following us at the funeral and god-knows where else."

"No shit?"

"No shit. I don't know how to tell Luce that my *ex*-girlfriend is a federal agent and she's been following us."

"Well, I'm your boss, so take my advice for what you paid for it. Tell her before she finds out another way. Then she *will* question your reasons for keeping it from her.

A slight chill fingered its way down Brooke's spine. She knew John was right, but what was the *right* way to break the news to your Yakuza girlfriend, who might venture over the line every once in a while, that your ex is a federal agent interested in your business dealings?

᰽᰽᰽᰽

Colby sat in her car, scribbling furiously. She wanted to make sure she remembered everything Brooke had said, which on the surface wasn't much, but it was more about what she didn't say that sparked an avalanche of questions for Colby. She smiled. Brooke looked good. She still had a killer body that looked like it needed a professional's touch, at least her professional touch. What was she saying? Brooke was with one of the most influential and dangerous woman in business and not on the open market. Colby had a hard time keeping her eyes on her pad and not on Brooke's rock hard body. Colby couldn't put her finger on it, but Brooke had changed. She had an edgy exterior to her now and Colby had to wonder if it was from her experiences in Eastern Europe, or was it being with Luce Potter. Luce lived on the fine line between law-abiding citizen and cold, calculating killer, which all had to have an effect on Brooke.

Women like Luce attracted women and men with their self-assured confidence and power. She wasn't kidding when she told Brooke power was a heady aphrodisiac. She had seen women throw their whole life away to be with a charismatic, sleaze-bag politician. Hell, she had seen it happen within her own organization. Men and women, selling each other out to get in good with the power-elite. Pathetic. Colby liked her women the old-fashion way, available, sexy and needy and if she could fill that need, all the better.

Looking back at the Financial Times building, she wondered if Brooke would tell Luce about her. Chances were Brooke was panicking trying to decide if she should or shouldn't. Luce was her next stop, but not before she went back to her office and prepared for her visit. Well, if Brooke didn't do it, it wasn't her fault if she ended up outing herself to Luce Potter.

Chapter Fifteen

Luce stretched and winced as the marks on her back reminded her of her visit to the Dungeon last night. She had asked for more and now she was paying the price, but her soul felt lightened. She couldn't explain it to the average person, and she wouldn't need to if someone was in the scene, but her head matched where her heart was now. Pulling her watch off the nightstand, she noted the time and calculated how much more she needed to get ready for a meeting with her crew. She planned to institute new changes at some of her businesses and they were sure to raise a few eyebrows. She didn't care, now that her grandfather was gone she only had herself to answer to. Luce was ready to leap ahead financially. She also intended to make a concerted effort deal with Petrov and Frankie. Frank had to pay for his deceit, and Petrov would pay for doing business in her city against her friendly advice. He was about to find out how ruthless Luce could be.

Brooke.

She suddenly realized Brooke wasn't at the house. They had been almost inseparable in the last year, but last night Luce had told Brooke she needed some space. She said she would call her when she was ready, but Luce wasn't ready and didn't know when she would be. Deception was a skill that cut deep and she was still bleeding from the gash her grandfather had given her. What did he think she would think about his *mistress*? Did he think she would welcome her with open arms? Brooke deserved better that the treatment Luce had put her through.

"Oyabun?"

"Yes?" Luce pulled at the French cuff of her shirt. Her immaculate look belied the turmoil boiling just underneath. "Come in."

Sammy peeked around the door, bowing as he entered her private sitting room. He kept his gaze down and slowly moved towards her, his outstretched hand holding an envelope.

"I'm sorry to bother you, but this came by special messenger. I figured it was important."

"How's your wife, Sammy?" Luce took the envelope and turned it over to inspect it.

"My wife?"

"Yes, Sammy, the woman carrying your child. I assume she's your wife, am I mistaken?" It wasn't uncommon in Japanese culture for men to have a mistress. Especially, handsome, young Yakuza men. They attracted women who loved the *bad boy*, dangerous image. Luce frowned upon the men, or women, straying if they were married. If they could cheat on their wives and lie about it, what would prevent them from doing the same in their business life? She needed ethical, hard-working Yakuza, not slimy, double dealing lowlifes.

"Yes, Oyabun." He bowed his head. "She's well."

"Is it a boy or girl?"

"We don't know yet."

"With all this new technology, you don't know?" Luce slapped him on the back and laughed. "I would think your wife would want to know so she could get that nursery she showed me in order."

"We didn't want to know. We, she, wants to be surprised."

"Hmm." Luce wanted children, but she wasn't sure her lifestyle would allow it. She and Brooke had talked about family often and both were very open about children. They wanted them.

"Will there be anything else, Oyabun?"

"No, thank you, Sammy. I'll be ready to do in a few minutes," she said, effectively dismissing him.

Studying the slim envelope, Luce looked for a return address and didn't see one. Grabbing her stiletto from her desk, she used it to slice the envelope open. Squeezing the sides, she peered inside, finding only a small note card. Tilting it, she slid it onto her palm and twisted her head to read the handwritten note.

Oyabun,

I use that term loosely. Now that your grandfather is dead, you're next. Everything you value will be taken from you, including that cute little reporter you love.

Frank

Well that's original, a death threat from the walking dead, Luce thought, examining the writing once again. Frank was working a tad too hard to push her buttons, but his threat against Brooke, now that earned him the top spot on her list of things-to-do.

"Sammy," Luce bellowed.

"Yes, Oyabun."

"I want you to call the delivery company and find out how they got this letter." Luce tossed it at Sammy in disgust.

"More bad news?"

"Naw, find out how they got the letter and a description of the person who sent it."

Sammy picked up the pieces of paper and read the note card. "I'm sorry, Oyabun. I thought he would slither away, but I guess now that your grandfather is dead, he's getting gutsy. Word on the street is he's been seen around town, throwing around money. I think he's trying to recruit a few members of the organization for the Russians, or maybe himself."

"Interesting. Well, he'll find it hard to recruit anyone from our family, but I have enemies, so maybe they'll join his candy-ass. It will come with a price though. Is someone still watching Brooke? I don't want her without protection and I don't want her around me, for her own safety. She won't understand, but that's the way it has to be," Luce said. She waved her hand at the door, directing Sammy to take his leave.

"What should I tell her if she calls again?"

"Tell her it isn't a good time and I'll call her back later."

"But she—"

"Sammy, just do as you're told. I want two people on this Frank thing. I don't want to be taken by surprise and I want him found."

"Yes, Oyabun." Sammy bowed and backed out of the door.

Luce rubbed her cold hands together, trying to warm them. She'd been chilled since the funeral. The only warmth she felt now were the lash marks that rubbed against her silk underwear. She absently-mindedly rubbed her thumb against the long scar that ran along the base of her palm. An accident that had a profound impact on her, without her knowing it at the time.

"*Kaida, you must respect the cold deadly slice of the steel,*" *her grandfather said, applying a gauze pad to the bleeding skin.* "*The gun sounds its impending death, the blade warns no one. Both deadly, but only one kills quietly.*"

"*I didn't realize how sharp the knife was, grandfather. Besides, I just pushed the button and it happened so fast,*" *Luce held back tears, not waiting to show weakness in front of her grandfather.*

"*Oh Kaida, you are so rambunctious. How did you get this?*" *He picked up the stiletto by the handle showing her the blood that ran down the edge.*

"*I asked Frank to get it for me,*" *she said, bowing her head.* "*It isn't his fault. I told him I had your permission, grandfather.*"

"*So, you've paid for your lie. For every action there is always a reaction. Sometimes it happens quickly and sometimes it is a dangerous reaction. Do you not agree?*" *He picked up her chin, stared into her green eyes and then studied the bleeding wound.* "*I think you're going to need stitches.*"

"*No, not stitches.*" *Luce pulled her hand away.*

"*Yes little dragon. The price you pay for handling something you weren't ready for.*"

Studying the scar, she recalled she'd often had to learn her lessons the hard way when she was young. Now though, Frank was going to learn his lesson the hard way. No one messed with Luce and those around her. No one. Grabbing the stiletto, she flipped it in the air a couple of times, before catching it and putting it in her inside pocket. Frank's death would be silent, she would watch his face as she pressed the tip into his chest and watch his life slip away, quietly.

Chapter Sixteen

M s. Potter, I'm sorry to interrupt—" Luce pressed a button on her phone, "Then don't, Ms. Wentworth."

Luce had moved Audrey Wentworth from employment at her home to her office. Brooke hadn't insisted, but Luce knew that once they were seeing each other on a regular basis, Audrey and her work outfit— or lack of one—would put her and Brooke into an uncomfortable position. Therefore, the easiest solution was a transfer within the organization. Besides, Luce could require different working conditions for Audrey, if she wanted.

"...but she says she has an appointment."

"Who is *she*?"

"Lucrecia Holtz," another voice blurted out.

"Audrey, send the persistent Ms. Holtz in please, then cancel my appointments until lunch."

"I only have you down for one appointment with Sasha."

"Call her and reschedule for this afternoon." She wanting to go over some new security plans now that Frank had made his intentions known, but it could wait. She was thinking of restructuring a few of her clubs and wanted to go through the beefed up security plan with Sasha. Sasha was her left hand, while Sammy was her right and she was starting to find both valuable assets to her new business model.

Pulled out of her thoughts when the door opened, she watched as a tall blonde walked towards her desk smiling, followed by her assistant, Audrey Wentworth.

"Ms. Potter, I thought you might want to see this immediately. I was going through the cards that came with the flowers from the funeral and it was mixed in with them." Audrey nervously laid the card face down.

"Thank you, Ms. Wentworth. Let me know when the thank-you cards are finished and I'll sign them."

"Yes, ma'am."

Luce clenched her jaw as she read the card.

Kaida,

Your grandfather can't protect you know. I'll take what you love one digit at a time.

Frank

"Bad news?"

"I'm sorry?"

"Well, from the look on your face, it must be bad news."

"And you are?" Luce tucked the card into the top drawer of her desk.

"Ms. Holtz, Ms. Potter. I'm so glad you remembered we had a meeting. It's a pleasure to meet you."

Luce studied the self-assured, lanky woman. The razor sharp creases of her business suit screamed anal-retentive, her Dr. Martens screamed dyke and her light makeup confused Luce. She took in the whole picture, surprised when the woman took the seat opposite her without invitation. Then a hint of recognition sliced through Luce.

"But we don't have a meeting, do we, Ms. Hotlz? I would remember someone as attractive as you. *Please* have a seat. I applaud your tenacity, so why don't we get to the point. What can I do for you?"

"Please call me Lucy, all my friends do. Oh Luce, Lucy, interesting don't you think? I don't believe in coincidences, so there must be something to our names being so close. I mean it was meant to be, you know?"

Luce shook her head at the babbling coming from clearly an air-head in a position of power, or maybe she wanted Luce to think she was stupid. The absence of a handshake kept Luce in her seat, the weight of her gun poking her back a reminder that she should've worn her shoulder holster instead or stuffed it into the top drawer of her desk. With Frank out there stalking her, she never went without a personal firearm or a weapon of some sort. Feeling its securely strapped to her reminded her of a time when seeing the stiletto had freaked out Brooke, making her even more nervous when Luce had slipped it out and tossed it open at the wall in frustration. Her excuse - it was better to let that fly than the person she was angry with. Leaning forward she re-positioned herself in her chair. She never let her guard down, and something about this woman made her uneasy. If something went sideways she wouldn't be caught by surprise.

"You're right, I didn't have an appointment. Every time I tried to make one, your very efficient assistant informs me that you are booked solid. I decided to take a chance and see if you would see me."

"Gutsy, Ms. Holtz."

"Please, Lucy."

"Yes, *Lucy*." Since you didn't have an appointment, and our names seem to match so closely, what can I do for you?"

"Honestly?"

"Yes, let's go ahead and lay our cards on the table, time is wasting."

"Well?"

Luce noticed how Lucy made a point of letting her gaze run up and down her body and then back to her lips before she licked her own. Luce knew when a woman was trying to play her and this woman was doing her best. "I could think of a few things, but perhaps another time."

Luce searched *Lucy's* face looking for a lie. She found nothing except a smile that didn't reach her eyes, perfect teeth and penetrating blue eyes. There was that pang of recognition again. She felt like she knew the woman from somewhere but she couldn't place where. She was great with faces, names not so much, but she was certain she had seen this woman recently.

"Well, now you have me, so again, what can I do for you?"

"I'm working for a charity that helps women get re-established in the work force." The woman reached inside her leather portfolio and pulled out a business card. She handed it to Luce. "As you've probably noticed, the economy is in the tank and women have been hit hardest. We're looking for a few women speakers for a fundraising dinner and your name was floated as a possible guest speaker."

"Really, who would float my name?" Luce cast Lucy a dubious glance. The recognition flashed in Luce's mind. This was the woman seated in a car with another person outside the Yoshida mausoleum when she and Brooke were at her grandfather's internment. She hadn't gotten a good look, but enough of one to place the blonde, slender features of *Lucy*. Was she a plain-clothes police officer, a fed, or something more menacing?

"I was recently at a charity dinner that you attended. I doubt you would remember me, but I did notice you and that very attractive woman on your arm. I saw her in the bathroom, you know how we women like to chat in the powder room. Well, anyway I was commenting about her date, *you*." *Lucy* smoothed out the lines on her slacks. Luce knew the diversion well, don't make eye contact and you'll be able to carry the lie further. "We spoke for a brief moment and I told her about my foundation... the long and short of it was that she thought you might be able to help. By the way, she is beautiful and can hold a conversation. That's quite rare these days."

"Thank you, I'll pass the compliment on to my dinner companion from that evening."

"Oh, she isn't your girlfriend? I'm sorry I just assumed the way you interacted you were involved. See what happens when one assumes?" Now *Lucy's* smile reached her eyes.

"Yes, one must be careful when they are stalking their future charity requests." Luce answered back.

"What? Me stalking? Oh absolutely, I know what I want and I'm not afraid to go after it. Don't you love the chase? I mean isn't that were the fun is for those of us who know exactly what we want?"

"I guess that depends..."

"On?"

"What you get at the end of the chase." Luce bantered back sending *Lucy* a smoldering look that should set her on fire. Luce could see a blush rush across *Lucy's* chest and then up her neck, spreading to her rosy cheeks.

"I can see your bad girl reputation is well deserved, Ms. Potter. So, is that beautiful little number I saw on your arm your girlfriend?"

"Does it matter?"

"I supposed not, what *honey* doesn't know won't hurt her now will it?"

Luce studied the woman and wondered where she was going with this line of banter. If she was working for a charity she was definitely going about it all wrong, but then Luce had a pretty good idea who the woman sitting in front of her was. If this agent was actually hitting on her that lent a whole new twist to the lengths the feds were taking to harass her.

Moving to the front of the desk, Luce reached for her hand and lightly caressed it, remembering the saying "*keep your friends close, but your enemies closer*". She knew she was assuming the control position looking down at *Lucy*. She always liked exerting her dominance on people, it made her feel in control and kept her visitor at bay. She let her thumb caress the back of the woman's hand as her gaze locked with *Lucy's*.

"Ms. Holtz, why don't we get back to the point of your visit, or would you like to talk about something else?"

"Oh, I think you've got my full attention, Ms. Potter."

"I hope so. It would be a shame to waste all this time talking about charity when we could be talking about something more interesting." Luce let the innuendo hang, waiting for her to take the bait. She was good at this and when *Lucy* didn't back down or at least drop her gaze she knew *Lucy* was measuring up. She suspected the woman was a player. The way she undressed Luce earlier with her eyes was a dead giveaway. Luce knew the competition in an instant. No, this wasn't a shrinking violet in any way.

"I would love to sit here and get to know you better," Luce took her seat again. "But I have a meeting I need to get to, perhaps another day, Ms. Holtz."

"Why don't I give you my personal number and if you change your mind you can give me a call. I'd be happy to discuss *anything* with you further if it would help you decide in our favor." Looking in her portfolio, and then patting her chest as if looking for a pen she said, "it seems I don't have a pen, might I borrow yours?"

"Of course," Luce said, opening an ornate box on her desk and handing the woman a filigreed pen.

"Wow, this is beautiful," *Lucy* said, turning the dragon pen with jade eyes over in her hand.

"It's a custom pen I have made. It's sort of an inside joke."

"It's beautiful."

Jotting her number on the back of the card, *Lucy* passed it to Luce with the pen.

"Please keep the pen," She studied the card and then fanned it against her fingers. This was going to be interesting, whoever Ms. Holtz, or whatever her name, was going to be the mouse to Luce's cat if she had anything to say. "It would be impolite in my culture to refuse a gift once it is offered. So I must insist since you can appreciate its beauty." Luce smiled.

"Well, if you insist. It is beautiful."

"It's a fine writing instrument and should give you years of writing *pleasure*. The cartridge is brand new so it should last for a while." Luce extended her hand. "It was a pleasure meeting you, Ms. Holtz. If I change my mind you'll be the first to know."

"Thank you for not kicking me out, especially since I stretched the truth a bit about having an appointment."

Luce pinched her fingers together. "Just a little."

"Yes, well thank you again for your time, Ms. Potter. I hope I didn't offend you with the fun little banter."

"Not at all. Have a good afternoon, Ms. Holtz."

Closing the door behind the imposter, Luce practically ran to her desk and phoned Lynn.

"Lynn, there is a woman coming down in the elevator. Five foot eight, blonde, wearing a grey suit and sensible shoes. I want you to follow her, but not to close. I think she's a cop or a fed. We'll know more when I activate the pen she took."

"I see her now, Ms. Potter."

"Good, let me know where she goes today, where she lives and if she meets anyone."

"Yes ma'am."

Luce ran her fingers over the ornate box that held her 'special' pens. These were 'gifts' she usually gave to those whom she wanted to keep track of, knowing their shelf life was most often limited. People were careless with their writing materials, but sometimes they stayed around long enough to impart valuable information on the subject using it. No one ever imagined that the ornate dragon with the jade eyes was in fact a voice activated, wireless transmitter catching everything they said.

"Ms. Wentworth, can you call Sasha and put her through when you have her?"

"Of course Ms. Potter. Anything else?"

Hmm, was there anything else Audrey could do for her? It had been a while since she had seen Audrey. What was she thinking? She was involved with Brooke, so the answer was obvious.

"No, Audrey that will be all."

☙ ☙ ☙ ☙

Colby took a deep breath and tried to steady herself. She had been prepared to be rebuffed by Luce Potter, instead Luce had practically pounced on her. She was still gripping the pen Luce had given her. Turning it over in her sweating hands, she studied the ornate instrument. Her phone buzzed in her pocket just as she reached the bottom floor.

"Agent Water."

"Hey, Water. I got some information I think you might find interesting."

"Okay," Colby said, sliding the pen inside her blazer.

"It seems my confidential informant told me that Luce Potter is opening three VIP men's clubs. She's looking for hot, young, dancers that can keep a secret."

"Interesting, is she converting her clubs or is she opening new ones?"

"New ones. Seems she's setting them up as invitation only clubs."

"We need to get an agent inside. Dancer, security, bartender, shit I'll take someone who can clean toilets." Colby nodded at a woman behind the security desk who had been watching her like a hawk. *Nice looking!*

"Well maybe you can apply to be one of the dancers. I'd pay to see that."

"Ha, ha, that isn't going to happen. Besides,

Potter has already met me, as Lucy Holtz, Foundation member for *Women Helping Women*."

"Are you still using that old ploy? Geez you need a new gig, Water."

"Hey, why change what works? Besides I'm sure we have a few agents that can go undercover and fit in nicely. I pull their files and interview them. Let me know when and where to send them. I don't want any screw-ups on this, Scarr. Hear me?"

"Loud and clear."

"Okay, so what are you going to do about your CI?"

"What do you mean?"

"I don't want any loose ends that could blow us out of the water. Get my meaning?"

"I'll put him on a bus with a one way ticket, a few bucks and a forty. That should keep him out of our hair for a while."

"And you're going to keep your eye out for him, just in case, right?"

Chapter Seventeen

Brooke picked up her cell phone for the fifth time in as many hours, checking and rechecking to make sure it was on. Still there was no missed call from Luce. It had been days since she'd seen Luce, bleeding, drunk and vengeful. Should she call? If she did, what would she say to Luce? Clearly she would voice the obvious - why hadn't she called?

Suddenly, she had a yearning for Korean food. If Luce talked to anyone now, it would be her auntie at the restaurant and Brooke wasn't a stranger anymore, she was family, wasn't she? No matter, auntie was the only family Luce had left.

Sliding out her door, hoping to miss Stella and her hundreds of questions, she walked right into her.

"Hey, where are you off to? You have a meeting at one thirty with John." Stella resettled the folders she had practically dropped when Brooke smashed into her.

"Oh, lunch. Hmm, tell John I might be a tad late." Brooke said, rushing past her assistant.

"Want some company?"

"No, I've got some work to do. It's a working lunch. No time for distractions." Brooke punched the elevator, wishing it would hurry. "Maybe next time."

Brooke threw herself into her Mercedes and slumped against the seat. Maybe this was a huge mistake. Maybe she should wait patiently by the phone until Luce called. Mentally shaking herself she thought about what she had said. What had happened to the strong, independent Brooke Erickson? The woman who challenged the status-quo? Somewhere she had lost sight of that woman; she was a mere figment of Brooke's imagination ever since she started dating Luce. Never one to turn her power over to another, here she was fretting over whether Luce Potter would call her, make her world start turning again, right it back on its axis. Fuck, who had she become? A slow simmer was turning into a full boil as Brooke retraced her steps leading her into Luce's life. Granted Luce was going through a tough patch and all, but clearly Luce didn't want Brooke to be a supportive girlfriend, someone she could lean on. No, she was patently self-sufficient and quite capable of handling her own shit. If they weren't a couple anymore Luce owed her an explanation, but Brooke wanted answers and maybe those answers could be found at a certain Korean restaurant, with a certain auntie who loved to talk.

⊰⊱⊰⊱

Darkness veiled the activities of those inside the restaurant as Brooke knocked on the glass door. A flash of white and a few whispers could be heard in the background.

"Brooke, what are you doing here?"

"Why is the restaurant closed, Auntie?"

"We had a private party earlier. Big mess. Come, come in, I make you something to eat. You're skinny as an alley cat."

"Thanks, I think," Brooke said, waiting by the door as her eyes adjusted to the semi-darkness.

"Oh, I don't mean anything by the cat remark. Come on, I put you in Kaida's favorite booth," Auntie said, pulling Brooke's hand.

Gazing around the room, the tables held the last vestiges of assorted kimchis, meat, rice and Soju bottles. *It must have been some party*, Brooke thought, noticing the karaoke machine still running. It's songs projected on the make shift screen covering a booth in the back.

"Sit, I'll bring something to drink. What you want?"

"Oh, Auntie don't go to any trouble."

"Trouble? This a restaurant. Food and drink are my business. So what you want?" Auntie stared at Brooke waiting for her answer. "Oh, I'll bring you something," she muttered, heading for the kitchen. "Damn skinny girls barely eat enough to keep my big toe moving. Bah."

Brooke smiled at the accusation. Auntie had a way with the English language that was endearing, if not humorous to the uninitiated.

A young girl brought out an assortment of kimchis, and arranged them in circular pattern in the center of the table and then bowed, leaving Brooke to stare at the arrangement. Anything red, Brooke knew meant hot and would screw with her stomach, so she picked at the potato and fishes that were mixed in with the other samplings. Spearing a cucumber, she barely had it in her mouth when Auntie set down a tall order of Soju. Staring at the sweating bottle, she cringed remembering the last time she had the high-octane drink. Luce had goaded her into "just tasting" the "Korean national treasure" as she referred to it. The hangover had been brutal. Worse, she had puked all over Luce's loafers before making it into the house.

"So, how you been, Brooke?"

"Good," Brooke said, pushing the side dishes around with her chopsticks. "Have you seen, Luce?"

Silence. The confirmation that the topic was going to be a measure conversation that would take a master to extract information from Auntie. Brooke smiled, and raised her eyebrows in question.

"Kaida, I talked to her a few nights ago, after the funeral, but not since. She okay?"

"I don't know, Auntie. I was hoping…maybe you…" Brooke set her chopsticks down and folded her hands in her lap. This was going to be a bit harder than she thought. She'd probably have better luck with the alley cat out back than what she was about to embark on right now. "I saw her that night, but she was in bad shape."

"Hmm."

"Do you know what happened?" Brooke gripped her hands together trying to control her nervousness.

"Kaida is a strong woman. She can handle her problems. Don't worry."

"But that's just it, I am worried. She sent me away. I saw the marks on her arm and I'm worried."

"What marks?" Auntie stern glance made Brooke her wish she'd put a gag in her own mouth. Now she had the old woman's full attention and she wasn't sure that was a good thing.

"Oh, it's…nothing. I'm sure they were just scratches or something. I mean…" Brooke looked down at her watch. "Would you look at the time? I've got to get back for an afternoon meeting."

"Sit."

Brooke did as she was instructed. She sat ramrod

straight, her eyes transfixed on Auntie. She didn't blink. Auntie had that gift most women of her stature and age often did, a command of those around her through fear and intimidation. While Brooke thought she could take the old woman, she would never be quite sure if it really came down to brass tacks.

"Don't bullshit an old woman. Now spill. Wait," Auntie said, holding up her hand. Nodding to someone behind Brooke the waitress appeared with a steaming dish of Bulgolgi, the barbeque meat dish common in most Korean restaurants, and two bowls of steamed rice. Bowing, she said something in Korean and backed away from the table and into the kitchen. The tinkling of bells alerted Brooke that the woman had probably left the restaurant leaving her alone with Auntie. "Okay, so tell me what happened to Luce? Eat."

Brooke sat wondering how she would accomplish both tasks at the same time. In amazement, she watched as Auntie wielded the chopsticks with an accuracy that one could only sit in admiration of, snagging the smallest of pieces from the side dishes and popping them in her mouth.

"Eat."

Slowly Brooke maneuvered through a few mouthfuls of meat and rice before she accidently dueled with Auntie's chopsticks reaching for the same kimichi piece.

"Sorry," Brooke said sheepishly, relinquishing her hold on the flaming red cabbage. It wasn't as if she would survive the peppery dish, but she tried anyway. Another sip of her Soju, eased the burning in her mouth only slightly as she caught sight of Auntie starring at her.

"What's wrong with Kaida?"

"I don't know. That's what I was hoping you could tell me."

More silence. It was damn aggravating. This wasn't a one-way street they were both careening down together. Auntie obviously knew something or she would come right out and say, I've got nothing, Brooke. She didn't mince words, more like she butchered them, but that was another issue.

"So…" Brooke raised her eyebrows in question again. "What's going on, Auntie? I'm worried."

"I told you, Kaida can handle her own problems," Auntie said, gently patting Brooke's hand. "Eat."

"You didn't see her, Auntie. Drunk, angry and cutting herself. I've never seen her like that, so don't try and tell me she'll be okay. I don't buy it." Brooke's voice rose in frustration.

"She didn't tell you anything?"

"She was cryptic and said something like, if I had any secrets I needed to share them now. Other than that, nothing and I'm worried."

"Do you have any secrets?"

"What? No! What the hell is going on, Auntie? And don't tell me nothing. I'm not buying it."

Auntie raised her glass of Soju to her frail lips and surprised Brooke when she slammed the empty glass on the table and burped. Filling it, she tipped her glass at Brooke and drained it, slamming it on the table, again. Expecting the follow-up burp Brooke waited, and waited, and waited, finally giving Auntie a questioning shrug.

"What?"

"No burp?"

"A lady does not burp."

"Oh, Christ. I'm going to kill myself," Brooke muttered. Her frustration with the Potter family was at capacity and she wasn't sure she could handle much more.

"Auntie?"

"Yes, dear?"

"Luce?"

"Yes, dear, what about, Luce?"

"Oh god, shoot me now."

Pulling her wallet from her oversized purse, she rifled through it pulling out bills.

"Stop."

"I should be going. This isn't getting me anywhere. I thought maybe you would be concerned for Luce's welfare, but clearly I was mistaken."

"I am worried for Kaida, but I'm not sure I can speak about what happened with her grandfather."

"So something happened?" Brooke probed. "Something happened that night? After the funeral?"

"Yes."

"What?"

"My Kaida feels betrayed."

"By who? Me?" Brooke pointed back at herself.

Auntie shook her head and looked beyond Brooke. Her mind was somewhere else as she was clearly trying to measure each word. Breaking Luce's confidence wouldn't sit well with her, but acting like a mad woman wasn't sitting well with Brooke.

"No, I wish I could tell you, but I owe it to Kaida to keep her trust. If I betray it she will never forgive me and if you know without her telling you, she may never forgive you."

"All of this is too cryptic for me. If she doesn't trust me to be there for her or support her during these bad times, then perhaps I'm the wrong person for her."

"Don't make decisions in haste, Brooke. Kaida is a proud woman and shoulders her own problems."

"Yeah, well that's just it. I was a strong, independent woman before I met Luce and now I feel like I'm being shown the door. Well, I know when the exit sign is flashing and right now I'm seeing it flash."

Auntie shook her head. "Nothing is ever easy with you young people. You make problems where none exist."

"Me or Luce?"

"Both."

"Stop talking in riddles, Auntie. We've know each other long enough that you can be direct."

"Luce is a prideful woman and I don't think— no I know—she doesn't want to burden you with her problems." Auntie shook her head. "It's not really a problem, so I'm not sure why she is reacting this way. Bah, you young people. In my day you took what life gave you and were grateful for another day."

"Auntie, please. What's happened?"

"I can't, child. I can't." Patting her hand again Auntie stood and started to clear the dishes. "I'm sure she'll come around in time, Brooke. Be patient."

"I wish I had your optimism, Auntie. I really wish I had it."

Chapter Eighteen

Luce looked down at the razor sharp creases of her black suit. She was still in mourning so she would continue with the black apparel, but in reality she always wore black because it was more intimidating. Today, she was having a meeting with her inner circle at one of the new VIP clubs she was opening. Her other businesses were booming, but Luce was switching gears with the new strip clubs. She was into information harvesting now and the clubs were the perfect vehicle. Beautiful women, alcohol and business men were a great mix for finding out what was happening in the world, especially in the business world.

Sammy, Lynn, and Sasha were now her inner circle. Luce relied on them to do their jobs and do them well. She had fired them in a fit of rage after learning of her grandfather's new "wife", an issue she allowed to infiltrate her business life. After calling each of them into the office and offering a brief explanation, things had settled out nicely.

As for her grandfather's wife, she was unfinished business Luce would take care of soon. She would need to calm her thoughts before a visit to the woman. In her current state, she wasn't sure what she would say, but she didn't want to dishonor the memory of her grandfather with a spectacle. The visit would have to wait.

"Oyabun," Sammy bowed and then stepped forward to shake Luce's hand.

"Sammy."

"Oyabun." Lynn bowed and waited to shake her hand.

"Oyabun." Sasha stood behind waiting, too.

"Sit, everyone," Luce said, pointing to a table with coffee and few breakfast items.

The club was dark by design, so turning on the house lights offered little help. The interior was more like a warehouse than a club, but she was doing some custom remodels on the club, especially the private rooms. The best sound system and cameras where being installed. This would allow her to monitor the discussions between the dancers and the clients. So private wasn't quite so private after all.

"Good morning." Luce looked down at her watch. "I appreciate everyone coming so early. I wanted to have a word with all of you before the girls start to arrive for their interviews."

Looking from face to face, she sized up her *family*. She had hand-picked Frank's replacements, opting for three instead of one. Picking two women to move up changed the nice orderly way of the traditional Yakuza. Luce was used to shaking up the status quo, and Lynn and Sasha had proven themselves in the warehouse last year when they saved Brooke's life. They'd had her back through the gunfire and she was proud to add them to her inner circle. Sammy on the other hand had proven himself without realizing it. Frank had betrayed him, Luce and the family. Sammy had lost a pinkie because of it. He had been loyal in spite of Frank's orders, now he sat at the table with her.

Luce thought her life now would be that of

teacher, her time of learning lessons over, but life wasn't built like that, not for her. Wisdom came through time and life, her auntie had shown her that. Her grandfather had shown her that patience and a level head could conquer youth and it's abundant energy. Her mother had shown her that love should be able to calm and civilize the savage beast, but she had paid the ultimate price for the love she shared with her father, JP. So her lesson in love had come from Brooke, whom she missed terribly, but pride kept her from mending the fence that stood a mile high between them. Luce's grandfather had called her prideful when she wouldn't accept his advice early in her business career. She had paid dearly for that lesson. In fact, one particular deal would have put Yoshida Enterprises in the top one hundred companies in the United States. However, Luce had passed on the deal because the CEO of the company had mistakenly called her Chinese. An ordinary mistake, but nonetheless a catastrophic error that had cost him millions for his company. Luce felt all he had to do was do his homework, as she had done. She had no tolerance for that type of mistake. Her grandfather had brushed it off. Saying only, *he will never make that mistake again, will he Kaida?*

"I've brought you all together to have a sit-down," Luce met each face and smiled. These were the only people she could trust now and they would know that by the end of the meeting. "I wanted to thank you all for forgiving my indiscretion the night of my grandfather's funeral. I'm sorry and wanted you all to know that. I received more bad news that evening and I didn't handle it well. Thank you Sammy for watching out for Ms. Erickson, I appreciate it. Ladies, I know you've been picking up the slack as her detail when

Sammy is working with me and I want to thank you."
Luce suddenly realized that if they were all here, who
was with Brooke? "Who's with her right now?"

"Paulie is at Brooke's house. He'll follow her to
work and then take up a position in the building until
I get back," Lynn said.

Luce knew the twenty-four hour detail was taking
its toll on her people, especially since she hadn't been
with Brooke. Normally that gave them a break when
the two women were together.

"Good." Cradling her hot tea between her hands,
she sat back.

"Right now here are my priorities. Frank hasn't
been found yet. He is priority number one. Directing
more resources towards finding him will flush him
out. While my grandfather was alive, he had been less
willing to see his old friend killed." *The new woman
in his life must have softened him*, Luce surmised. "I
respected my grandfather, but Frank betrayed this
family. Period."

"I want to catch that bastard bad, Oyabun."

"Don't beat yourself up, boss. We all trusted
Frank." Lynn said

"Me too, Sammy. Thanks, Lynn." Luce was glad
to hear everyone was on the same page.

"Here is my second priority – Petrov. He was
following Brooke the night of the funeral, and I'm
pissed at myself for being so careless. I overlooked the
fact that Petrov might make Brooke a target because
of our relationship." Luce watched the tea swirl in
her cup before continuing. "Priority number three,
Brooke. Sadly, I've regretted not making Brooke
priority number one, but this is business and in the
Yakuza world, family and business were synonymous.

Fingers of the same hand. I've beefed up the protection around Brooke, but I haven't really spoken to her since the night of grandfather's funeral."

"We'll keep an eye out for her, Oyabun. Don't worry, we've got this. Right?" Sammy said, looking around the group.

She missed Brooke, but right now she didn't have the time or words to tell her how fucked up she felt about that night. She had hoped time would smooth things over, but that would mean she would have to take action she wasn't sure how to take. However, her self-isolation was taking its toll on Luce. She missed talking to Brooke, sharing her day, making love with unabashed abandon, but the intimacy was what she really missed. Brooke had softened her rough edges when they were together. She found a way inside Luce's cold heart and sparked a fire that only she could keep banked. Brooke was the yin to her yang, the light to her darkness, and yet she couldn't find the words to say that would pull Brooke back into her embrace. Her shame was so great it paralyzed her. No one had ever stymied Luce in such a way.

"I appreciate you picking up the slack while we work things out. I need more time to and then we'll be back to business as usual. I'm worried that Frank or the Russian's might try something, so be on your toes." Luce leafed through her spiral bound pad looking for her notes. "I need all of you to be on the lookout for Frank." Luce pulled the two notes and tossed them on the table for everyone to see.

Lynn picked up the cards and read them. "What the fuck?" She passed them on to Sasha.

"That's ballsy. Frank's a dead man," Sasha said, sliding the notes to Sammy.

"I'm not worried about myself, but everyone's life is being threatened. We have to be on point no matter where we are or what we're doing."

"Umm, Oyabun?"

"Yes, Sammy."

"I think we need to talk about the Russians." Sammy looked like he had swallowed a stone and it was caught in his throat. That worried Luce.

"What's going on, Sammy?"

"I wanted to tell you the night of the funeral, but I didn't because you weren't exactly in any condition to talk. There was an issue that night with the Russians."

"What do you mean an *issue*?"

"I had taken over for Lynn that night. Brooke decided to go out for a drive. I knew she was headed here when she didn't hear from you. On the way over a Russian got in between Brooke and I in the downtown area. She picked up on at least one of us, because she pulled a pit maneuver that Mario Andretti would be proud of. She lost the Russian quick, but the problem was she lost me, too. I tried to stay back far enough not to be seen by the Russian, and I lost her in the downtown traffic."

"I see, but you brought her here that night. I'm confused." Luce squinted and concentrated on what Sammy was telling her. All that mattered was that the Russians were still hanging around, but Brooke had lost them. At least that night.

"Brooke called me in a panic. She had turned down a side street and ducked into a public garage to hide." Sammy finished the details of what happened that night. It didn't matter to Luce, she was already seething. "I'm sorry, Oyabun. I couldn't believe I lost her."

"She's a pretty good driver. At least you found her."

"Is it possible it was Frank?"

"It's possible, but not likely. I caught a glimpse and he was Caucasian."

"Those guys are like flies on shit. Let's make sure we don't get any on our shoes that they can track. I want everyone to start taking different routes home and to the club, and I want someone on Brooke at all times. I'll have to do something drastic and push Brooke away for a while. Don't be surprised if there's a public blowout between us. It's for her own good." Although they nodded in agreement, she could see their disapproval, even if they tried to hide it.

Now Luce felt worse. She had pushed Brooke away that night without finding out if she was okay. Hell, she didn't even have the courtesy to reject the sex Brooke had willingly offered that night. No, she was the ultimate dog, the kind that screwed and used and then pissed on those around her. Shaking her head, she wished she had called Brooke just once that night. Then none of this would have happened.

Wisdom.

She lacked it in spades.

☙ ❧ ☙ ❧

"So tell me..." Luce looked down at the application sitting in front of her. "Kathleen. Why do you want to dance here?"

"Kat."

"Kat?"

"I like it better than Kathleen."

"Kat, then. Why do you want to dance for me?"

The way the dancer looked at Luce made her smile. If she could look at men that way, Kat would be very popular.

"I'm good at my job. I like to dance and I've got a great work ethic."

"Interesting accent you have. Where are you from?" Luce asked, studying Kat's lips. The slow, deliberate smile didn't reach her eyes. Another telltale sign of a professional who knew how to work a man, only Luce wasn't a man, so she didn't have a dick to do her thinking for her. Kat took her time, let her tongue flick across half her lip and then smiled again.

"New York."

Cocking her head to the side, Luce narrowed her gaze at the woman. "Hmm, I don't think so, it sounds more foreign."

"There are lots of foreigners in New York. You never know what you'll pick up there.

"Are we still talking accents or skills?"

"Depends."

"On?"

"If I make it to second base."

Luce was intrigued enough to give the sexy redhead a pass to the next level. A hard ass body like that would put men on their knees and they would spend more money than they had sense. The trick was could she get them to talk when they were alone. Luce had nothing to lose. If nothing else Kat could dance and be eye candy for the club.

"Yeah, you can make it to the next step. However, I should warn you, it's a little tougher than standing up there looking good."

"I can handle whatever you wanna throw at me."

"I can't wait to see what you've got. Why don't you

have a seat over there and wait. Next." Luce scribbled a few notes on the applications. Without warning, Kat stood in front of her, straddling her legs, her arms on each side of the easy chair.

Sammy and Sasha jumped up and grabbed Kat's arms, but before they could remove her Luce waved them off.

"Is there something else?" She admired Kat's well-shaped cleavage before she looked up into green eyes she was sure could bend metal.

Kat slid warm lips against hers. Luce tasted spearmint Lifesavers on her tongue. A moment later Kat's warm breath caressed her ear. "Thank you, you won't be sorry."

"I'm never sorry."

❧❧❧❧

Pushing her pen the bartender had gotten the whole exchange on digital. She had been hired that morning and by the luck of the draw, her first morning happened to be at the same club Luce was working. The new bartender captured the entire exchange on digital.

"Damn, I hope the rest of the job is this easy," she said, pushing the pen again to record as Luce's hand ran up the dancer's thigh and then cupped her ass. "The boss is gonna love these pics."

"Hey?"

"Yeah," she said, acting as if she was writing something.

"The Oyabun wants a dirty Martini."

"Yes sir. You got it. Vodka or Gin?"

The man whispered something in Luce's ear. She

nodded and then called for another dancer to the front of the stage.

"Vodka."

"You got it."

Slipping her pen into her pocket, she made sure the pin hole was facing forward. Lucky for her, she had played bartender in her underage days working her way through college. Now it was paying off. She pulled a glass and made sure it was stain free, tossed some ice in it and swirled it around before sending more into the metal shaker. Pouring the alcohol without looking she watched the action play out on the stage. The Yakuza leader had a way with women that would make men envious. The cool, aloof, bad girl attitude gave her an air of mystery and danger and chicks dug that shit. Hell they ate it up as much as they did women with badges and uniforms. *If you were into that kind of thing*, she thought. She shook the drink and studied her new boss. Slender and angular, Luce was feminine with a touch of butch, all mixed into a tall drink of woman.

Tossing the ice out, she filled the sweating glass, leaving just enough room for a toothpick with an onion and a couple of jumbo green olives speared through. She placed it on a tray and swung around the bar. Delivering the drink might get her in position for an up close shot of her new subject. "Ma'am."

"I would have picked up the drink," Sammy said. "Next time just call me and I'll come and get it."

"Of course, you looked busy. I didn't want to bother you."

"No one gets close to the Oyabun. Remember that."

"Of course."

Luce didn't look up at the confrontation behind her. Trusting, maybe a little too trusting of her inner circle, she thought. *Arrogant asshole*, the bartender muttered under her breath. When the time came, she would take pleasure in making sure the Man-ass got his.

☙☙☙☙

Luce was ready to move into the second phase of interviews. Women talked a good game, but could they dance? This wasn't Dancing with the Stars, but it was considered a profession. Since most bimbos off the street thought they could dance around a pole, this was where she would separate the, *I've danced for my boyfriend, so how hard could it be,* from the true talent.

"I'll see one girl at a time. Show me your best stuff. If you can't get me excited how will you get the clients horny? Remember, a horny client spends money ladies. Since I sign the paychecks, you should consider me a deserving client. Don't leave it out here, bring it and let me see what you've got. Understand?"

A chorus of yes's echoed through the club.

"Good, now go get changed and remember, men like a woman who smells good, but not like a whore. So go light on the perfume."

The line of women made their way back to the changing rooms as Luce stood and sipped her martini. God, she loved her job today. Sexy bodies, willing women and legs for days—what more could a hot-blooded lesbian ask for?

Brooke.

Funny how looking at beautiful women made her think of only one. Brooke. Guilt was eating at her now that she hadn't called Brooke. How would she explain to Brooke that her grandfather hadn't trusted her enough to let her share in his happiness? That he had kept a woman on the side and didn't tell her. Finding out about it after his death cut her to the quick, left her wondering why. Trying hard to bring fonder memories to the front and push back the feelings of betrayal wasn't working. The fact that it had consumed her meant she had let it control her, and not the other way around and she was always in control of herself. Frank's betrayal hadn't cut her as deep, but then she hadn't trusted the asshole from the beginning. This was family and she could only surmise that her loyalty to her family might have been one-sided at least this time.

"Oyabun, they're ready for you."

"Be right there, Sammy."

Slamming her drink, she walked the empty glass to the bar and ordered another. Luce had turned hiring the bar staff over to Lynn, willingly delegating the mundane task to her subordinate. The bartender was one of those new hires and looking more closely, she could see why Sammy had bit her head off earlier. She was...hot.

Brooke.

"What can I get for ya, boss?"

"Huh?"

The bartender pointed to the glass and asked again. "Another?"

"Yeah, exactly like that one. What's your name?"

"Cher, short for Cheryl."

"Like the entertainer. Interesting."

"If I had her money I wouldn't be working here."

"Really?"

"I didn't mean it like that, I meant—"

Luce waved her hand to stop the bartender before she said something stupid. "I know what you meant."

"Sorry, that didn't quite come out the way I wanted."

"No problem. So where'd you learn to bartend?"

"You've probably never heard of it. A little dive down in the Castro that's out of business."

"Why do you think I wouldn't know a lesbian bar in the Castro?"

"I dunno, I guess it just doesn't seem like your kinda place. Besides, I didn't say it was a lesbian bar." Looking around the bar, she shrugged. "This is just... swankier. You know what I mean?"

"Oyabun. The dancers are ready."

"Be right there. You can send my drink to the diamond room."

"You got it."

Luce wondered if the bartender realized she hadn't outed herself as a lesbian, but that Luce had in fact called her out when she referenced the lesbian bar. What other little secrets did the bartender have? Now she was being paranoid. *Thank you grandfather, I'll never trust anyone again.*

Chapter Nineteen

Colby sat in Deputy Chapel's office strumming her fingers on the arm of the uncomfortable chair. She hated being called to the principal's office yet again for something she didn't know she'd done. The folder sitting her in lap grew with each day of investigation. Adding the Russian component had increased it substantially, still she was hard pressed to connect the Yakuzas and the Russians. In fact, she would be hard pressed to connect Luce's group to the drug cartel's or the Russians.

"Agent Water. I hope I haven't kept you waiting long?"

Standing, Colby extended her hand. Deputy Chapel only looked at it and continued to her desk.

"No, not at all." *I love sitting here and wasting twenty minutes on your fat ass,* she thought.

"Good, I wanted to touch base with you on the investigation and impart some information I received through an anonymous source. Interested?"

"Of course, Deputy Chapel, if it pertains to my investigation, I'm always interested."

"Good. I thought you might."

Colby sat watching Chapel as she thumbed through some papers, rearranged a few stacks that seemed to grow each time she touched them, and then blindly pulled out a folder without looking at it. *Is that what happens when you've done desk duty to long, your fingers turn into homing devices?* she wondered as she watched the deputy's eyes scan the piles again.

"Ah, here it is." She pushed through another voluminous pile. She plucked one from the bottom of the stack. Colby wondered when it had last seen daylight, considering how deep it was buried. "It seems you're on the wrong track with the Russians."

"Really? What makes you think that?"

"This," Chapel said, tossing the file towards the end of the desk as if handing it to Colby would spread a communicable disease.

Colby scanned the first pages and then quickly thumbed through to the last page.

"Where did the information come from?"

"Are you doubting its reliability?"

"It just seems to lead in a totally different direction than all the information I have." Colby scanned the print again to make sure she wasn't seeing things.

"A CI dropped a dime on a member of the drug cartel and outed his boy. Apparently there's some bad blood between gangs and he wanted them out of the way."

"He could be killed for this."

"He's willing to risk it. They burned his tattoo off." Deputy Chapel talked as if she were discussing baking recipes with her bridge group.

Colby pulled a picture from the paper clip that held it to the folder. Damn nasty, she thought, staring at the huge scar the kid would carry for the rest of his short life. When word got out, and it always did, that he was a snitch, the next picture she would likely be looking at was a shot from the coroner to ID his body.

"So you think cutting off his tat is more important

than his life?"

"He's in county lock-up right now, solitary confinement. He isn't worried about his life, we are, and yes, the information he's provided has panned out thus far."

"This is DEA stuff, we're DOJ. We should pass this on to them and work together. They have more intel on the cartel than we do." Colby stared at Deputy Chapel and waited for the rebuttal she knew was coming.

"Hell no, this is our case," Deputy Chapel thumped her finger on her metal desk. "We're going to make this case and we're going to make this case stick. Understand?"

"We?"

"This is a team operation, Agent Water. One falls, we all look bad. We have a lot of time invested in this case. We're just changing the focus based on the information from a credible CI."

Since when was a drug dealer a credible informant? Colby thought.

Glancing back at the short stack of paper, she studied each paragraph committing it to memory as if her life depended on it. The drug cartel was the worst organized crime syndicate. They made the Yakuza look like the local church choir who helped little old ladies cross the street. The cartels had no loyalties, no honor, they only honored the color green. The money these young kids made put them at the top of the food chain in their neighborhoods, kings in their little kingdoms. Who knew teenagers could be so ruthless? So cold and calculating, able to kill the way most kids ordered a cheeseburger at the local burger joint like it was nothing.

"So you think the drug cartels and the Yakuza are bosom buddies, working hand in glove?"

"I think the Russians are old news. We haven't seen hide or hair from them in months. Don't you think that's suspicious?"

"Hmm, not really. They could be underground for a reason." Colby closed the file and handed it back.

"I think the Yakuza have run them from the city. I think you need to focus on this new information. Gangs are moving in where the Russians were and they're gaining a foothold in places we haven't anticipated. There's a link between the new clubs the Yakuza are opening and the influx of drugs into the city. They are moving lots of product and I've been told that product is moving out from the clubs."

"Maybe." Colby was skeptical about this new information. She wasn't sure how deep into the investigation the deputy had inserted herself, but she couldn't disobey a direct order. Then again, she hadn't been given a direct order to drop her investigation on the Russians.

"I think this is big enough that I want you to drop your investigation on the Russians and focus on the cartel and the Yakuza. I've handed you a direct link between the two and I expect you to follow that up. Understand?"

She'd spoken to soon. Now she had a directive and being the good little soldier she was, Colby would do what she was told—almost.

"What about the threat on Brooke Erickson's life by Petrov?"

"Got anything to back that up?"

"Yes. Agent Scarr followed one of his guys who tried to follow Ms. Erickson to Potter's. She lost 'em, but who knows what would have happened had he gotten her on that deserted road."

"Petrov's got a grudge he wants settled is my bet. Besides, may I remind you that Petrov hasn't been up on the radar in a few months?"

"But the funeral—"

"Look, I know you have a hard-on for Petrov, but he isn't part of this investigation now. Focus on the money and the drugs. Both lead to Potter and the cartel."

"Whatever," she whispered.

"Are you being insubordinate, Agent Water?"

"No ma'am. Just thinking about all the investigation time down the drain."

"Well, tie this package up in a nice bow and you'll have all the time in the world to tie up the Russians so tight they can't run if they wanted."

"Yes, ma'am," Colby said, standing. "Will there be anything else?"

"No, that should do it. That gang member is down in lockup waiting for transport to a safe house. We had to escort him out of Mexico. I don't want to keep him in one location too long. You know how word travels, even in this agency."

"Yes, ma'am."

Colby knew what Deputy Chapel was implying, but she didn't want to admit D.O.J. had dirty officers. It pissed her off wondering why people who served her country would dishonor it by being dirty cops.

❧❧❧❧

Colby checked her weapon and badge at the cage. Without them she felt naked amongst the riffraff of society, or should she say the misunderstood criminal element? Perhaps that was more politically correct. She knew the weapon was prohibited. The deputy checking her in explained that her badge could inflict injury or death in skilled hands. Looking at the hulking deputy standing next to her, she noticed the embroidered shield on his shirt. *Geez, it's gotten that bad*, she lamented, wondering when society had lost its civility, even amongst criminals, Then again she didn't deal with this level of criminal. In fact, the criminals she dealt with considered themselves better than everyone else. They just worked a different angle than the average citizen.

The cool dampness of the cement assaulted her body as her nose wrinkled at the smell of chlorine and sweat. The days were short enough that the wetness hung in the air. By summer the building would be doing a different kind of sweating and she was glad she didn't work corrections when the animals heated up. Like snakes in the sun, summer and longer days meant more activity.

The door behind Colby slammed with a bone-jarring thud. The sound of metal against metal signaled the bolt was down and she was locked inside with her informant. Something didn't settle right with her as she stared down at the gang-banger. Maybe it was the peach-fuzz face sporting the light caterpillar mustache that had her confused.

Instead of a gang hardened *cholo* sitting in front of her, was a kid who should be thinking about his first date. That was the image she grappled with, until he opened his mouth.

"What the fuck you lookin' at, bitch?"

Oh, so there was a gang-banger under all the soft

baby skin.

"My name is Agent Water, and I'm here to talk to you about your drug connections with the cartel and the Yakuza." Colby said, setting her pad on the cold steel table. She kept a death grip on her pen. She'd heard stories of prisoners using a writing instrument to kill people and she wasn't taking any chances with this gutter mouth. "You kiss your mother with that mouth?"

"You ain't my mother, bitch." The sneer was a permanent fixture, plastered on for intimidation. She didn't flinch.

"And clearly I'm not your English teacher, either. Don't you have a more extensive vocabulary than that or do you save it for your *familia*?" Her condescending tone seeped out with each word. She wasn't about to stoop to this little pint-size punk's level, but his use of the words "bitch" and "fuck-you" were grating on her nerves.

"Fuck you, bitch. You ain't my family, either," he said, trying to reach past his cuffs chained to the table. "Guard, get this *puta* outta here. I'm done talking." Looking her in the eyes, he tried to sound as menacing as his puberty voice allowed. "I ain't talking to you. Got it?"

Colby smiled. "Oh, if you think you're getting that deal you were promised, you'll talk to me."

Scribbling some notes, she waited for the information to sink in. If he was turning on the cartel, he knew his options were slim to none in this race, meaning he better choose wisely. He was leaving for the safe house tonight after the DEA had secured his family. The little puke didn't need to know that, though, and it wasn't her job to tell him.

"What the fuck, we had a deal."

"Oh the one where you rat out the boys of the cartel and link 'em to the Yakuza? That deal?"

"Yeah, those assholes burned off my colors." He pulled his orange jumpsuit sleeve up and displaying the ugliest burn she'd ever seen. "Bastards took a heated butter knife and burned it off. They can take my colors, but I'll always be…" He flashed a W with his right hand and howled. "Weess siiidde. But fuck those *pendejos*, they threatened my family, and my family is, my family."

If Colby hadn't seen it with her own eyes she wouldn't believe the peewee was still so loyal considering they had probably threatened to kill his whole family if he ratted. As usual, kids like this thought life was like a video game, play hard-die hard. Life wasn't meant to be lived into old age for guys like this. He knew he'd be lucky to see his twenty-first birthday and celebrate a legal drink. What did it matter this kid had done everything already and so a few more months were extra in his book. No milestone to mark his life, a headstone yes, but he didn't have any more milestones to tick off signaling his ascension into adulthood. He was way past that.

"So tell me, how much product were you sending to the Yakuza?" She studied the little worm as he smirked. Already sick of his foul mouth and attitude, she wanted to end the interview, but this might be the only chance she had to verify what she'd read in the report earlier.

Puffing up his chest he bragged, "Five, ten kilos a week."

"That's a lot. Where'd you deliver it?"

"Behind the club."

"What club?"

"The one those chinks own."

"Chinks?" Colby repeated the disgusting slang. "The Chinese?"

"Naw man, fuck, ain't you listenin'? Those Asians bitches."

She was ready to climb over the steel table and tear his head off. It took all she had not to beat this "bitch" to death. "One more *bitch* and I'm going to help your digestion by knocking you teeth down your throat." Too late, Colby's anger got the best of her. "I want to buy a vowel and get a clue here. Asian meaning..."

"The Asian mafia. Fuck and they say you assholes are the smart ones."

If he listened closely, he would hear Colby's molars grinding. He was so caught-up in his own gang shit he only had eyes for himself, ignoring the potential danger that only lay a few inches from him—her.

"I. Need. More. Than. That."

"The dude with his pinkie cut off, man."

"Now we're getting somewhere." *Lucky for you douche bag*, she thought as she twirled the pen absently between her fingers. "Okay, what did this *dude* look like?"

"I don't know, they all look alike to me. Slanty eyes, black hair, no pinkie."

One quick jab in his neck and if she were lucky she would strike his jugular killing the little shit. Slipping the pen into the inside pocket of her blazer, she stashed the impending opportunity for the sake of her job.

"Tall, short, fat, skinny. Good dresser, jeans and t-shirt. What?"

"The dude wore a suit."

"Old, young?"

"Older than me, I guess." The kid squirmed in his restricted position.

Everyone was older than this kid, except his siblings. So far, Colby hadn't taken any notes. Nothing worth wasting the paper on had proved useful.

"Tats."

"Yeah, the dude had some ink. I saw it poking out of his shirt and on his hand."

"What did it look like?"

"Fuck, I don't know. Why you askin' me all these questions. I already told the other dude everything."

"Because I'm new to the case and I like to do my own work. So this club, where was it and when did you meet this guy?"

"A club down in the financial district. On Geary, I think." He bit down on one of his nails and pulled off a slim piece, spitting it on the floor.

Geez.

"And?"

"And what?"

"What time did you meet with this guy?"

"After closing, said his boss didn't want anyone accidently seeing the delivery being made."

"Did you ever see his boss?"

"Naw."

"Did you see him go into the club with the drugs?"

"Yeah…I mean not really. Me and Gordito just got the fuck up outta there. Fucking cops are everywhere."

"You don't say?" She shook her head, not surprised by his lack of respect. "Tell me what kind of shoes he was wearing?"

"Shoes? I don't know like every other fuckin'

Yakuza. Nice shoes. Polished." Suddenly pleased with himself, he sat up a little taller as if he was the observant one of the brain delinquents.

"You've met a lot of Yakuza?"

"A few." He sat even straighter. His truthfulness in question suddenly put his nose out of joint.

"Hmm."

"What? You don't believe me?"

"Let's just say I've had better information from dead informants." She really wanted to say snitches but the conversation, if that's what you could call it, hadn't yielded any noteworthy nuggets yet.

"How come you ain't takin' any notes, dude?"

Great, now he's a mind reader.

"'Cause you haven't told me anything yet, *dude*."

Looking like he had a secret he wasn't going to share, he sat back crossed his arms and smirked at Colby.

"Look, I don't have time for this, so if you have anything else you want to say now's the time, because when I leave today I'll report back to my boss what a waste of space you are and that you don't have shit. I'm sure she'll rethink your deal."

"I don't think so."

"Oh, I think so."

"Naw, I ain't tellin' you everything. It's my, how's that sayin'…ace in the hole."

"Let's not bullshit each other, *dude*. You're marked, and even if you get out of here and into a wit program, you and I both know you won't stay down. You can't, you like the action, the money and a job at a fast-food restaurant won't cut it. So, you'll pop your greasy little head up and it'll get popped off."

"Maybe, maybe not."

"Where's Gordito?"

"I don't know, I ain't his mama."

"Did he take your position?"

"Huh?"

"Is he the one running the drugs now?"

"Probably."

Strumming her fingers against the steel table, she was just shy of an aneurism at this point in the questioning. "What does he look like? Where can I find this fat bastard?"

"Who?"

"Gordito?" Colby gripped her hands together trying to control herself from strangling the little shit.

"He ain't fat."

"Christ, why the name, Gordito then. It means fatty right?"

"Yeah, but we call him that 'cause he can put the groceries away."

"Great. What's his real name?" Colby looked down at her watch. It was going to be a very long day.

Chapter Twenty

Luce relaxed in the comfortable chair and waited for the next part of the interview process to start. Another drink was deposited on the small table next to her.

"Let's do this, Sammy."

"Bring in the first gal." Sammy motioned for the door.

The bass of the music broke the quiet as a young girl in tall platform shoes swished her hips walking towards Luce. She couldn't help but smile at the seductive way the young gal worked herself in Luce's direction. *This is going to be such a hardship,* she thought as the woman glided effortlessly onto her lap. She gyrated in time to the pounding bass, her tight ass rotating on her long legs. Leaning back against Luce, she grabbed one of Luce's hands and wrapped it around her middle to caress her flat toned stomach. Dipping Luce's fingers just at the waistband of her bikini bottom, she rolled her head towards Luce's and whispered, "So, how'm I doing so far?"

Spice. Her perfume was the second thing Luce noticed. *Not bad.*

Luce looked down at the small firm breasts partially exposed by design and smiled. "So far so good."

"Good, I'd hate to disappoint my future boss."

"I'd hate that, too."

"So, did you have a rough day at work?"

"Not so far."

"Hmm, you smell good," she said. She stood and turned to put her knee on the arm of the chair. She pushed her breast just under Luce's nose, her hips rotating suggestively over Luce's lap.

"That's funny, I was just thinking the same thing."

"What? That you smell good?"

"You're good."

"Thanks. I'm told I'm a natural pleaser." She whispered close to Luce's ear.

"I see that."

Luce pushed the petite girl up and smiled. "I think you hired."

"Really?" she squealed. Clapping her hands, she leaned down and kissed Luce on the cheek. "Thank you."

"Sammy? Send in the redhead."

"You got it."

"What's your name?" Luce asked the girl still leaning over her.

"You can call me Candy, since you can never have enough."

"Let's work on the name. This is a VIP club, not a porn studio. Okay?"

"You got it."

"Good. Now go get changed and see Sammy, he'll tell you when to report for training."

Another quick kiss and Candy was gone. Her tight little ass flashed and she ran down the hall to the changing rooms.

Kat strutted down the hall towards Luce like a cat edging closer to her prey. The sexy glide kept Luce entranced, her gaze wandered all over the tight, muscular body. The string bikini looked more like postage stamps trying to cover her intimate parts— *barely* covering, the optimum words. The Lucite shoes made her taller, allowing her to tower over the seated Luce. In fact it put one of the postage stamps at face level and it was all Luce could do not to grab the tan ass and pull her close enough for a lick.

Brooke.

There she was again, slipping into her mind at the most inopportune times. Pushing the memory back into the dark recess of her mind, she reached up and slid her hand along Kat's swaying thigh. Kat worked her way around the chair, her hands wandering down Luce's chest as she lightly rubbed her breasts against Luce's head. Moving back to the front, she let her cocksure body slowly move back and forth before grabbing both of Luce's hands and rubbed them the length of her body.

"So..." Kat purred.

"Yes?"

Luce watched as Kat pulled her hand up to her mouth. Flicking her tongue out Kat ran the tip of it across the tip of Luce's finger then pushed it past warm lips. Kat's slippery tongue rolled against her finger sending a charge through Luce's body. Hypnotized by the seductive act, all Luce could do was press her thighs tight and try and control the surge through her spiking center. Full, red-coated lips worked Luce's finger like a hooker worked a client. The friction was a torturous pleasure for Luce. The last time she had her hands full was the night of her grandfather's funeral and Brooke had satiated her hunger. The vibrating music pounded Luce's body and added to the tension she hungered for at that moment.

The slow grind against her thighs coaxed Luce

further into the tight little web Kat was spinning as she pulled Kat's mouth down closer to hers.

Luce flicked her tongue out and begged for entrance into the tight, wet place her finger currently occupied. Threading her fingers through the soft, red locks she tilted Kat's face, pulled her finger out and replaced it with her tongue. Luce felt like she was practically devouring the dancer as she pulled her onto her lap.

"You're playing with fire." Luce whispered as she steadied Kat's hips.

"I'm not afraid of a little burn. Are you?"

"Oh, I'm never afraid of a little fire."

"Good, then we're speaking the same language aren't we?"

"Somehow..." Luce continued her travels along Kat's body. "I don't think we're talking anymore."

Luce jerked Kat's ass across her lap and groaned as she felt the hard muscles come into contact with her. Standing, she held Kat tight against her body before lowering her onto her acrylic platform shoes. Soft breasts tightened at the contact and a hush was pushed out between the two women. Now Luce was faced with a decision, take advantage of the offer being extended or keep her distance between employee and employer. Obviously, if Kat could work her into a frenzy she would be an asset to the club.

"Well, since I'm your boss now. I don't think it would be appropriate to cross the line."

"Maybe you could wait to hire me for an hour or so." Kat leaned her body against Luce, running her hands over the lapels of her suit jacket.

Luce captured the hands and held them tight. She could easily unravel, but she had unfinished business with Brooke. If Brooke would talk to her after all this time.

"I'm flattered, trust me. You're very talented and I think you'll be an asset, so I hope you'll take my offer. I'm sure we can come to some acceptable terms."

"Oh, I'm not worried about the terms, but I am interested in the fringe benefits that come with the offer." Kat let her tongue wet her lips again and scorched Luce with another fiery look.

"I'm sure you'll find our benefit package quite generous," Luce said, letting the implication hang. She wasn't about to position herself any closer to the beautiful woman, but if she needed something later, she would keep the hook baited.

∾.∾.⁊.⁊

Standing in front of Luce's newest club, Brooke took a deep breath and held it. Confrontation wasn't something she enjoyed, but she'd crafted her own style as an investigative journalist. She fingered the diamond necklace Luce had given her, sliding it back and forth on the gold chain. Exhaling, she slipped into journalist mode, grabbed the door handle and rushed inside before her nerves made her turn around and go back to the office. The music was seductive and sexy, and no doubt made for erotic dancing. Nothing prepared Brooke for what she saw next. Walking towards the music, she stopped and watched as a tall, leggy, red-head wrapped herself around Luce, grinding against her lover, make that ex-lover. She stood, just as mesmerized as Luce appeared to be, as the dancer worked herself around the Oyabun. Luce smiled as the dance got more intimate, more tactile, more...more...

sexual. She'd never seen anyone put themselves that close to another's lips without having a relationship, and this was crossing the line. Panning around the room, everyone was focused on the scene playing out before them. Standing still in the darkness kept her out of sight. Well almost everyone.

"Can I help you?" a soft voice whispered in her ear.

Without looking back she shook her head.

"Are you here for the dancer tryouts?"

Brooke only shook her head. She couldn't stop herself from staring.

"Why don't I make you a drink?"

Brooke felt herself being pulled towards the bar, her gaze never wandering from the dancer's lithe body, undulating to the music. If she had been here for any other reason she would be turned on by the scene. Clearly, the woman knew how to dance and loved to do it with an audience. The only thing Brooke could be thankful for was the fact that she still had her clothes on. Sliding her necklace back and forth she stood stunned as Luce reached up and pulled the dancer down for a kiss.

"Here, you look like a Cape Cod kinda gal."

A drink was pushed towards her. Brooke automatically took a sip, the alcohol burning on the way down.

"Geez, you don't make 'em light do ya?" Brooke said, coughing lightly.

"I want the customer to get their money's worth."

Brooke finally looked at the bartender, who gave her one of those apologetic smiles someone offered when they knew something bad was about to happen.

"Thanks."

"Your boyfriend over there?" Cher said, tossing her head towards Sammy.

"No," was the only thing Brooke could squeeze out.

Suddenly she saw Sammy, whisper in Luce's ear. Luce shaded her eyes and scanned the darkness, helping the dancer off her lap. Brooke started walking towards the door and felt a hand grab her arm.

"What are you doing here, Brooke?"

Brooke was pulled back towards the bar. She couldn't say anything she was to stunned. This wasn't happening to her. It couldn't be how things would end, not after all she and Luce had shared.

"You weren't returning my phone calls. I was worried."

"So you thought you would come here and spy on me?" Luce's voice started to rise in anger.

"No…no…I just needed to talk to you, but—"

"But what? You just couldn't let it go could you, Brooke? You're so selfish. I needed space and you just couldn't give it to me could you?" Luce's face was gnarled as she spit her words through grinding teeth.

Brooke snapped out of her desperation. "Oh, it looks like you'll get your space. I can see you're all broken-up about your grandfather. Stupid me, I thought you were distraught with grief and that's why you weren't calling me. You just couldn't end it respectfully could you? You had to go to the gutter and let some tramp slam her shit all up in your face. Did she make you feel better? Guess you couldn't call me with your face full of pussy."

Brooke flinched as Luce raised her hand. Luce had never hit her in anger before and she was shocked to see it raised now.

"I don't think so, boss." Cher said, clutching Luce's forearm. "No one hits a lady when I'm around."

"Take your hand off or you'll pull back a stump," Luce said, without looking in Cher's direction.

A crowd has gathered around the two women. Brooke wished she had stayed away, but what was done, was done. Sammy stood on one side of Brooke between the bartender and Luce. Lynn stood closest to Brooke, her arms crossed over her chest, towering over her. Just as she was going to say something the dancer sauntered over and wrapped herself around Luce's arm.

"Everything, okay?"

"Everything's just fine, Kat." Luce kissed Kat and caressed her face. "Why don't you go get dressed. We're done here. As for you," Luce said, pointing to Brooke. "I told you were done, now get your ass out of here. I don't want to see you around my clubs anymore. You got it?"

Before Brooke could say anything, Luce was escorting Kat to the back of the club. Brooke tried to swallow. She felt as if a wad of cotton was stuck in her throat. A wave of nausea washed over her, her face flushed and her knees buckled. Thankfully, Sasha picked her up before she could hit the ground, making a spectacle of herself.

"She doesn't mean it, Ms. Erickson. She hasn't been herself since she lost the Oyabun." Sasha tried to comfort Brooke.

"No she meant it. I've…I've never seen her so… vicious." Brooke accepted the bottle of water that was offered.

"You better get her out of here," Cher said, running her hand over Brooke's head. "I'm sorry."

"Why are you sorry? I don't even know you and you're sorry?" Brooke shook her head.

"Get back to work," Sasha snapped.

"Yes, ma'am." Cher saluted, taking up her post behind the bar.

"Don't, she didn't do anything wrong. Unless you thought Luce should have slapped me?"

"Of course not. I'm sorry Ms. Erickson, I need to get you home." Sasha guided Brooke towards the door.

"I'm not going home. I need to go back to work. I can find my own way, thank you," she said, wrenching her arm from Sasha's grip. "I'm not your responsibility, now please take your hands off me, I know the way out." Brooke startled herself when she slammed the door. Taking one last look over her shoulder, she couldn't believe it had ended like this, demeaning and ugly. This was a whole new Luce Potter. One she was shocked to meet.

Chapter Twenty-one

O yabun?"

"What?" Luce snapped at Sammy.

"I need to see you for a moment." Sammy cleared his throat. Bowing he stepped outside the door and waited.

"I'll be right back, Kat. Maybe we could have dinner soon," Luce winked, her grin hid the anger simmering just under the surface.

"Of course, I would love to be your dinner date." Kat ran her fingertips down the front of Luce's body. "Hurry back."

"Hmm."

Luce pulled the door to the dressing room closed behind her. She didn't want Kat to hear what she had to say to Sammy.

"Where is Brooke?"

"She's gone."

"Good, did Sasha take her home?"

"No, Oyabun."

"What, why not?"

"She said she was going back to her office. I'm sorry Oyabun, I know it isn't my place, but...I mean... well I just..." Sammy shuffled from one foot to the other his head bowed, afraid to make eye contact with Luce.

"Spit it out, Sammy."

"Are you ill?"

"What? No, why do you ask?"

"I've never seen you raise your hand to Ms. Erickson. I understand you're still grieving for the Oyabun, but—"

"Things are happening that I can't explain, Sammy, but it's for the best that Brooke find someone else. She deserves someone better than me." Luce said almost apologetic. "Just make sure that someone is watching her for the next couple of weeks and then hopefully things will have calmed down and we can get back to normal." Luce twisted her neck. A pop echoed in the hallway. Twisting it to the other side, she felt another pop. The tension sat squarely on her shoulders where it belonged. As long as someone was after her, she would be knotted up, until she solved her biggest problem, Frank.

Chapter Twenty-two

Colby swung into the office complex, familiar with the layout from her previous trip. Smiling down at Stella, she slid a hip onto the assistance's desk and leaned down admiring her cleavage.

"So, what's for lunch?"

"Are you my lunch date today?"

"Could be, but I hear that you're not into girls."

"Hmm, who said that?"

"Your boss."

"Really, well she doesn't know everything. My personal life is my personal life."

"Oh, good to know, but I should warn you I don't have the ability to commit to anyone right now. Job constraints pretty much have me all over the country at any given time, but I am into beautiful women who like to have fun."

"I like fun." Stella said, moving closer so Colby could peer down her cleavage.

"So, I see."

"Stella?" Brooke's voice echoed out of the office.

"Duty calls." Pushing the intercom button on the phone she responded. "Yes, Ms. Erickson."

"Could you bring me the hedge fund notes, I need to make some changes to the article before you type them up."

"Yes, ma'am." Stella wrinkled her nose and

cocked her mouth. "Guess I better get back to work."

"Why don't you give me that file? I'm here to talk to Ms. Erickson and it'll save you a trip. Besides, you can pick out a restaurant for lunch." Colby winked at the blushing assistant and grabbed the offered folder. "Wish me luck."

⚜⚜⚜⚜

The footfalls behind Brooke didn't bring her around. She reached up for the folder she had asked for. The weight of the folder in her hand, she thumbed through it and pursed her lips. The numbers didn't seem to make sense. Preoccupied, she didn't see the person walk behind her and reach for her shoulders.

"Fuck," she screamed, jumping forward out of her seat and away from the hands trying to strangle her. "Stella."

Seeing Stella at the door, frantic, she ran around the desk away from the person behind her chair. "Who the fuck is...Colby?" she patted her chest, as if it would slow her racing heart.

"Hello, Ms. Erickson. I'm sorry I thought you saw me when I handed you the folder."

"Thank you, Stella. I'm fine. Please close the door behind you," she said, trying to catch her breath.

Thud.

"What the fuck are you doing here? Fuck, Colby."

"Ooo, salty language, I like it. Kind of a turn on." Colby sat herself on the couch and waited for Brooke to calm down.

"Knock it off, Colby. I don't fall for your shit anymore. What do you want?"

"A date?"

"Not a chance."

"Okay, how about some answers?"

"What makes you think I have answers you need?"

"A hunch." Colby patted the couch, but Brooke just stared at her and shook her head. "Okay."

Brooke watched Colby pull out what looked to be a dragon pen, similar to the ones she had on Luce's office desk, and scribbled something on a piece of paper.

"Where did you get that pen?"

Looking it over, Colby threw a smile at Brooke. "I don't remember," she lied. "Would you like to see it?"

"No, it's beautiful. I was just admiring it." Brooke crossed her arms, leaning against her desk. She wasn't in the mood for a verbal sparring match with Colby about the pen. Obviously she had already been to Luce's place, the pen proof of the visit. She still had hours ahead of her and it was already four in the afternoon. After what had happened at the club she wasn't in the mood for a stroll down memory lane. The sooner she could get her ex out of her office the sooner she could get back to work.

"So, what do you want, Colby? Obviously this isn't a social call and I have work to do."

"I'll try not to take up too much of your time, then."

Brooke watched Colby spread photos across the table. She couldn't see them from her vantage point, but she would be damned if she was going to look at photos to identify dead people. Standing her ground she locked eyes with Colby, her hands and body tightened and she visibly clenched her jaw. Clearly, she wasn't moving.

Neither woman moved, each not wanting to bend to the other. Brooke followed Colby's eyes to the photos and then looked back at her. She knew what Colby wanted. She could wait out the best of them. Brooke was an investigative journalist with the constitution of a brick wall. She did her best work while waiting for a lead to come through. *Bring it on,* she thought, staring down Colby.

"Have you talked to Luce lately?"

"Is that why you're here? I can save you the trouble, Colby. I saw Luce this afternoon and it wasn't a pleasant experience."

"Huh."

"Did you girls have a fight?"

"It's none of your business, Colby. Now, see I told you I probably couldn't answer your questions. If you don't mind I have a lot of work to do."

Brooke swung around her desk and plopped into the leather chair that had surely molded itself to the shape of her ass, she'd spent so many hours in it lately. Pulling her keyboard tray towards her, she worked on her hedge fund report that was going to print at the end of the week.

A photograph of Luce and the redhead from earlier landed on top of her hands. The woman, actually she looked like she was barely old enough to drink, was straddling Luce's lap and exposing her barely covered tits mere inches away from Luce's face. Luce definitely looked like she was enjoying the up-close display. A wide smirk Brooke had come to recognize as part pleasure, part flirting, was plastered on Luce's face.

"What's your point here, Colby? I already told you, Ms. Potter and I aren't an item. Clearly, these photos prove that. Now will you leave me alone?"

Another photo landed on top of the last. This one had the redhead planting a kiss on Luce's neck, her finger threaded through the black locks. Luce's eyes were closed, and her mouth open in obvious ecstasy. Brooke swore she could almost hear her low throaty moan. Her heart raced. Her mind bounced around trying to formulate excuses for what she was seeing in the photos, although she had seen the real thing only hours before.

Another photo sliced through the air, this time landing on the desk next to her. Luce's face buried in between the woman's abundant cleavage. Another of Luce's arms pulling the woman higher on her lap. Another of the redhead biting Luce's chin. Another landed with the woman's tight, naked ass hovering over Luce's lap, and finally one with Luce's grabbing the tight ass with one hand while the other ran up the woman's back. All the while the redhead's face smiled in obvious delight. They were having a good time, it was clear, but...it didn't matter, Brooke was done. Scooping up the photos, she tapped them on her desk, organizing them and handed them back to Colby.

"And?"

"You see this beautiful woman all over Ms. Potter and all you got is, *and*?"

"Yep."

"Wow, you really have changed, Brooke. So can I ask you about the drugs?"

"Drugs? What are you talking about?"

"Look I know you and Ms. Potter were an item and you probably still have loyalties to her, but drugs, Brooke? Really?"

"I have no idea what you're talking about, Colby."

"You're going to sit there and tell me that Ms. Potter hasn't been getting drug deliveries to her clubs and she hasn't been using the clubs as a front for dealing drugs?"

"That's exactly what I'm going to tell you. I've never heard Ms. Potter discuss drugs, ever."

Brooke was surprised at the allegations of drugs. Luce had never, ever talked about drugs in any context in the past year. Not using, not experimenting, or even the money surrounding the drug trade. Brooke somehow expected that it went against Luce's moral character. The nasty smell of addiction didn't set well with Luce, whether alcohol, drugs or something else, she didn't need a crutch and didn't condone those that did. Something didn't pass the smell test here and her journalistic instincts were flaring.

"So what makes you think Ms. Potter is involved in drugs?"

"I have my sources."

She raised an eyebrow at the pictures "So I see." It was Brooke's turn to be skeptical of Colby's intentions. Throwing around accusations of drug dealing, prostitution or money laundering weren't below Colby, she just seemed to be reaching. "Where would you get such an idea that Ms. Potter would be mixed-up in drugs?"

"Brooke, let's cut the Ms. Potter crap. I know you two are lovers, you all but said so the last time I was here." Colby sat back down on the couch with a huff. "My source is reliable, besides, he puts the drug delivery at the club with a Yakuza. All inside stuff."

"He?"

Thinking about who could link Luce with drugs wasn't coming together. Luce wasn't in the habit of dealing with lowbrow, bottom feeders, not to mention she was trying to legitimize most of her operation, but the VIP clubs were a new business Brooke knew nothing about. Clearly, or the pictures wouldn't have caught Brooke by surprise.

As for the drug trade, Brooke knew the Russians and the drug cartel were making deals to export through Russian channels, it was all over the streets. Most capitalistic bastards with enough money were trying to squeeze into the barely legal side of the import/export trade in the hopes that they could land a lucrative deal in the process of shipping high volumes overseas. The Russian involvement made it easy to ship drugs out to the motherland, with the promised connection of wider distribution in Eastern Europe, which was even more attractive to the cartels. The drug trade from Afghanistan though was competing with the U.S. – Russian connections. The trade route over land made it easier to move drug mules than the ocean route between the U.S., Columbia and Russia. Arms for drugs, and vice-versa made it all a nasty, bloody business, and one Brooke hoped Luce hadn't gotten mixed-up in.

"Look, you want to come clean, let's lay all our cards on the table then." Brooke leaned on her desk. "You tell me what the hell is going on and I'll see what I can find out."

"It's not that easy, Brooke. I'm working a case with your lover as the prime suspect. I can't tell you who gave me the drug information and I can't tell you what I know. I won't compromise my investigation."

Brooke shook her head. "Wait, you think you can walk in here, ask me a bunch of questions and *I'll* spill *my* guts, you must be out of your mind."

"No, I had just hoped that you wouldn't want to see your girlfriend go to jail. We're talking major time here Brooke. Drugs, prostitution, gambling and whatever else Luce is involved in will get her major time and that doesn't even count what I think happened to JP Potter."

"I see, so you think you can play on my emotions for Luce by showing me some pictures of her in a compromising position. I'll be so jealous that I'll coming crawling back to you and confirm everything? Is that right?" Brooke's voice trembled with anger. How dare Colby try and take advantage of what she perceived to be a weakness in Brooke—jealousy. "That threatening to expose Luce or send her to prison will get me to spill my guts, is that it?"

"I'm hoping you'll see reason and do the right thing, Brooke."

"I've told you that Luce and I aren't together and even if we were, I wouldn't trade what I had with her, for you, ever. You have no concept of loyalty, Colby. The closest thing to loyalty you have is using the same brand of deodorant for the past ten years. So, don't try and come in here on your flag waving, high horse and tell me that I should do the right thing for my country. That's your job, not mine. So get your happy ass off my sofa and don't darken my door again. Next time you come, bring a warrant and a shit load of agents, because if I see you here again, I'll file a harassment lawsuit. You've stepped way over the line this time, Agent Water."

Pulling the door open, she practically dumped Stella on the floor.

"Did you get an ear full, Stella?" Brooke directed her attention to Colby. "Now get out."

Colby grabbed her folder, shoved the pictures into it and hoisted it up under her arm. She put her pen in her blazer. "Don't make this harder than it has to be, Brooke. Be smart, think about yourself, because obviously Luce isn't. At least not according to these pictures." Walking in front of Brooke she stopped short and turned close enough so only she and Brooke could hear each other. "You're in dangerous waters and you don't even know it. The Russian's have a man on you twenty-four, seven and it's only a matter of time before they do something deadly to get at Luce." Brooke looked up into Colby's softened eyes. "I can't protect you all the time."

The pain Brooke saw made her wince. Colby didn't soften easily, and for her to almost plead for Brooke's safety was offsetting.

"Good-bye, Agent Water. Stella, please see that our guest makes it out of the building." Brooke followed Colby out to the hallway. "And if you leave with her, Stella, you're fired."

She knew that it was a low blow to call Stella out like that in front of Colby, but she had lost her patience with the situation. Colby would use Stella to get information. It was in her DNA, just like being a womanizer. It all came down to sex with Colby. If it met her needs, she used it.

Colby turned to plead Stella's case for her, but thought better of it when Brooke slammed the door.

"Fuck, fuck, fuck." Brooke heaved against the door and waited. What had Luce gotten herself into now?

Chapter Twenty-three

I'm going to see that bitch my grandfather married," Luce said smugly.

The sting of the slap caught her solid on the cheek. The sound only now assaulted her ears. Without thinking, she touched the heated handprint left from the assault, as she bolted to a standing position, warning off her man.

"You're lucky, you're my auntie, otherwise someone would be mopping up your blood off the floor." Luce warned between grinding teeth.

"Do you think you can scare me, Kaida?" Auntie stood in front of Luce trying to stare down her niece, who towered over her slightly stooped body. While she wasn't physically imposing, she had a reputation of kicking ass and not taking shit from anyone.

If the grimace on Luce's face was any reflection of her mood, her auntie didn't seem to care.

"You weren't raised to be disrespectful. I'm ashamed to call you my niece." Auntie's dismissive tone left Luce standing by herself. Looking over at her second-in-command, she saw Sammy's hand still rested on his weapon under his jacket.

"Go sit down, Sammy. What are you going to do? Shoot my auntie?"

"But, Oyabun, she hit you. You have a quite a welt on your cheek."

Luce's ire was peaking with each word Sammy

spoke. She had been shamed in front of her second and Auntie knew damn well he had seen everything. Family elders had a way of shaming the younger generation and did it with flair. The fact that Sammy was reminding her of the incident, only added to her discomfort.

"Did your mother never slap you?"

"Of course, but only once. Soon I was taller than her and I think it frightened her."

"Trust me, she wasn't afraid of you, she was afraid for you. If she didn't want your father getting his hands on you."

In Japanese families, boys were golden. In some families, they were allowed to run rampant in their young years with little to no boundaries. While girls were groomed to be silent, demur and withdrawn, often requiring other women's company for companionship. Luce had watched as Japanese women dropped their eyes, laughed behind their hands and almost blended into the wallpaper when men were around. She would never be that woman, never.

"You might be right. He was a mean drunken bastard." Sammy rubbed a phantom bruise on his chin. It was pretty common knowledge that Sammy's dad was a mean drunk, but they all ignored his behavior out of respect for Sammy's mom. Luce's grandfather had gone over to Sammy's house when they were young children. He wanted to straighten out a young Sammy, but had ended up laying down the law to Sammy's dad instead. The stupid bastard had greeted him at the door drunk and brazenly threatened to kick his ass. That was the last time anyone had seen Sammy's father drunk. Many said that the Oyabun beat the man to within an inch of his life. It didn't matter what happened. He got sober and straight with his family and then he was gone. A note was left behind explaining that he was going home to the motherland and no one ever saw or heard from him again. The only exceptions were the monthly checks he sent to take care of his family.

Luce sat back down in the booth and rubbed the growing welt. Spying her Auntie walking towards her with something in her hand, Luce jumped to her feet not wanting to be caught sitting when her aunt swung again.

"Relax, Kaida," Auntie grumbled, wiggling the ice pack. "It's for your cheek."

Bowing her head automatically she responded, "Thanks." Luce flinched as she placed it against her face.

"You're lucky, that's all you got. You're not so big that I can't put you over my knee and whip your smart ass, still."

"Oh, I think we are way beyond that, Auntie."

"Humph, we'll see. Talk like that again and you'll get the same. Oyabun or not makes no difference to me."

"Auntie, Auntie." Luce couldn't think of anything to say to her swinging aunt.

"Your grandfather would be disappointed in you. He raised you better than that." Auntie speared a piece of tofu floating in her soup. "Perhaps your biological father is coming out in you now?"

Luce was sure Auntie knew she was pushing buttons that would send her into a fit of rage if she continued with her rant about JP. Luce would rather cut off her last two fingers than be anything like JP. He had disgraced and disowned her when her mother died so he had no influence on how she was raised. If they shared a genetic trait she was sure it was her quick temper and her propensity to use violence to solve problems.

"Are you making a point, Auntie or just trying to push my buttons?"

"Is this how you honor the memory of your grandfather? By disrespecting the woman who made his last years livable?" Luce didn't need to look at Auntie, she could feel the disappointment rolling off her.

"I feel like I didn't know my grandfather at all, Auntie. How do you live with someone for ten years and not tell your only living heir? How?"

The question stung even as it left her lips. She asked herself the same thing over and over for the past week and answers still escaped her. At the moment she felt she had more in common with the bastard who'd fathered her that the man who raised her. Betrayal was a knife that cut so deep, she doubted the wound would ever heal.

"What good would meeting her do, Kaida? Huh?"

"You don't think I deserve to meet the woman who inherited millions from my family?"

"Is this about the money? Is that why you're hurting?"

Luce stared at her auntie. Money? This wasn't about money, this was about something else, but before Luce could vocalize it her Auntie interrupted.

"I didn't think so. You want to make this woman pay for your grandfather not telling you about her. You think that confronting her will make you feel better. Well it won't, Kaida."

"Have you met her?"

Silence lingered at the table.

"No."

"Auntie..."

"No. I heard rumors but I never asked. It wasn't my place."

There it was again, that silent, demur woman Asian culture was so revered for. Luce would never be that silent, that invisible, ever in her life. She would be a force to be reckoned with and that type of woman came with the demand for answers. A demand to be seen and dealt with.

"I see..." Luce wondered why her aunt who usually made it her business to know everyone else's had decided to suddenly take a pass on her grandfather's. "Why?"

"Why what?"

"Why didn't you ask? It's not like you to leave things alone."

"Your mother was my best friend. Besides, I didn't want to know. Your grandfather was an honorable man. He would never dishonor your grandmother's memory, never."

"But what about me, Auntie?"

"Quit acting like a spoiled child who thinks she deserves everything."

"I was his—"

"He was your grandfather, not your boyfriend, Kaida. He didn't owe you anything. Did you ask his counsel when you found out you liked girls?"

"Of course not."

"Of course not? Why not? He was your grandfather, didn't he have a right to decide what was best for you?"

"I don't understand where you're going with this, Auntie?"

"He was a proud Oyabun. Did you think about how this might affect him and his life?"

"Of course, but it was my life, Auntie," Luce grumbled at the turn the conversation was taking.

"Exactly, he let you live your life and he needed to live his. Perhaps he didn't tell you because he knew you would act like this, Kaida."

"But she didn't even come to the hospital."

"Where you at the hospital every minute? Didn't you have business to attend to? Perhaps he didn't want…how do you young people say it…all the drama in his last days."

"But this could have all been avoided if he had just told me years ago." Luce tried to assure her aunt.

"Perhaps, but perhaps you would have made him choose, Luce. Her or you. Could you have allowed another woman into his life?"

"I want to say yes, Auntie." Luce shook her head. Faced with the possibility of sharing her grandfather with another woman, could she, would she have understood his need to be with someone other than her grandmother? It was a question she would never know the answer to now.

"He made the choice so you wouldn't have to. Let him rest in peace, Kaida. His soul deserves to find solace and comfort with your grandmother. Don't deny him that."

Luce didn't say anything. The wisdom that came with age trumped anything passion brought into life. She would never be a woman of advanced years or an abundance of wisdom. Her passion would bring a different kind of senility.

Bowing her head, she said, "I bow to your wisdom, Auntie."

"Hmm, the day you bow to me is the day I should retire my young dragon," Auntie said, patting Luce's folded hands.

"Do you doubt my sincerity? You're the only family I have left, Auntie. You mean the world to me." Luce threaded her fingers and regretted the tone her questions had taken.

"Speaking of family, how is Brooke?"

"I don't know, Auntie. The last time we spoke it wasn't good."

"Why am I not surprised, Kaida? You're famous for burning bridges. Don't burn this one. She's been good for you."

"I know, trust me, I know."

Chapter Twenty-four

L uce picked up the phone on the first ring. "Yes," she said, looking down at her watch. It was barely seven, but she hadn't been sleeping well since Brooke had stopped staying at her house.

"Good morning, Oyabun."

"Good morning, Sammy. Checking up on me? I'll be at the office as soon as I finish a few things here."

"I'm sorry Oyabun, I wasn't checking up on you. We...um...it seems we have a problem."

Luce wasn't sure she was ready for another problem, especially this early in the morning. "What is it, Sammy?"

"You know that mic you put on that fed who came by your office?"

"Yes."

"Well, we picked up some stuff I think you're going to want to hear."

"Why don't you give me the *Readers Digest* version, Sammy?" I don't have time to come downtown right now." She had been planning to get a tattoo over her scars. The remnants of her cutting incident the night of the funeral.

"I'm sorry, Oyabun, but I think this is something you'll want to hear with your own ears."

"Fuck, Sammy, just give me the details. I told you I've got an appointment." How bad could it possibly be, she wasn't doing anything the feds could pin directly on her, at least she didn't think they worked that fast. The rumor was if the federal government was involved in an investigation, you could move to a whole new location before they even got the warrant to search your place. And as usual, the feds broke down the door to the wrong house and lost out on what could have been prime information. Now local cops, that was different. They worked fast. So back to her original thought, *how bad could it be?*

"Spill it, Sammy, or you could lose another digit if you're not quick about it."

"It's Ms. Erickson…"

"What about Brooke?"

"She's on the tape, Oyabun."

"What do you mean, she's on the tape?"

"She's being questioned by the woman with your pen and it looks like they know each other."

"Fuck, like *how* do they know each other?"

"I'm sorry, Oyabun. I think you should hear the tape for yourself. It's sounds like they have history."

"Shit," Luce whispered. History, what did that mean? History like a journalist who had government connections her stories, or history like they have, or had, a relationship? If that was the case why didn't Brooke tell her she knew a federal agent? Didn't Brooke think that was something Luce needed to know before continuing their relationship? Oh fuck, maybe Brooke was working for the feds. Maybe she was just using Luce to get dirt on her so the feds could put her away. Luce couldn't handle more betrayal, not from Brooke, too.

Luce exploded, punching her fist through the closest wall.

"Oyabun, are you okay?" Sammy asked. His voice

laced with fear.

"How do they know each other and don't sugar coat it, Sammy. Not if you value your job. I'll shoot you myself if I find out you lied," Luce threatened. "Are they a current item?"

"No, it clearly sounds like Brooke doesn't want anything to do with the Agent."

"What's the agent's name?"

"Agent Colby Water."

"What agency does she work with?"

"I'm not sure."

"Okay."

"There's more, Oyabun."

"Fuck, what else?"

"Agent Water thinks you're selling drugs through the VIP clubs."

"What?"

Where the hell was that coming from? Drugs were a dirty business and she didn't like to get her hands that dirty, even if the money was good. Besides, the drug cartels were like rabid dogs. They bit the hand that fed them and had no loyalties to anything but the almighty American dollar. Hell, they killed their own people if it made them more money and if family got in the way it was their funeral. No, the drug business wasn't one she wanted anything to do with, period. But why did Agent Water think she was involved with the drug cartel? Something wasn't adding up, or *maybe* she was being *set-up*.

"Has anyone else heard that tape?"

"Just myself and Lynn."

"Good, put it in the safe. I'll be right down. Who's on Agent Water?"

"Sasha."

"Good, call her and see where our little Agent Water is right now. I want eyes on Brooke too."

"You got it."

She couldn't see Brooke to get the answers she needed, not now that the feds thought she was selling drugs. Luce slammed the phone down on the desk and looked at the hole in the wall. Slamming her fist she added a matching one next to it.

"Somebody's got a lot to answer for," Luce said, rubbing her skinned-up knuckles. "I wonder what the going rate is for a federal agent?"

Pulling her gun from her shoulder holster, she popped the clip out, checked it out of habit and slammed it back in place. Someone was setting her up and she was going to find out who. If Luce was into guessing games her first guess would be a fucking Russian and the worm who betrayed her family.

✄ ✄ ✄ ✄

Colby shifted in the front seat of her government issued SUV. Gone were the days of the standard white or black sedan. These days the government spent money on more SUV's since they often did double duty as tactical vehicles as well. Colby was sitting in just that kind of vehicle: tinted windows, her gear in the back, a change of clothes and a blanket. The blanket had come in handy on the days when she had some *rec* time. Right about now she would kill for some *rec* time with a particular brunette who came to mind. Unfortunately, Colby had her working undercover at the VIP club Luce Potter had just opened last week. *Dang!* She had gotten lucky when Cheryl was picked up as a bartender, but she had stacked the deck in her favor with more than one qualified applicant for various positions at the club. The only problem was it put her light on resources for keeping an eye on Luce. Now, it only left her and Agent Scarr. He'd done his fair share of sitting in a car, making it her turn.

For the past week she'd been Luce's shadow, but she hadn't seen anything that confirmed the information from her informant, nothing. You could set a watch according to Luce's schedule. At seven-twenty, she left her estate, arrived at her office complex exactly at seven-fifty. She took her lunch at eleven-thirty, choosing either sushi or a quaint Korean dive in Korea town. Back at the office by one and out by four with her usual stop at one of her clubs. Lately, she had been stopping at her newest VIP club for a lap dance or two from the hot red-head from the photos. Colby was running the dancer's information and hopefully the government gears wouldn't grind to a halt before she got her information. Potter had distanced herself from Brooke, and on some level it pissed Colby off. Colby remembered the look on Brooke's face the last time she'd seen her. The shock had been brief and well concealed after a moment, but it was obvious Brooke had no idea what Luce was into lately. Brooke definitely had a career in acting, because she played it off well.

Getting out of the car, Colby stepped to the curb and casually brushed some phantom lint off her blazer as she checked the area making sure none of Luce's goons were around. Lucky for her, Luce's offices were near a great little coffee shop that she had become quit fond of lately.

"Hey, Colby, how are you? The usual?"

"Hey, DC how are ya this cold morning?"

Colby had spent enough time looking more like

a local employee who liked to take her breaks at the coffee shop. Her cover – a relocated tech employee who lived out of the local hotel. The tools of her trade were carried around in her messenger bag. She had the latest in GPS surveillance, her back-up weapon and magazines and a laptop.

Unless she accidently left her bag behind, no one would make her for a federal agent, except Luce or her employees. Luce didn't seem to have the coffee habit. *Lucky her*, Colby thought as she quickly calculated all the money she had spent since the advent of the *new* coffee shop. Hell, by her own math she could have come close to affording a nice little BMW convertible if she gave up her addiction. Naw, then what would she do with her free time? *More sex!*

"Black with a kick?"

"You know me so well already." Colby smiled, dropped a five and walked to the doctoring station. Three sugars, a chug of half-and-half and it was passable as coffee.

"How's the apartment hunting goin'?"

"Slow, who knew it was so damn hard to find a decent place in the city?"

"Yeah, it took me months to find a place that took me, my dog *and* had parking. That gets ya..."

"Wait. I had no idea places charge extra for parking."

"Yep, covered and locked parking is even more." DC said, wiping down the counter for the third time in ten minutes.

"No shit. Hell, I'm thinking if I find some place close to work I might just sell the car and ride my bike. Now, I think you've convinced me to part with my SUV. That and the price of gas is strangling me."

"That's a tough one."

The barista had bought her story hook, line, and sinker. He was fresh from the mid-west and a little too trusting. A few years in the city would fix that soon.

"Well hey if you hear of a place let me know," Colby said, flipping open her newspaper. "The sooner I get one, the sooner I'm outta your hair."

"Are you sick of me already? Geez you blondes are all alike. Love 'em and leave 'em." He shot Colby a toothy smile. He'd flirted with her every day for the past week and a half. She didn't have the heart to burst his bubble, besides a love-sick man helped build a better alibi.

"I'm not the one with the dog and the girlfriend," she flirted back, her throat tightening as she spit the words out.

The sound of the bell over the door stopped the barista before he could finish his flirt. Thankfully, Colby pulled the newspaper closer and pretended to read it while checking out the newest patron in the coffee shop.

Short, stocky, Caucasian. The bulge under his left armpit signaled a possible weapon. She could barely make out an accent as she tried to listen in. Definitely not American by birth, she figured out quickly. Pulling out a pad and a pen, she jotted down height, weight, hair color, and eyes. The scar on the back of his left hand and his pasty complexion made it obvious he didn't tan easy. He had all the characteristics of Eastern European, but she'd never be sure without confirmation.

Trying to be as stealth as possible, she walked her coffee cup back over to the doctoring station and waited. As he pulled the door open, she snapped his picture at the same time as the bell overhead rang, hiding the imitation sound of a lens closing on her phone. She'd have to figure out how to turn that off. The sound was damn irritating when she was on stake out. It was amazing how loud things sounded when you were trying to hide. Following him, she watched as he jumped into a Caddie. Typical, mafia car with tint and rims. Punching his license plate into her phone she sent it to Scarr, in hopes he would identify it as a license plate and run it.

To her surprise, he didn't leave the parking lot, instead he parked in the next lot over, dropped the driver's window and lit a cigarette. While that didn't label him Russian mafia, it definitely added to the growing list of possibilities. Moving her stuff closer to the window, she flicked the paper open and watched Mr. Black Caddy over the top. He flicked his ash and she watched as he chain-smoked a whole pack before getting out of his car again and stretching.

Interesting, coffee, smokes and yoga, next he'll be... Colby stopped in mid-thought as another car pulled up next to the black Caddy. *Fuck me,* she whispered. A young woman got out of the car and walked over to Mr. Black Caddie. However, it wasn't just any woman; it was the hot redhead from the VIP club. The fact that they were meeting in such close proximity to Luce's offices didn't escape Colby. Pulling her phone, she frantically pushed through the menu hunting for the camera app.

"Damn, technology," she said, finding the app in time to snap several pictures before they retreated back to Mr. Black Caddy's car. The tinted window went-up and Colby stayed glued to her seat. If she left now, she would draw their attention. Worse, she would miss an opportunity to gather more information on the dancer, namely her car license plate. Chances are it would come back just like the Caddy's, registered to a no-name business front. Now Colby's hunches were getting the best of her. Maybe, Ms. Dancer was just having a liaison with Mr. Caddy? It was just a coincidence it was in front of Yoshida Enterprises. Right? Not likely. As if things couldn't get worse, movement on her right caught Colby's eye. Luce's right-hand man, Sammy Lew, was walking towards the coffee shop.

"Shit," Colby cursed, snapping the paper up again.

"Hey, DC my man. How are you?"

"Hey, Sammy," DC slapped the offered hand. "How you been?"

As the two chatted, Colby stayed glued to the Caddy. They had probably seen Sammy come across the street as well, because Ms. Dancer quickly jumped out of one car and into hers. Quietly, she exited the lot and rolled over to the Yoshida business offices.

"Interesting," she said, watching the black Caddie roll out behind her and shooting down in the opposite direction. Colby packed all her gear up, folded the newspaper and shoved it under her arm to make a bee-line for the door.

"Excuse me, Miss?"

Chapter Twenty-five

Brooke was finished waiting for the ever-elusive phone call from Luce. She was going to push the issue, or they were done. She had waited long enough for a response to her messages and texts, now she wanted closure. Work had kept her busy enough, and while she hadn't sat around waiting by the phone, it had been aggravating and she deserved better than what Luce was giving her—nothing.

"Hey, gorgeous. What's got you so cramped up?"

"Huh? Oh, John. I'm seriously done."

"You're quitting? You're not serious. If it's because of the travel voucher, we'll get that straightened out, trust me Brooke, it's just a computer glitch." John nervously loosened his collar as he slumped down in his chair. He stressed easily and lately the economy had him practically broken out in hives.

Brooke sighed, rubbing her forehead. She'd made a decision she hoped she could live with. Now all she needed to do was confront Luce and tell her.

"I've made a decision about Luce," she said, sliding back against the chair. "I'm done waiting for Luce to return my call. I've called, I've texted her." She used her fingers to tick off each chore. "I've emailed her, I'm done. She doesn't want to talk to me, fine. Besides, I think she's seeing someone already."

"What? No way." He couldn't have looked more surprised, which shocked Brooke. Hadn't John been the one to warn Brooke away from Luce in the beginning? "How do you know she's cheating?"

"God, John, I am an investigative journalist. Besides, it all makes sense. Her grandfather died, she's had an epiphany and now she's wants to be single. Live life to its fullest before the rug is pulled out from under her."

"Proof, Brooke. Do you have proof?"

Brooke reached into the top drawer of her desk and tossed a photo in John's lap. "Yep, here's the proof." One of the photos Colby tossed at her from her last visit had slipped under her desk and gone unnoticed until the cleaning crew put it on her desk. What a *thoughtful* surprise she walked into that morning. She'd spilled her coffee all over her new suit. The burns were the least painful thing she would encounter that day. A beautiful woman sprawled out all over Luce and Luce couldn't look happier with the experience. Her gaze was firmly focused on the woman's *assets*. Her smile wasn't only genuine, it was one Brooke had seen often.

"Ouch." John grimaced, peering over the edge of the photo at Brooke.

"Yea, *ouch*, that's what I was thinking when I saw that little exchange. She beautiful isn't she?"

"Look, I'm sure Luce can explain this. Where'd you get this photo?" John turned it over looking for something to indicate its owner.

"I have my sources." Brooke snatched the photo back and stared at it for the umpteenth time. "Here I thought she was broken up about the death of her grandfather. Color me stupid."

"Call her, Brooke."

"I've tried, John. I'm done."

"Call her," he said with a little more emphasis.

"She's a proud woman, Luce. If what you told me about the night of the funeral is true, then she might be ashamed of her behavior and doesn't want to admit it."

"I'm her girlfriend, John. Besides, she doesn't look to broken up in this photo does she?"

"Sometimes things aren't what they seem, even in a photo, Brooke. You better than anyone should know that."

She crossed her arms and avoided looking at John. "I've told you, I'm done. Clearly, she's moved on," she said measuring each word. "Unlike you, I know when to call it."

"What do you mean by that?"

"Nothing, I'm just frustrated and taking it out on you. Ignore me. I'm just being a bitch right now."

Reaching across Brooke's desk, John grabbed her phone and punched the intercom. "Stella, can you dial Luce Potter's office for me? Thank you."

John cradled the phone between his shoulder and cheek. Ignoring Brooke, he picked at a finger nail and then made a show of looking at his manicure. "Ms. Potter, please. It's John Lloyd from the *Financial Times*. I'm sure she'll want to speak to me. Tell her it's important." Pausing, John got comfortable. "Thank you, I'll wait."

"What are you doing, John?"

"Calling Luce."

"I see that, but she won't speak to you, so put the phone down."

"Aw, Ms. Potter how are you?"

Brooke couldn't hear the response on the other end, but she was sure it wouldn't lead to anything.

"I do need something, could you hold for a second?" John passed the phone to Brooke, shaking it and raising his eyebrows. "You said you couldn't get through, well you're through. Talk to her before she hangs-up."

"No," she whispered.

"Brooke," he whispered back.

Yanking the phone from his hand, she covered the mouth piece. "I'm going to kick you're skinny ass."

Waving his hands at her, he whispered. "Just talk to her."

"Hello, Luce. I'm sorry. John has butted his nose into something he shouldn't have. I'm sorry to bother you." She paused, and nodded her head. "Yes, I'm fine and you?"

Brooke could feel the strain of the conversation in her body. She tensed as silence echoed through the phone.

Finally, Luce said something.

"Ms. Erickson, how are you?" Luce's distant tone meant she wasn't alone. It was their code when they were dating and they called the other's office.

"I see, you have someone in your office?"

"Yes, would it be possible to call you back? When's a good time?" Luce's all-business manner was different this time.

Before Brooke could respond, she heard a woman's voice in the background. "No, no, give me just a minute and I'll be right with you." Brooke heard the muzzled explanation Luce gave her guest.

"I see you're busy. Well, I mean I can't see, but I can hear that..." Brooke stuttered and then just slammed the receiver down.

"Why'd you do that?" John said, reaching for the phone.

"Don't. Don't pick up that phone again."

"I told you she has moved on. Damn it, John, she's moved on." Brooke buried her head in her hands and tried to control the sob she could feel starting to break out.

Chapter Twenty-six

The cold, musty confines of the warehouse enveloped Luce as she walked in. She flashed back to the last time she had been here.

"Take it off. Let him breathe." Luce said, opening the cylinder and dumping the empty cartridge into her hand. Putting the last four bullets into the cylinder she could smell the coppery odor of blood and cordite mixing, filling the room. She steeled herself for what was about to come. She owed her father nothing, the fact that he had contributed to her biology was a footnote on the long list of things she and her mother had to endure at his hand while they were a family. Some things couldn't be forgotten or forgiven, not to Luce. Remembering how at peace her mother looked as she lay in the mahogany casket, buffeted any feeling of empathy she might have for her father. No matter what she did, he would always be with her. She would never be able to forget him because every time she looked in the mirror, he would be staring back at her.

Stepping back to avoid the blood pooling at JP's feet, she gave an order to wrap his legs with tourniquets. They would slow down the flow of blood and minimize the mess that the cleaning team would have to take care of later. The pallor of death covered JP's face, the grey tone replaced his normally pale coloring. His head flung forward as he passed out from the shock of being shot.

"Nuh, huh, you don't get off that easy, you bastard.

Wakie, wakie. I want you to be experience everything, Daddy. Like mom did when you hung her." Slapping his face to bring him around, she ordered Sammy to bring her some water. Pouring it over his head, he pulled up, gasping as he breathed in the liquid. *"Good, now are you taking me serious? Or would you like another example?"*

"I told you—"

"Stop."

Luce slapped his face, a hand print appeared on his cheek as the water enhanced the stinging of the slap. She was losing patience with JP and if he didn't know it yet, he soon would. Pulling his head back, she bent down and whispered in his ear.

"Listen to me, I know your working with Petrov. In fact, I know you bragged about being able to deliver me, dead or alive. Now, the question is, do I deliver you to him, dead or alive?"

Releasing his head it slumped forward, his chin practically hitting his chest as it bounced. A maniacal laugh bubbled up from his despair, confusing Luce. Had he lost his mind, or was the pain so great that it clouded his judgment? Tossing his head back he roared in laughter.

"You are so fucking screwed and don't even know it. You play right into our hands."

"What're you talking about?"

Luce stayed calm. She had seen JP try to weasel his way out of things through lying, so she wasn't playing along this time. Waiting, she absent-mindedly rolled the cylinder on the revolver, the clicking echoing through the office. The muscles between her shoulders bunched together as tension filled her body. JP continued to laugh, so she reached over and hit him with the butt of the gun, making him pause before shooting her a dirty *look. She smiled at the dirty, tear soaked face that, after tonight, she would never see again.*

"Hmm, the way I see it, the only one screwed is you, JP. You have two holes..." Looking down at his legs, she corrected herself. "Make those three holes in your legs and the night isn't even over. So, if you even think you have any leverage here, you might want to reconsider your options."

"You're a little girl playing in a man's world, Luce. You have no idea what you've gotten yourself into do you?"

"God, you are so dramatic, JP."

Rolling the cylinder, she placed it against his temple and pulled the trigger back one click. Taking a deep breath, she steeled herself against the rage that was building deep inside, trying as hard as she could to temper it with patience, but it was no use. Closing her eyes, she saw her mother's beautiful face. Her soft, almond shaped eyes seemed to close more when she smiled and Luce would often giggle and ask her mother if she could still see her when she smiled. Her mother's response was, "Of course, Kaida. You are always in my mind." Then she would bend down cup her face and kiss each of her pudgy cheeks. How she missed her mother, and thanks to the bastard that sat in front of her, taunting her, she would never see her again, never kiss her good night, never feel herself wrapped in a warm loving hug, ever. Her life had been replaced with the cold, hard reality that letting someone in might get them killed, so she adjusted her life accordingly. It was all his fault and she owed him nothing but her hatred. She felt tears threaten but swallowed her pain. She would be damned if he would see her cry, he didn't deserve that pleasure.

"*Any last words?*" *The cold, dead tone in her voice made JP turn and look at her. If he thought he would find hope in her eyes he was wrong.*

"*Wait.*"

"*You have no life lines, no friends to call, no one to help you JP.*"

Killing JP, was inevitable. He had been the sperm donor, but never the father she needed after her mother's death and she hated him. Her pulse sped up as she anticipated Agent Water's impending, *come-to-Jesus*, moment. It'd been a while since she'd brought anyone over to her way of thinking. She hoped she wasn't out of practice.

The room looked like a scene right out of a Hollywood movie. Agent Water sat tied to a chair with her hands behind her back, a gag shoved in her mouth and a blinding light overhead. Sammy and another man sat off in the corner. The glow of their cigarettes signaled their position in the darkness.

Pulling off her gloves, she slapped them against her palm. She noticed Colby jerked at the sound.

"Put those damn things out. This place is a firebox waiting to go up."

Snuffing the butts out on the dirt floor, Sammy apologized. "Oyabun, I didn't think you would mind. We've been waiting for hours."

"I got delayed at the office."

Luce noticed Agent Water didn't show the usual signs of fear she was accustom to seeing. In fact, she looked rather relaxed. When their gazes locked, Agent Water squared her shoulders, sat up straight and shot her a dirty look.

"I guess I should be thankful looks can't kill, shouldn't I, Agent Water?" Luce squatted down and ripped the gag from Colby's mouth. "Or is it, Lucrecia Holtz? Which part are you playing today?"

"Fuck you."

"Ah the indignant ingénue. Agent Water, did you think *I* was stupid enough to fall for that little act you pulled in my office? *Seriously?*"

"Well, I had to give it a try."

"Clearly you don't know me as well as you think you do," Luce said, standing and tossing her gloves at Sammy.

"Oh, I think I know *you* better that you think," Colby sneered.

"Really."

"Hmm," Colby licked her chapped lips, rolled her eyes and sighed. "I know all about you, your grandfather and his mistress—" The sound of knuckles meeting flesh resounded throughout the warehouse. "Oh, hit a sensitive spot? Let me guess it was grandpa's mistress?"

This time Colby's head jerked with the next blow. Luce rubbed the back of her hand in satisfaction. A trickle of blood oozed from the corner of Colby's mouth. She glared at Luce, but being tied up eliminated her ability to intimidate. Luce just smirked at the hatred seething off Colby.

"Guess that was it, huh?"

"I guess you like getting smacked around, don't you?"

"Naw, but I know you do," Colby said, smiling around bloody teeth.

This time Luce slapped her with the palm of her hand, the crisp sound echoing throughout the warehouse again.

"Glad to see you like to do your own dirty work,"

she said, spitting blood.

Why was Colby pushing her buttons? Didn't she notice the power dynamic wasn't in her favor?

"I don't mind getting my hands dirty if that's what you mean." Luce patted her hands together as if they were dirty. "In fact, I prefer taking out the trash, too."

"Well, you realize I'm a federal agent and killing me puts the death penalty on the table."

"What makes you think *I'm* going to kill you? You're too valuable to me alive. Besides, you haven't told me how you know Ms. Erickson."

"I suggest we compare notes about Brooke after all of this is done and over." Another wicked smile from Colby and she was going to leave with a few less teeth and a lot more bruises.

"Which means what?"

"Let's don't play games Ms. Potter. I know you and Ms. Erickson are involved. I saw you two together at the funeral and weeks before that when I was doing background on you." Colby spit again, this time it landed closer to Luce's polished loafers. "It would take a blind man to miss how —" Colby couldn't say it. It suddenly hurt to put it into words.

"How what, Agent Water?"

"How in love with you she is, that's all."

"You act as if you've see her in love before. Now, that wouldn't be possible would it Agent Water? I'm sure Ms. Erickson would have mentioned that one of her ex-girlfriends was an Agent with the DEA." Luce picked at a piece of peeling paint that had popped up on the old table.

"DOJ."

"What?"

"I'm a DOJ agent."

"Awe, Treasury. What are you looking for now? A RICO violation, tax evasion, what?"

"Do you mind loosening these?" Colby pulled against her own cuffs. They had gone through her things and cuffed her when they found them. It was degrading to be locked up with your own equipment, but that was the least of her problems right now.

"No, there's something sexy about you sitting there all tied-up with no control. We call it being a submissive, so get used to it. I think you're going to be like that for a while."

"Someone's going to miss me. I do have to check in and I give a report to my boss, Deputy Chapel, at four p.m.," Colby lied. No one would miss her for a couple of days. "So, let me go and we'll call this even. I won't say anything to my buddies at the agency or... Brooke." Colby let Brooke's name go low in the most dramatic whisper she could muster.

"Deputy Chapel, huh?" Luce sat on the end of the table she had just been picking at the paint. Her leg swung back and forth close to Colby's chair, close enough to push it over if she pissed her off again.

"Yea, know her? I guess when you've been around organized crime as long as you have, I'm sure the name has come up a time or two." Colby shifted her shoulders trying to loosen her wrists in the cuffs.

"A time or two, but not in the way you might expect."

Luce saw Colby stop moving when the comment finally came to rest in her brain. Slowly turning towards Luce, she narrowed her eyes, the lips of her mouth formed a thin line as she pursed them tightly together.

"I don't like what you're implying, Potter."

Luce smiled. It was her turn to surprise Agent

Water with information she wouldn't like hearing. "No, I don't suppose you do." Luce slipped her glove on and pulled her gun from her shoulder holster, placing it on the table. She nodded her head towards the door and made sure Sammy and the other man left the room before she continued.

"You're the only one out of the loop here, Agent." Luce's stare didn't waver. She'd had more than a few dealings with the ladder-climber, Deputy Chapel. She wasn't sure how she figured into all of this, but Luce knew if her name was connected, it wasn't good.

"So why are you on me?"

"I have no idea what you're talking about, Ms. Potter."

"Aw, the innocent agent, who *just happens* to be following one of the most powerful women in the country, nice."

"Wow, you don't have an ego do you, Potter?"

Luce smiled at the statement. She was many things, but humble wasn't one of them.

"Look, we both know that you've been following me for a while. Let's cut to the chase." Luce braced herself on each side of Colby's shoulders and went nose-to-nose with the Agent. "Why me? Why are you following me?"

"I'm just doing my job, Potter."

"I hear there are drugs on the street and you're trying to connect them to me." Luce let her foot rest on the chair, between Colby's legs. "Let me save you the trouble, I don't do drugs."

"Hmm, what makes you think I'm looking to hook you on a drug charge? You're up to your neck in so many other *opportunities*, why limit yourself to the drug trade?"

"Exactly, why *limit* the opportunities. Like you, I bet you avail yourself of lots of opportunities."

"Well one can never have too many opportunities." Colby's swollen lips barely cracked a smile.

"So, back to my question. Who told you I was connected to the drug trade?"

"No one—"

The quick slap sent Colby teetering on two of the wobbly chair's legs. Luce put her foot back between Colby's legs and stopped it from tumbling over. Leaning down close to Colby's face again, she rolled her eyes and let out a deep, long sigh. Running her hands along Colby's neck, she let her thumbs roll over her swollen lips and smiled.

"Are you flirting with me now, Potter? It won't work. I'm not into bad girls. I like mine a little more wholesome."

"Don't flatter yourself, Agent. But you are doing something to me, seeing you all tied-up like this, sure you don't want a quickie?" Luce leaned back and laughed. The look on the agent's face was priceless and Luce's wicked sense of humor couldn't resist the taunt.

"Well, I guess that's the only way you can get off, huh? You like your women trussed up like a Christmas turkey. Is that how Brooke likes it now?"

"Ah Brooke, is she part of your job?"

Luce couldn't ignore the broad smile breaking across Colby's face. It took all she had not to slap it off, but she wouldn't be goaded again if she could help it.

"Who?"

"Agent Water, you know that cute little pen you picked up in my office?"

Colby twitched slightly as she looked over at her blazer.

"Yes, that pen." Luce walked over and slapped at the jacket looking for the pen. Pulling it from an assortment of pens in the inner pocket of the blazer, she held it up for Colby's inspection. Pulling it apart, Luce dumped a small wireless transmitter in her hand for Colby to inspect. "I've heard everything you said. In fact, I have it recorded, would you like to hear it?"

Colby looked past it and ignored the taunting tone of Luce's voice. Luce knew she was doing a mental run through trying to figure out what she might have said when she had the pen.

"So, want to tell me how you know Ms. Erickson? It's clear she isn't just someone you would visit to for a story." Luce pulled Colby's face forcing her to look Luce in the eyes. "Look you can either tell me what I want to know or I'll pay Ms. Erickson a visit, and I think you know I can be very persuasive. Just look at your face."

Luce knew her threat was hollow, but Colby didn't know that and if her reputation played out in her favor, Agent Water would spill her guts. Luce was betting the Agent wouldn't risk Brooke's safety, regardless if she was an ex or not. No one was that heartless, well except her, but she knew when to apply pressure and Agent Water didn't earn her compassion. She was sure Agent Water felt the same way about her, as Luce felt about feds: they were expendable if they got in her way. Right now, Agent Water was in her way.

"You wouldn't hurt Brooke," Colby said, shaking her head. "She deserves so much better than a low-life like you. What she sees in you, I'll never understand."

"And what, you're the alternative?" Luce laughed. "From where I'm standing, you got nothing."

"Big talk when my hands are tied." Colby

struggled to get free, but only succeeded in cutting into her wrist more with the tight cuffs.

Luce flicked her wrist at Colby. "Oh don't worry about that, I'm sure you'll be free soon enough and then we can have a go at it. Now, want to answer my question?"

"Which one?"

"I know you think I'm involved in the drug trade, that much I got from this," Luce said, holding the small device between her index finger and thumb. "I just didn't have you tagged for an idiot. The cartel and the Russian's are butt-fucking on that side of the fence. So why are you looking to me for drugs?"

"I got nothin' better to do." The flip remark slipped easily from her lips, just as Luce's hand reached around her neck. Thumbs pushed against the flexible windpipe, as Luce's gripped tightened, cutting of the blood flow to her head. Bulging eyes, the gasps for breath didn't stop Luce from apply more pressure. The glazed look on Colby's face signaled she was just about to pass out, so Luce let her grip loosen.

"Want to try again? Who put you on me?"

Colby didn't say a word, she didn't even try. Luce tightened her grip again, watching Colby's face turn a deep shade of red, her eyes glazing again.

"Op, op, op. Don't go to sleep on me, Agent Water." Luce slackened her grip again bringing Colby around. "Okay, one more time. Who put you on me?" Luce raised her eyebrows in question. "Agent Water?"

"Gang-banger," she whispered barely coherent.

"You're sitting your fat ass on me because of a gang-banger? God, so now you're using gang-bangers as CI's. What happened, run out of tweakers?"

"Fuck you."

Chapter Twenty-seven

"Good afternoon, Ms. Wentworth, is Ms. Potter in?"

Audrey ran around her desk trying to intercept Brooke before she reached the door to Luce's office.

"No," she grabbed the handle and put her back against the door. "You just missed her, she had a meeting and I don't expect her back until tomorrow morning. How are you Ms. Erickson? I haven't seen you around the office for a few weeks." Audrey didn't move.

Brooke stood so close to Audrey she was sure Audrey could smell her perfume, up close and personal. Something was up, Audrey didn't stop her from going into Luce's office. They were way past that and Audrey had known Brooke for almost two years.

"Audrey?"

"Yes, Ms. Erickson?"

"Why are you blocking the door? Is Luce inside and you're running interference for her?"

"Oh, no Ms. Erickson, I promise," she said, running her fingers across her heart. "She isn't in there. She really is at a meeting."

"Hmm."

Suddenly, Audrey was pulled back as the door opened and a stunning redhead stood behind her. But this wasn't just any redhead, this was the one out of the photos Colby had surprised her with earlier. The one she had seen practically fucking Luce at the club.

"Good afternoon," Brooke stuck out her hand. "I'm Brooke Erickson, investigative journalist and you are...."

She'd set the snare so easily, now it was time to see if she could lure her prey into it.

"Hello, my friends call me, Kat." Kat smiled, not the kind that reached the eyes, but the kind that made someone want to slap it off her face. Suddenly, Brooke wasn't so sure she wanted to talk to the woman who seemed to have her ex-girlfriend wrapped around her finger. She was coming out of Luce's office, wasn't she?

"Well, since we aren't friends," Brooke pulled her hand away. "Is Kat short for...Katarina...Katlin...?"

"Kathleen." Kat pushed her jacket over her arm and wiggled around Audrey.

"I didn't catch your last name," Brooke said, standing in front of Kat.

"That's because I didn't throw it. Now if you'll excuse me I need to get to work. Please tell Ms. Potter I'll see her later." Kat looked Brooke up and down, then walked past her without saying a word.

"Ms. Erickson, would you like to leave a message for Ms. Potter?"

"She's not in there, really?"

"She left a few minutes before you arrived." Putting up her hand Audrey stopped Brooke. "I don't know why she didn't leave with Ms. Potter."

"I do." Brooke tried to smile but just couldn't muster the energy. Seeing Kat in Luce's office left her with no other conclusion but that Luce had moved on.

"I wouldn't jump to any conclusions, Ms. Erickson. I've known Ms. Potter a long time and she doesn't let something like that replace someone like you."

"Really? Well I think it just happened, but thank you for the vote of confidence, Audrey. It's nice to see you with some clothes on." She smiled and patted Audrey's shoulder. She suddenly felt sick to her stomach. The realization felt like a sledgehammer hitting her. Her knees started to buckle.

"Ms. Erickson?"

"I'm fine, I think I just need to sit down." Cold and sweaty, Brooke felt lightheaded and swayed slightly before sitting down in the offered chair.

"I'll call Ms. Potter."

"No," Brooke yelled. "I'm fine, do you have some water?"

"Of course. I'll be right back."

Waiting for Audrey to disappear she stood, wavered slightly but made her way to the door to the waiting area. Quickly pulling her phone she hit speed dial and waited.

"Good John, you answered. Can you come pick me up at Yoshida Enterprises? I'm not feeling well, that's why. I'll meet you down in the lobby. Hurry."

Looking back into the offices, Brooke slinked towards the elevators trying to avoid Audrey who was making her way back to an empty chair. Just as the elevator doors opened she heard Audrey calling her name. She didn't answer and pressed the close door button before anyone else could get in. It wasn't like she was going to ever see Audrey again, so no harm, no foul sending her on a wild goose chase for water. Her head still swimming, she bolted out of the elevator and hit the door just as John pulled up.

He ran around to the passenger and opened the door. "God, Brooke you look awful. What happened?"

Before she could answer, she felt her body go limp and sway towards John.

"Shit, what did Luce Potter do now?" he said, easing her into the car.

❧❦❧❦

"Brooke, honey. Brooke wakie, wakie."

A gentle pat on her face roused her. Shaking her head, she tried to clear the fog in her brain.

"Brooke, what happened?" John's voice pushed Brooke further into consciousness, the last place she wanted to be. Acceptance, she would need to *accept* her new *reality*. Luce had moved on and now she had to as well.

"If you were straight, I would ask if you were pregnant."

Brooke smiled at the ludicrous statement. *If only*, she thought.

The moving car was starting to make her nauseous.

"Pull over, I feel like I'm going to puke." Brooke leaned her head over and hit the window button, hoping the fresh air would settle her stomach. Her mind, that would take something else to settle.

"Do...Not...Puke...in my car, Brooke. This baby is almost paid-off and I would hate to take it out of your paycheck." John joked easing the car off the road.

Skidding in the dust cloud of dust, John jumped from his side and opened Brooke's door, practically pulling her on to the dirt.

"Relax, I'll get out." She swung her legs to the side and sat with her head cradled between her knees.

"What are you doing?"

"Putting my head between my legs. Isn't that what they teach you in first-aid? *When the subject feels light-headed put their head between their knees and tell them to breathe,* so I'm putting my head between my knees and breathing."

"Do not puke. I'm a sympathy puker and one whiff of you puking and I'll puke, so no puking." John stepped back and paced like and anxious husband watching his wife have contractions, helplessly waiting for the impending climax.

Brooke smacked her lips, suddenly realizing her mouth felt like it was packed with cotton balls. "Do you have any water?" she asked, looking up at John standing in the sun.

"What, water?"

"Uh, yeah, that liquid stuff that comes in bottles," she said, shading her eyes to get a better look at John. "Really, John? You look like shit."

"I look like shit? You look like shit. I'm not the one who suddenly faints and almost goes splat on the cement at Yoshida Enterprises. What happened? Did you and Luce have a fight?"

Brooke shook her head and scrubbed her face, wishing she could wash it all away. "No, I didn't see her."

"Huh?"

"I didn't see her," Brooke said, standing, still a bit wobbly. "I did see that hot, redhead though. She was in Luce's office when I got there. *Kat,*" she said, almost purring the name.

"As in kitty cat?"

"No as in Kat, not Kate, not Kathy, not even Katlin, but *Kat.*"

She leaned against the fender and clutched her

stomach. The name made her nauseous again. If she could spit it out and cleanse her mind she would puke 'til she couldn't puke anymore, but that wouldn't exorcise her from Brooke's memory.

The car dipped as John slid up on the fender and hugged Brooke. Resting her head on his offered shoulder, she started to slowly crumble under the weight of the realization that she and Luce were done. Oh, she'd floated that possibility time and again in the past week or two, not really choosing to believe it could happen. Seeing Kat come out of Luce's office made it real.

"So that's it? It's over?"

"Yep."

"Are you sure it was the same woman?"

Arching an eyebrow and leaning back, she looked at John's optimistic face. Her eyes teared up and she nodded., John pulled her into his strong embrace.

"I'm pretty good with faces. Names I suck at, but faces I've got."

"I'm sorry, Brookie."

"Me too."

Chapter Twenty-eight

Luce let her hand rise and fall as the weight of her gun settled into it. Agent Water was more than a pain in her ass. She was a problem that had to be dealt with, now. The people she'd killed deserved to be killed, that was how she reasoned their deaths. Luce wrestled with her inner demon on this one, though. Agent Water was poking her nose in things that could get her killed, but an agent's death, that was a little more unsettling, it was almost un-American.

"If you're going to kill me, get it over with, will ya?"

"Why, you have someone waiting on the other side for you?" Luce sniped back.

"Not really, but I'm not the type that likes to drag things out. I'm not really into long term commitments."

Colby's attempt at humor didn't surprise Luce. She'd seen the biggest men grovel at her feet for their life. Everyone handled it differently, but she had yet to shoot a woman, federal or not, and it rattled her a little.

"Who says I'm going to shoot you?"

"If you take it out, you'd better use it. That's what they tell us when we get our first weapon. Or haven't you taken any firearms training, Potter?"

"Oh, I've had plenty of practice. Trust me, I'm sure I've killed—" Luce clamped her jaw tight realizing she was about to incriminated herself.

"Killed what, men?"

"Targets," Luce said so nonchalantly that someone would have thought the two women were close to getting along.

"What is that?" Colby said, jutting her chin towards the iron in Luce's hand.

Luce jerked her head back, surprised. "This?" She turned the gun over and then back again. She wasn't sure where Agent Water was going with the question, but she'd play along, for now.

"It's a Berretta Nano, 9mm." Luce laid it on the table, crossed her arms and continued. "Polymer housing, stainless steel frame, no rattle, double-action trigger pull, no manual safety, and I can put a five shot pattern in the size of a quarter. There's enough weight at the end of the barrel controls any muzzle flip. The flat top design means I can sight my target in without having to use the sites, but I wouldn't recommend acquiring any new bad habits if I were you, Agent Water? Does that answer your questions?"

"Looks like a Glock knockoff to me, but hey what do I know. So, do you shoot?"

Just as Luce advanced towards Colby her phone rang, the tune signaled it was her office calling. She pulled it from her blazer and eyed the number out of habit.

"Luce here. When? Is she okay?"

"She seemed fine. I hope I didn't do something wrong," Ms. Wentworth said.

"No, you did the right thing, when Brooke gets a bug up her ass you can't stop her. Thank you, Ms. Wentworth, I appreciate the heads-up." Pausing, she leaned into the phone.

"Unfortunately your visitor was still in your

office when Brooke arrived."

"She was still there? Shit."

"I tried to explain, but she wouldn't listen. I'm afraid you're visitor wasn't much help either."

"There was nothing you would be able to say to explain that. Don't worry she's going to come to her own conclusions."

"I just thought you would want to know, Ms. Potter."

"Thanks again for letting me know. I won't be coming back to the office today, so please feel free to take the rest of the afternoon off." Luce snapped the phone closed.

"So, Ms. Erickson was at your office today. Interesting."

"Tell me again, Agent Water, how do you know Ms. Erickson? Professionally or personally?"

"Does it matter?"

"You don't have to tell me, I have ways of finding out."

"You hurt Brooke and I'll kill you. She's a nice woman and she doesn't deserve to be treated like crap by someone like you."

"I'll take that as a threat against my person."

Colby strained against her restraints and almost stood until Luce pushed her back a little too hard, toppling her chair over. Colby grimaced in pain and tried to roll to her side. Luce pressed a foot on a chair leg kept her in place. Luce sneered as she straddled Colby, lying on the floor, smashing her hands.

"I wouldn't hurt a hair on her head, just for the record. You on the other hand...by the way, are your hands hurting?"

"Fuck you."

"Hmm, you're not really my type."

"Yeah, I've seen your type. Redhead, slutty and straddling a pole, or was that your thigh I saw between her legs?"

Colby tried once more to roll to her side. Luce jerked her up almost breaking the chair. With a thump, the two were face to face.

"You've been pushing me all day. I don't suffer fools lightly, so keep it up." Luce slapped her again, pulling it slightly so this time it stung more than hurt. "Now where were we?"

⬩⬩⬩⬩

Colby turned her head and spit another mouthful of blood and then stared at Luce. She wasn't going to be offering any information to the off-kilter Yakuza. The cold, dusty confines of the room didn't leave Colby many options. No one would be walking by, so screaming wasn't going to get her anywhere, and the two guys who had brought her to the warehouse spoke mostly in Japanese. She didn't speak a lick of Japanese, Korean yes thanks to her mother, so she didn't have a clue what awaited her.

She had flexed her wrists when the Yakuza had put her own handcuffs on her, and now twisted them in what little wiggle room she had. Her left shoulder popped when Luce had pushed her on her back with her arms pinned behind her. Colby wouldn't be surprised if it had become dislocated. Lucky for her it wasn't her shooting hand. The pain firing through her upper body kept her mind alert and looking for an opportunity to take back control of the situation.

"I'm not going to ask how you know about Kat.

I'll assume you have someone inside my organization, a mole, but he won't last long. Once I put the word out he'll be gone, so to speak." Luce fingered the boxy semi-automatic as if she were touching a lover. Colby imagined those fingers stroking Brooke and suddenly worried for her safety. If the phone call was any reflection of her concern, something had happened to Brooke at Yoshida Enterprises.

"Look let's cut the bullshit and get right to the point," she said, trying to work her wrists out of the cuffs. She shifted in her chair trying to make it look like she was getting comfortable. "How is Ms. Erickson?"

"Hmm, you're concerned for Brooke's welfare. Touching."

Luce acting aloof was surprising, she was more comfortable with the aggressive, dismissive crime boss. *That* person she could deal with, the unknown was harder to plan for. If Luce got physical, Colby could hope that the chair would break in their struggle, allowing her could gain the advantage. Now she had to provoke the raging lion.

"At least she didn't see me getting humped on by that cute redhead."

Luce swirled towards Colby. She swung wide enough that Colby leaned back, avoiding the punch, but she knew that wouldn't satisfy the aggressive butch reloading for another try. The left hook caught her by surprise, catching the tip of her chin and toppling her sideways. She felt the chair give a little as it hit the floor. It was rickety when she was pushed down on it by the two meatheads earlier, so it was only a matter of time and she was a patient woman. Luce kicked Colby in the stomach, her black boots becoming a blur as Colby wretched at the contact.

"What's the matter, your mouth writing checks you ass can't cash?" Luce squatted down and stared at Colby. "No snarky comeback? Well, color me surprised, Agent Water."

"You have me at quite a disadvantage. Me on the floor, cuffed, and you standing there smug and cock-of-the-walk. Oh it's *so* hard to be you." Colby chuckled, hoping it would move Luce to pick her up again and right her on the old wooden chair.

"Yes, well it sucks-to-be-you now doesn't it?"

Luce leaned against the table and stared down at her. This wasn't going to work, so Colby needed to take another tactic sure to blow Luce Potter out of the water. She noticed Luce rolling up her sleeves exposing a small white gauze pad taped to her forearm. It was too small for a tattoo, which she knew Luce was partial to, so jabbed at her.

"What happened to your arm?"

The *fuck you* look Luce gave Colby only made her more curious. Like a dog with a bone she wasn't about to let this opportunity not help her in her plan to get free.

"Did you get a paper cut at work?"

"Fuck you." Luce's clenched her jaw, the muscles bunching.

Colby could practically hear Luce grinding her teeth. She'd work the Yakuza boss one way or the other. Women like Luce were hard to figure out, but given an opening Colby knew she could exploit it for her own benefit.

"So you're a cutter, huh?" The faint line of a scar on the inside of her other forearm made it impossible to be wrong. It was old, but old habits die hard, especially with high-strung women like Luce Potter. Lately, she'd gone through a lot of pain. If Colby were guessing, Luce was using her own pain to neutralize the pain induce by the death of her grandfather.

Silence. Colby had enough nonverbal communication training to know this was a tacit admission.

"Does, Brooke know you're a cutter?"

Luce cut the distance in two strides, courtesy of those long, muscular legs that now straddled Colby's own. Luce leaned within inches of Colby's face. When she spoke, Colby felt her warm breath.

"Don't try and psychoanalyze me, Agent Water." She dropped her voice to an icy whisper. "You might not like what you find when you peel back the layers." The slow methodical deployment of the threat sent a chill down Colby's back. For the first time this afternoon, Colby understood she had pushed the limit with Luce Potter. It was all in the eyes.

Colby started to open her mouth to say something, but saw the punch coming at her. She clenched her jaw to steel herself for the blow, and wasn't disappointed. One of the back supports snapped when the chair toppled again. She pressed it to her back to keep the chair together as Luce set her upright.

What had kept her hands anchored and secure was now mobile. Colby let go of the back support. She needed one more drop to the floor to be able to disguise slipping her cuffs between the gap of the broken slats.

"So, you never answered my question...wait, don't tell me...Brooke's into cutting too?"

"You, fuckin—" Luce leaned into the punch with all she had and hit Colby square in the abdomen. Colby couldn't suck air in fast enough before the blow forced the wind out of her lungs. She felt herself starting to get light-headed, on the verge of passing out. *Keep it together, fuck, keep it together*, she chanted as the lights dimmed slightly. Biting the inside of her mouth, the fresh coppery blood coated her tongue. She rolled to her side, curled into a ball and waited for the next onslaught.

"Oyabun?"

"What?" Luce spit out, straightening just as she was going to reach for Colby again.

This was her one and only chance.

"I have a phone call for you."

"Why didn't they call my phone?"

"I'm sorry Oyabun, I don't know."

"It's your lucky day, Agent Water."

Luce walked out the door and closed it behind her, taking her second in command with her. Colby quickly slipped her hands under her ass, pulled them in front of her and waited. When nothing moved she looked around for her blazer. Inside the blazer was her cuff key. It looked just like a pen and if no one knew any better, they would've overlooked it. She found the blazer and shuffled the garment until she found, her pen, aka cuff key. *Thank god they're as stupid as they seem*, she hurried fumbling with the lock. With her left eye nearly swollen shut, it was hard to focus. She felt the pop of the cuff on her right hand and began working on the left when she heard voicing coming closer. She grabbed her jacket and unscrewed the single light hanging in the room. If Colby was going out, she was going out fighting.

Chapter Twenty-nine

Brooke paced the front porch of her small Craftsman bungalow. If her nerves didn't get the get best of her, she was on her way to forgetting Luce Potter. A slight buzz, courtesy of her abundant glass of wine, added to her anticipation for the evening. She refused to sit home and cry over Luce Potter, but she if she stayed home that's exactly what she would do. Her ride pulled up to her driveway.

"Stella." She waved her office assistant over. "Drink?"

"What are we drinking and who are we drinking to? Wow, you look fucking hot." Stella whirled her finger in a circle directing Brooke to turn around. "I love that little leather number. Where'd you get it?"

"Just something I picked up recently. I thought I'd be using it for something else, but…" Brooke hefted the wine bottle. "Wine?"

Brooke avoided the question of *who*. She didn't want Luce's name to linger on her lips or her mind. She poured Stella a generous glass of wine and finished the bottle off in her glass. The leather squeaked as Brooke lowered herself into the wicker chair. The smell of the leather enveloped her as the warmth of the evening relaxed her—or was it the wine? It didn't matter she needed *this*. Smiling that giggly little drunk smile she got when she was feeling good, she looked at Stella. "Are you ready for tonight?"

"Sure, but I have to be honest, I was surprised when you called me and said you wanted to go to The Dungeon. After the last time, I figured Luce took care of all of those little..." Stella squirmed in her chair, tucking her feet under her, leaving her high-heels behind. "...needs."

Brooke's *last* time at The Dungeon, Luce had taken over her initiation into the bondage scene. She had gone as part of her research on the subject of BDSM after seeing Luce in a compromising position. She wondered why a woman with such power would allow someone to control her in such a way. After her visit Luce had taken her places she had never thought were possible to go, all based on trusting the one you love. Giving consent had been like giving up her virginity, it was hard, but once done it was freeing. She'd never been so sexually stimulated in her life. She knew that her *enlightenment* had been because of Luce and her expertise.

Luce didn't own The Dungeon and just because they weren't together now shouldn't stop Brooke from flexing her *new* muscles. She didn't know why she had a sudden urge to visit the club; probably because Luce wouldn't approve of her attending alone. *Fuck her!* Besides, it was like her body was demanding to be freed, let go. Let go of Luce, let go of her worries, let go of her pain. It was as simple as that.

"Well, I think I'm interested in seeing what The Dungeon has to offer. I hear it's ladies night." Brooke smiled and wiggled her eyebrows. "Besides, I'm feeling a bit...naughty."

Stella practically sprayed the sip she was starting to take. "*Naughty*? Did you just say, naughty?"

"Hmm."

"I don't think I've ever heard you use the word naughty before. Who are you and what have you done with my boss?" Stella looked Brooke up and down, smiled and took another sip. She wiggled her finger at Brooke.

"Well, tonight I'm not your boss, and what happens at The Dungeon—"

"Stays at The Dungeon," both women said, laughing.

"Wow, I've got to say that I've never seen this side of you. Whatever's happened has really changed your stripes. I like it." Stella leered at Brooke.

"Okay, I'm still your boss when it comes to afterhours play time. Besides, I'm on a mission," Brooke said. She stood, her leather creaking again as she walked to the door. "I'm ready to try someone thing new, something—"

"Don't say it, naughty."

"Something hot and sexy."

Stella's gaze roamed over the tight leather cat suit Brooke had poured herself into and smiled. "Honey, I'd say you're gonna get a whole lot of trouble tonight. By the way, I love those shoes. Where?"

"You know that sex shop over on Eight Street?"

Stella let her head swim around dramatically before she opened her eyes and stared at Brooke. "Wait, you went into a sex shop and didn't invite me? What the fuck?"

"Anyway, like the shoes?"

"Um, yeah. I just said that, what are they...eight inch heels?"

"Almost, but I love the platform. I feel... intimidating." Brooke smiled and strutted across the porch showing off her new confident walk. The leather suit moved like liquid motion, as Brooke swayed her hips ever so gently and then spun on the ball of her foot.

"If Luce could only see you now, trust me, she'd be on her hands and knees panting."

"Luce who?"

"You know, Luce Potter."

"Stella, we're over. Didn't you know? She has a new girlfriend, this stacked red-head."

"What? No way, Luce is gaga over you." Stella shook her head and sipped her wine.

"I don't want to hear her name tonight, got it? It's done and over with. She's made her decision and I've moved on, just like she did."

"But—"

"Auk, zip it or I can go by myself tonight if you'd rather chase Luce around?"

Stella smiled, "No, I think I'd rather watch you tonight. Besides, ladies night at The Dungeon is always a circus."

"Good. Finish your drink and let's go. The cab is here, no drinking and driving for us. If someone wants to leave early, you can."

"Oh no, I'm in it for the long haul." Stella tossed back her wine. "Someone has to watch out for you, lookin' like someone set you on fire. Oh, this is going to be hot."

"Let's go then and see how many eyebrows we can scorch tonight."

"Right behind you. Right behind you." Stella said, watching Brooke's tight ass bounce down the walk.

☙☙☙☙

Colby crouched down in the dark corner, holding one of the broken legs of the chair. She slid against the wall, feeling for a door, anything that would take her out of the room. With only one eye barely open she had to move by touch. Boxes lined up against the wall made her path that much slower. Just as she slipped around one of the boxes, she heard two men's voices.

"Hey, did you turn the lights off?"

"No, I thought you mighta hit the switch."

"Find the switch and let's get rid of this bitch. The Oyabun wants us to dump her outside of town."

"She's getting soft in her hold age. In the past she would shoot the assholes, but now she wants us to dump this one. I don't get it."

"She's the Oyabun, you're not supposed to *get it*. Do what you're told. Now find that damn switch."

Colby could hear the men running back to the door and flicking the switch back and forth as she crept away through the darkness. As she ducked and crawled along the wall she felt a door handle nudge her shoulder. Thank god, she whispered and pulled on the handle. The faint click paralyzed her for a moment. She waited. The men still argued.

"Damn light must have gone out. Maybe the Oyabun busted it when she beat the shit out of that agent?"

"You idiot, why would she do that? Find the light and see if it's broken."

"You find the light."

"There's an agent in this room and we need to take care of business or the Oyabun is going to kick our ass. Got it?"

Geez, men, Colby thought.

Before she heard another word, the door gave

way and she fell over a lip and onto a landing. She kept a death grip on the door handle as her ass hit the floor and held her breath trying not to make a sound. Hearing nothing, she stood and eased the door shut. The ledge she found herself on was only wide enough to stabilize herself. She leaned against the door. If the two Yakuza's searching for her opened the door, she'd fall ass over and down a good ten feet. It wouldn't kill her, but she could do without the broken bones, and it would add to her torn-up face and wrists.

"I can't find her."

"Fuck, we're dead. Find that bitch or we're going to lose a digit."

Footsteps moved closer to the door. Colby grabbed the handle and held it with everything she had. Someone jerked on the handle. A thud against the door and then another jerk of the handle and he was gone.

"This door's locked, so she's gotta be over there, somewhere behind those damn boxes."

She heard him whisper to his buddy. "You go that way, I'll go this way and we'll push her to the center."

"Got it."

Looking around, Colby realized she was stuck. No way down, no way up, just stuck until the Yakuza left.

She tried to wipe her dripping nose with the tail of her shirt. The dampness and smell of chemicals in the warehouse were making her sinuses flair up. *Great, all I need to do now is sneeze and they'll find me, sure as shit.* She wiped at her nose, flinching at the contact. She assessed her injuries. Her left eye was swollen shut. Her shoulder wasn't dislocated as she'd thought, but it would be a while before she could lift it above her waist. Running her tongue over her teeth she felt a loose tooth or two, but none missing. The taste of blood was still present and she ran her tongue along the inside of her cheek, finding a long gash run the inside of her mouth. Pulling her jacket more tightly around her, she sat, letting her legs dangle over the side of the stoop. She owed Luce Potter and she would damn well collect on that debt, if it was the last thing she ever did in life.

Colby pulled her sleeve back to look at her phantom watch. It was gone, along with her service weapon and her ID. If she reported it to the agency she could guarantee she would be taken off the case at a minimum, if not lose it completely. Something Luce said, though, didn't make sense. How did Luce Potter know Deputy Chapel? Luce hadn't been around *that* long, and Chapel hadn't been off a desk in years. Something didn't add-up.

She leaned her head against the door and listened for movement in the room. It felt like she had been sitting for at least an hour. The drip, drip, drip of liquid somewhere down below kept a rhythmic pace in her head. The chemical smell burned her nose, and added to the difficulty she was already having breathing. Taking a deep breath confirmed at least a cracked rib, but it kept her focused on her circumstances, for now. She wanted to close her eyes and rest, just for a few minutes and gather her strength back before getting up. No. She was sure she had a concussion, so no sleep for her. Not till she saw a doctor. Trying to stay lucid, she mentally went back over her notes on the case. Yakuza, Russians and the drug cartel all made for interesting cocktail talk, but she was still having trouble linking Yakuza with the drug cartels. There wasn't even a thread she could grasp to weave them into the same world, let alone the same dirty business trade.

She cupped her ear to the door one more time and listened, hoping the silence wasn't a trap. Gently pulling the handle, she peered inside the dark room. Listening, she still heard nothing. Sliding over the lip of the threshold, she closed the door and laid on her stomach. The cool cement, sent a shiver through her aching body. Inching her way across the floor, she stopped and listened again. Nothing. A few more inches, and she waited. She slid behind some boxes stacked against the wet wall, waiting. Her vision was nearly non-existent in her right eye, and still she tried to look around. Nothing moved. The tap of her head hitting the box jerked her wide awake. Colby realized she must have dozed. She needed to get out of the warehouse and somewhere safe. Slipping further into the darkness, she gingerly slipped past an office where she could hear the two men arguing.

Without stopping she slid on her stomach to the only other light she could see. The dusk peering into the warehouse. Staying in the shadows, she sat just inside the wide door. After one last look around, she gathered as much strength as she could as she slipped outside the door. The alleyway grew darker the farther she went. Taking in a lung full of fresh air caused her chest to spasm as a coughing jag started. Colby clenched her muscles tight to hold the cough, her ribs screaming at the torture.

Nothing moved behind her, nothing in front of her. She was free, finally.

ﷺﷺﷺ

Colby searched the street, squatting behind a

car trying to make sure she couldn't be seen. No cell phone made her realize how dependent she was on technology and remembering a time when a pay phone was practically on every street corner, bar and gas station. Now, she couldn't find one to save her life. She tried to stand and almost fell to her knees, doubling over as her stomach muscles cramped up. Her head felt as big as a balloon and her left eye was now completely swollen shut. She had her bell rung before, but it had been a while since she had it thumped this bad. Gingerly she licked her split lip and wet the cut, the taste of blood still oozing. Her ID wallet, badge, cell phone and weapon were gone. How would she explain the loss of her government issued equipment? That problem was beyond her right now, instead she was more worried about staying covered and getting help.

She spotted a deli with no customers inside. Slipping in, she hid behind the door and looked out the length of window.

"Hey, you can't stay in here," came a voice behind the counter.

Colby tried to ignore the irritating voice, but it called to her again.

"Hey, did you hear me? There's a soup kitchen down the street and around the corner. They'll help you out."

Colby turned to say something to the woman when she heard her gasp.

"Jesus, what the hell happened to you? If you're in trouble we don't want any of that here."

"Relax, I'm a federal agent," Colby said, swooning before she leaned against the door.

"Do you have ID?"

"I just got the shit kicked out of me, what do you

think?"

"I think you need to go before the thugs that did this come back."

"Can I use your phone?"

"Well...I don't know...I mean how do I know you're a federal agent," the woman said, looking Colby up and down.

"Call this number," Colby rattled off Scarr's phone number. "Tell him Agent Water is in danger. If I'm bullshitting you'll have your answer soon enough."

Colby clutched her stomach and fell to her knees.

"Hold on there, Agent Water. Bill...Bill come quick." A short, squat man came running from the back. "Give this gal a hand while I call her friend."

"What the hell happened to you, young lady?" His gentle voice was nothing like the shrill one of his wife. "Here, let me help you to a chair."

"I really don't want to be a bother, but can I just get a drink of water?" Colby let him pick her up and deposit her in the closest chair. Luckily, her location hid her from anyone looking inside the deli.

"Sure, sure," he said, rubbing the back of her hand. She flinched at the touch. "Oh sorry, I didn't mean—"

"No, no, that's all right, I'm just..." She pulled back the sleeve of her blazer and exposed her raw wrists.

"Oh." He rotated her arms and looked at both sides. "I'll get you some salve for those and some ice for that face."

"Please, I don't want to be a bother. I'll just wait for my friend to get here."

"Marge, did you make that call?"

"He's on his way," she shouted from the back.

"Said to lock the door just in case whoever did this comes back."

"Okay. Marge can you bring some ice for the agent and some of that salve you put on burns."

Colby reached for his arm to stop him, but he was moving faster than she expected for someone so stout. Taking a sip of water, she let herself relax for a brief moment. She'd trade a hot bath for all the money in her bank account, if she could. She jumped at the sound of a distant car door slamming. Ducking down behind the table she peered out towards the door. She wasn't going back to that warehouse without a fight.

"Okay, let's see those bruises," Bill said, staring down at Colby. "You okay?" He studied the door and then Colby and then back at the door again. "No one's coming, besides I locked the door," he said, pulling the shade down on the door.

"Just jumpy, I guess," Colby said, sitting back on the chair.

He gently applied an ice pack to her swollen face. "Here, hold that and let me look at your wrists."

Where was Scarr? She flinched at the pain of the Iodine swab brushing against her wounds.

"Sorry, I bet that smarts, huh?" Bill blew on the Iodine, just as her mother did when she was child. Strange she would remember that at this very minute. The smell, it quickly took her back to her childhood. *Why couldn't life be like that now? Simple, easy and carefree.*

A light tapping on the door caught her by surprise. Colby jumped to her feet and leaned against the wall behind the door as Bill pulled back the shade just enough to see out.

"Sorry, we're closed."

"You called me, I'm Agent Scarr." The deep voice was barely above a whisper.

Bill looked over at Colby, waiting for an answer. She nodded and limped over to the chair, sliding in, allowing the exhaustion to finally set in now that back-up was there.

"Jesus, Water. What the fuck happened to you?" Scarr stood over Colby, grimacing. She knew he was making a quick, tactical assessment. "Who did this? Why didn't you call me? We need to get you to the hospital. I need to call this in." Scarr pulled his phone and was just about to hit a speed dial when Colby snatched the phone from him.

"No." She slumped back down and felt like collapsing, but figured if she did, Scarr would take this to the deputy. Colby wasn't ready for questions about what happened. She wanted time to formulate a feasible story—not necessarily the truth—but something close. "No, you need to get me out of here. Whoever did this could still be roaming out there."

"Geez, Water, what the fuck happened? Why didn't *you* call me? Where's your gun and badge, agent?"

Colby bit her tongue. She hated it when someone called her, *agent*. It was a way of distancing themselves from the humanity of the person and she knew Scarr was doing *just* that. Her chain of command could get away with that, but a peer or subordinate couldn't, not with her.

"I had just enough time to stash it, for safe keeping," she lied.

Colby wasn't about to disclose that Luce had taken her professional identity. She was certain Luce was trying to demoralize her in whatever way possible.

"Thank you for your kindness Bill. I'm sure there'll be questions, but not right now. I need to get home. Scarr." She tried to stand, but could barely hold her own weight.

"I'm double parked out front." He looked over at Bill and tossed his chin in Colby's direction. "Do you mind giving me a hand, sir?"

"Oh, not at all, I put some Iodine on her wrists and some ice on her face, but I think it would be a good idea if you got her to the hospital. She should have that eye looked at. It's closed shut and looks pretty—"

"I've got from here, sir. Thank you." Scar cut him off and practically picked Colby up off her feet as he put her in his SUV.

"Oh, of course. I didn't mean to imply that you government types don't know how to do your job. I was just sayin' that—"

"Thank you, Bill. I appreciate your help," Colby said, barely extending her hand.

"Oh, I hope you catch the creeps who did this, take care."

"Thanks again." Scarr slammed the door and stalked over to the driver's side mumbling under his breath.

Chapter Thirty

The Dungeon was slammed. The crowd wrapped around the front and down the dark alley, each patron attired in their choice of accoutrement imaginable for a bondage club. The smell of marijuana drifted through the air. A contact high was possible, but Brooke and Stella wouldn't be waiting in line. They had *special* privilege, Brooke intended to use this one last time.

"Hi, JJ.," Brooke said, stepping up to the bouncer wanding the few people who would get the chance to strut in The Dungeon tonight. Thanks to the latest mommy porn book, people— especially women— flocked to the club in droves. Brooke felt like an old pro now that she had been more than a couple of times to the club, but that didn't quell the butterflies she still got when she arrived. She wasn't scared. No, she knew what to expect, but for some reason she still could feel a giggly school-girl hiding underneath her leather.

"Wow, what's with the line tonight? Seems longer than usual?"

"Hey, Brooke. Where's Luce?"

"I'm on my own tonight. You know how it is, JJ, sometimes a girl just wants to stretch her muscles, alone."

"Nice muscles," he said, checking her out as he patted her down, too.

"Careful there, Samson, she's taken. Remember?"

Stella piped up, protectively.

"No worries there, Precious. I got time for you," he said, running the wand over Stella. "I wouldn't mess with Luce's woman. Now you...I would...well you know...you look good tonight." He winked at Stella.

Stella rolled her eyes at Brooke, but Brooke could only shake her head. Stella liked to flirt, but she needed to be the one to initiate, otherwise she wasn't interested in an easy catch.

"What's going on JJ?"

"Oh, it's a special show or something tonight. You have a mask? They're making everyone wear a mask tonight."

"No shit?" Brooke looked at Stella shrugging. "Guess we should go."

"Naw, don't worry they've got some inside." He thumbed them through. "See ya later, precious."

"Come on, precious." Brooke grabbed her arm and tugged Stella through the crowd.

"Why do men have to be such pigs?"

"Come on you'll get us kicked out before we even get a drink."

Stepping through the dark hallway into the club, Brooke was stopped before entering.

"Mask?" A woman said, pointing to a table of masks ranging from porcelain white masks, to freakish, to downright scary.

Brooke fingered the painted paper mache masks and studied them all before choosing. "You don't have anything that isn't so...so...freaky?"

"Honey, it's a bondage club, if you want a nun's habit, you'll need to go to the party store down the street. So pick already."

"I guess I'll take this one." Brooke picked up

the devilish mask and winked at Stella. "What do you think? Is it me?" Brooke slipped it on.

From the look of the room, it was clear that anonymity was the game tonight. She couldn't describe anyone outside of the mask that they wore. Her eyes were instantly drawn to the masks, bouncing from disguise to disguise, she could only focus on the garish, as her gaze swept the room.

"I think it is tonight." Stella selected hers and looked at the inside. "This is going to fuck-up my makeup," she said, sliding it on.

"Well the glittery porcelain look works for you." Brooke grabbed Stella's hand and pulled her towards the bar. "I need a drink...with a straw." Brooke stuck her tongue out of the slit.

"Oh that is so cute."

"Hey, why don't you grab a table? We'll have a few drinks, first."

"Okay, Cape Cod for me."

The music vibrated through Brooke as she bobbed her head to the beat. She was still buzzing from the wine earlier and she didn't want to lose it any time soon. Tonight, she just wanted to be a voyeur. Watch and learn, or maybe she would throw caution to the wind and submit to the play in one of the rooms. She would play it by ear, or libido. Grabbing her order, she weaved through the growing crowd.

Stella stood and grabbed two drinks from Brooke. "Wow, two?"

"Have you seen the crowd around the bar? It's three deep and I barely made it out with the drinks."

"Yeah, it looks like it's going to be a wild night, huh?"

Brooke slipped the straw through the slit in

her mask to savor the fruity drink. There was more alcohol than mixer, but Brooke didn't care. The plan was to drink to forget, not play it safe. Stella was her safe word. The crowd was electric tonight. The energy that buzzed around the room was making Brooke giddy, or was it the alcohol? It didn't matter, her switch was flipped and she was ready for the night's entertainment. She had heard someone talking about it being demonstration night, something the Dungeon used to generate business for the backrooms. Sounded good to Brooke. She couldn't wait to see what Dr. Williams had up her sleeve this time, with the forced anonymity of the masks. A few men strutted their stuff in leather thongs barely big enough to cover their packages, and some women were exhibitionists by nature and shame wasn't a word heard in the Dungeon on nights like tonight. The smell of sex floated in the air like an aphrodisiac, that warm musky smell when bodies were rubbing together, mixing.

"Ladies and gentlemen."

The lights in the club dimmed and the pounding music lowered a beat or two, to something more manageable for conversation.

"Please be seated or grab someone's lap and have a seat. Tonight we are thrilled to have some great entertainment. If it makes you want to try it out, even better. We are looking for a few volunteers. Do I have any volunteers?" the husky voice boomed.

Brooke searched but couldn't find the person talking. Her interest peaked when she caught a glimpse of a few people coming down from the stage wearing capes.

"Oh this is interesting," she whispered to Stella.

"Hmm, looks like that movie, *Eyes Wide Open*,

with that couple who are no longer married. I never knew what she saw in him. She just towered over him, and she was so beautiful. I mean if I—"

"Are you nervous, Stella?"

"Why?"

"You're babbling."

"Oh gosh, I guess I'm just, oh I don't know, excited."

"Ladies and gentlemen, we are looking for a few volunteers. If you raise your hand one of our Seekers, will find you."

Stella's hand shot right up.

Brooke reached up frantically to pull it down. "What're you doing?"

"Volunteering."

"No, you can't, I mean, you're my safe word."

"What?"

Before Brooke could say anything more, someone in a black cape was beside them looking down at her. She could barely make out a smile behind the long-nosed mask, but there was something familiar about the eyes.

"Me, me, pick me," Stella pleaded.

A hand reached out and grabbed Stella's while the mask never stopped looking at Brooke.

"Yea, me." Stella said, gleefully like a child who'd been selected for the chocolate factory visit.

Brooke sat frozen to her seat, the gaze still holding her firmly. She didn't move as roughened hands helped Stella to her feet and led her to the stage.

"Wonderful, we have our volunteers for tonight's show. Now we're going to send them back stage to change, so don't wander off. You'll miss all the excitement."

Brooke felt her pulse quicken thinking about the stranger in the mask. Something about him made her wish she had been picked instead of Stella. As she sipped her drink someone touched her shoulder.

"This is from the Dom that was just here. Compliments of the house." The waitress set the smoking martini glass on the table.

"Wow, what is it?" Brooke could see the dry ice floating in the glass. The soft light in the bottom of the drink made the liquid glow, only adding to the spectacle.

"We call it, Aphrodite, it's supposed to be an aphrodisiac, but the club makes no guarantees that this drink will improve your love life."

"Interesting." Brooke picked up the glass to inspect it from all angles.

"Careful, it's intense." With that warning, the waitress in latex was gone.

Brooke watched her exposed ass shimmy in the spanking skirt she was wearing as she finally disappearing in the crowd, leaving Brooke to the steaming drink. Closing her eyes and dipping her nose into the rising vapors, she wanted to experience the full effect of the drink's performance before all the dry ice melted. She couldn't smell anything, but felt the wet steam moisten her upper lip and nose. Gingerly, she raised the glass to her lips and took the smallest sip, barely wetting her upper lip. Snaking her tongue out she sampled the drink.

Melon, with a hint of sour. Not bad, she thought venturing further. Tipping the glass, the ice floated to the other side before it finally let out its last puff of steam.

"I hope that's not a sign of things to come," she

said. The layered taste of the drink surprised Brooke and before she knew it the glass was empty.

"Ladies and gentlemen are you ready?" The loud speaker spewed again.

The patrons in the crowded room began clapping and a low hum vibrated in Brooke's chest and soft light filled the room as the curtain was pulled back. Stella stood, practically naked, her body intricately covered in a knot pattern Brooke had seen before. She couldn't force herself to look away as a woman walked out onto the stage carrying a suede leather flogger. Brooke had never seen one so big as the Dominatrix, still wearing the mask from earlier, held the handle in one hand and cradled half of the length in the other. The long strips swayed with each step the Dominatrix took. She had thought the cape hid a man, but it was really a she. The energy she gave off bowled Brooke over. Only a top had that kind of energy, that kind of presence.

Brooke looked from Stella, who winked at her, to the woman about to put Stella through her paces. Short leather gloves, barely big enough to cover her fingers and palms, slapped against the flogger. The muffled sounds echoed in the room silencing everyone. Her body slinked in a high-necked latex dress, cut open to her belly-button. Brooke could see the small round edges of her breasts peeking out. She was sure an adhesive of some sort kept them in place.

A man whispered behind her, "God, I'd call her mommy and let her spank me. Hey, I've been a bad boy, Mistress. I think I need a spanking."

The Dominatrix looked out into the crowd, and smirked. Brooke could swear she was looking right at her, but her the man behind her yelled, "I'm next, baby."

Shuddering at his boyish bravado, Brooke refocused her attention on Stella and the stage. She noticed for the sake of modesty, Stella's nipples wore pasties and around her hips a leather device of some sort, Brooke looked closer - a fucking chastity belt with lock - wrapped what was left of her sex tightly.

The crowd surged with excitement as the Dom, wheeled the flogger across Stella's middle. Brooke wanted to tell them all to look away, but she sat entranced at what played out before her. Nothing was sexual but damn close played into the way the Dom caressed Stella's body with the end of the flogger, running it between her legs and over the locked chastity belt. Brooke leaned in on the next slap of the leather across Stella's breasts. Her mind whirled at the times Luce had done this very thing to her. The trust she had given Luce when Luce asked her to submit. The thought that she would no longer share that trust she enjoyed with her lover made her well-up with tears.

Oh.

The crowd pulled Brooke back into the scene being played out on stage. The dominatrix walked around Stella, touching her pink skin that was amplified by the overhead lights. She whispered something into Stella's ear. Stella nodded her head and a blindfold was added to heighten the experience. Brooke nodded along. It was electrifying to see how the Dom worked the flogger with precision across the lilywhite skin of Stella's back. Brooke suddenly wished it was her and not Stella taking the lashing. Her body tingled at the thought of finding release from her inner demon tonight. Luce had been her demon for the last two weeks and she was ready to exorcise that demon for good, tonight.

The lights dimmed, plunging the club into near darkness. Brooke had missed the last part of Stella's show daydreaming about Luce. Damn, she looked around to see what was happening. Nothing. People buzzed about, the energy near palpable. A few more acts like that and a sexual frenzy would be unleashed.

"Hey, how did you like the show?" Stella said. Her smile so big she looked almost Cheshire. The dominatrix stood next to Stella, helping her to her seat.

She leaned down and whispered in Brooke's ear. "If you'd like the same treatment, I'll be in a reserved room in about twenty minutes." The soft leather of the glove the woman wore, slid against Brooke's cheek. *Oh fuck*, she thought closing her eyes and imagining those hands performing for her. "See you then," she said. The command couldn't be missed and Brooke felt her body weaken at the thought.

She didn't say anything, only looking away instead to avoid committing to something she wasn't sure she wanted now. Brooke could feel the electricity humming off of Stella. The woman practically vibrated as she fidgeted in her seat. Stella finished off the watered-down drink she had been nursing before she was the evening entertainment. She downed the second drink with gusto. Brooke wondered what it felt like to be the main attraction in front of possibly hundreds of people.

"How was it?"

"What?"

"Being on stage, in front of all of these people?"

"Oh...well...when you're up there you don't even notice anyone, but that hot Dom. I mean she was just...magical. I can see why you like to come here, if she's on the menu, I'd order her every time."

"Did you see her face? Who was it?"

Stella shrugged her shoulders. "I don't know. They gave me a choice of outfits to wear and then brought me out on stage."

"Wait, you picked that outfit out. Are you kidding me?"

"What?" Stella shifted from side-to-side, her flogging inhibited her ability to sit still. "It isn't like I'm going to see these people ever again."

"Umm, hello." Brooke waived her hand. "You know me."

"Yea, but you're a freak, too. I mean come on, don't tell me you haven't been back here since that one time I brought you for *research*," Stella said, making air quotes.

Brooke didn't respond to the accusation. She should have just kept her mouth shut.

"Besides, I heard what the Dom said and it looks like...a...you might be staying after school. Besides, you said you were ready to get freaky tonight anyway, right?"

The loud speaker interrupted Brooke's response, announcing the start of another show. Brooke couldn't watch. The sound of a hand against flesh made her tingle each time she heard it. Had it been twenty minutes? Another sip of her drink. Would she take the invitation from the Dom? Another drink. Was she ready to let someone else touch her like that? Another drink. Her mind morphed at all the questions as she finished the last of her third drink.

Yep. She had come to The Dungeon with those exact ideas in mind and now an offer had been extended. Screw Luce, her loss, she wasn't anyone's property. She was going to set the night on fire and let it burn.

"You'll probably need to catch a cab tonight, Stella."

"What?"

"I'm going to take that sexy Dom up on her invitation. Who knows how long it will take? See ya." Brooke headed for the back before she lost her nerve.

"Have fun."

"Oh, I will."

❧❧❧❧

Brooke made a slow, hesitant path through the cavernous hallway, peeking into each room where a door was open, looking for the Dom who had made the offer. Her mind raced at the possibilities that awaited her, but the idea scared her, too. She'd never been in this part of the club without Luce and now she was venturing deeper into depravity. She stopped. Three doors remained in this hallway. Brooke could let fear rule her head or she could let pleasure rule her mending heart. Heart won out. Peeking to her left, she saw the Dom sitting relaxed, her arms outstretched resting on the arms of the chair, open and beckoning her to come forward. Brooke could barely make out a smile behind the mask. This mask was different. One side was white, while the other half was red, cut just at the upper lip. Ruby red lips smiled at her. Studying the Dom from the doorway, Brooke noticed she had changed into a leather. The luxurious scent filled the room. Her long black hair was pulled tightly back into a pony tail. One gloved hand slapped a flogger against the inside of her thigh. The contact surely heightened the Dom's own pleasure, as the leather-on-leather contact echoed in the room adding to the surging emotions. Brooke's heart raced. The alcohol was barely a buzz and shedding fast as her adrenaline ate it up. Pure energy pulse through her.

Without a word, Brooke moved forward and knelt before the Dom, resting on her heels and bowing her head. This part she knew. This part she had seen done dozens of times with other subs and dominates. The Dom ran her fingers through Brooke's hair, stroking her head. A low voice asked a question. "So, what's your deepest, darkest, deviant fantasy, my pet?"

The slow strokes against Brooke's scalp kept her focused on the contact. Not wanting it to end, she moved her head against the touch. She was tactile, she loved the way women melded together and couldn't get enough skin-on-skin contact with she was with a woman.

"Hmm?"

"I don't know, ma'am," Brooke purred.

"Perhaps you like electricity torture?"

Brooke shook her head. "No ma'am."

"Hmm, perhaps, you like cutting?"

"No. I can't stand the sight of my own blood, or anyone else's for that matter, ma'am."

"Perhaps you prefer men?"

Brooke heard the Dom chuckle after making the statement. Confused, she shook her head again. "No."

"Do you like to be spanked?"

A slight nod escaped Brooke before she stopped. She wanted something, but going through the shopping list of some of the most extreme torture made her realize she was on the grey scale of BDSM.

"Do you know what I like?"

Brooke shook her head at the question.

"I like the soft skin of a woman, the way she

smells, the sweet way she tastes." The warm whisper on Brooke's ear made her close her eyes. Her body on alert the closer the Dom's lips moved towards to her ear. Her hard nipples strained against the tight leather, almost painfully. The promise of release made the pain pleasurable. "You know what else I find sexy?"

Brooke shook her head again. This was going to be a long evening, if the slow arduous questions were the way the Dom was torturing her.

"I love the look of red lips wrapped around a ball gag. The way a woman's body reacts to being tied up, and how she writhes in pleasure as she's being touched. I love to run my tongue the length of her body when she's just at that point of climax. You know...when her skin is prickly with the start of an orgasm and you slip your finger inside of her only to find her dripping wet...and yet...I stop. Her face begs me to continue, to finish her off."

Brooke could barely swallow. The vivid descriptions were doing what the Dom had intended. Mental foreplay. Her mind struggled to keep her thoughts together. All she could think of were the images, looping over and over again. Then she felt the handle of the flogger run up her body over her breasts, or was she imagining the contact?

"I love a woman's body, the soft curves, the simplistic form that has inspired great works. Can you think of a more beautiful sight that two women engaged in the wondrous act of making love? There is no greater intimacy than when a woman goes down on another woman, opening her, tasting her, loving her in that moment. The completeness of true togetherness when a woman shares herself. The connection two women share when they communicate with their bodies. It's the ultimate giving of one's self."

Brooke felt as if the Dom was stroking her body, seducing her with words – like fingers that reached across the taut leather and undulated over her skin. Brooke's body anticipated the response to the caress as the Dom slowly, methodically fondled her with her velvety voice. Sitting with her hands on her knees, she wanted to crawl into the woman's lap and demand she stop talking and do something, but there were rules, and they needed to be followed, to the letter.

"I see you're shaking, are you cold?" The Dom rose and walked around Brooke, the long tendrils of the flogger trailing over Brooke's back.

"No, ma'am."

"Are you afraid then?"

Brooke shook her head.

"Do you want to leave?"

Brooke nervously cleared her throat. Without thinking, she gently, almost unnoticeably started rocking back and forth. The movement caused the leather to press against her clit, stimulating her further.

"Stop, let me do that." The Dom put her hand on Brooke's shoulder and held her down, stopping her movement. "I'm sure I can take care of that...need for you. Of course if you'd rather just sit there and *talk*, we can do that as well.

❧❧❧❧

Luce let the leather strips trail across Brooke's body. How she wished it was her hand. How Brooke hadn't figured out it was her was beyond Luce. The waitress informed Luce that Brooke had been drinking heavily throughout the night, and that someone had sent over a special drink called the Aphrodite. The combination of alcohol in the drink were enough to send a full-grown man over into his cups, but Brooke sat here alert as far as Luce could tell.

Brooke rocked back and forth like a small child comforting herself. Luce wondered if the tight leather outfit was adding to her *enjoyment* of the evening. The moment Brooke entered the club, someone had pointed her out to Luce. Liquid sex, was all that came to Luce's mind. At first blush, Luce was pissed. *How could Brooke come here?* It wasn't as if they had been here a lot lately, but the thought of Brooke seeking out pleasure with someone else made her territorial. Brooke was hers to pleasure, period. Then Luce's light bulb moment flashed. She had seen to it that Brooke thought things were over between them and that Luce was involved with Kat. Just watching Brooke walk in wearing that outfit brought out Luce's more animalistic instincts. She wasn't about to let someone else claim Brooke tonight, not if she had anything to say. She'd been deprived of Brooke for far too long and she craved her like a junkie craves a hit. Staying away had been for Brooke's own good, to protect her, but it had come at a price. Nevertheless, Luce had instantly come up with a plan to be alone with Brooke tonight, and it was working beautifully, so far.

Inhaling deeply she recognized Brooke's scent, a mixture of sweat, leather and Luce's favorite perfume. Mixed together, Luce's body reacted the only way it knew how, sexually. The visceral response made her body tingle. Her skin felt as if it were on fire and the urge to touch Brooke took over.

"Stand," she commanded.

Brooke stood, her head down, still submissive.

"Reach-up and grab that tie-down bar." Luce tossed the flogger on the seat and stood behind Brooke, admiring her. She removed Brooke's mask and replaced it with a blindfold. If Brooke hadn't figured out who her Dominatrix was, she wasn't ready to let the cat-out-of-the-leather, so to speak. Running her nose through Brooke's soft locks of hair, Luce inhaled deeply and held her breath. Brooke's essence singed every nerve vibrating in Luce. It took all she had not to reach around and pull Brooke's body close. She slowly let her fingertips glide down Brooke's arms and down her back. Squatting, she finished her travels down Brooke's tight thighs and calves and then back up to her leather-encased ass. Squeezing it with both hands, without thinking, she gently bit one cheek. It tightened under her lips and a faint squeal slipped out of Brooke.

"Spread your legs wider," Luce instructed. Still squatting, she let her hands roam over one leg, sliding up to the top of the thigh to linger at Brooke's center. She gently palmed the crotch of Brooke's leather pants. "Did you paint these on or...?" Luce let the question hang out there for a moment before moving to the other leg and repeating the action. This time she let her right hand stay between Brooke's legs, cupping her as Luce stood. She reached around to touch Brooke's tight abs. Luce could hear Brooke's short pants as she continued to stoke her stomach with one hand and between her legs with her other. And then it was time.

"Don't move, do you understand?"

"Yes, ma'am."

The sound of a zipper slowly sliding echoed through the room. Luce slipped her gloved hand into the cat suit and stroked Brooke's bare midriff. Raising her hand, she rested her forefinger against Brooke's lips.

"Bite the tip," she said, not wanting to stop what she was doing between Brooke's legs.

Brooke bit it as Luce pulled her hand from the short glove.

"May I touch you, intimately?"

She could feel Brooke's body quaking, the groan from deep within her throat evidence that she was within reach of an orgasm.

"I won't if you don't want me to, but..." Luce pressed hard outside of her leather, massaging the firm clit underneath. A thin leather barrier separated her from what she wanted: The soft, succulent essence of Brooke, hidden between folds of skin. The taste of her lover, kept from her for weeks was within reach, was hers if she was just patient.

Brooke caught her quivering lip between her teeth to stop it. She was on the verge of coming. Luce wanted to help her get there, but only with permission. Those were the rules.

Brooke didn't say anything. She didn't move, so Luce withdrew her hands and took a step back.

"What are you doing?" Brooke's voice sounded pleading.

"You didn't answer my question. So, I withdrew my favor." The haughty sound to Luce's voice showed who was in control at the moment. "Do you wish to continue?"

"Please."

Placing her hands back in their original positions, Luce asked again. This time it was a low, sensual whisper in Brooke's ear. "May I touch you... *intimately?*

Chapter Thirty-one

Colby sat on the gurney curled under her blanket. If hell had a feeling, she was sure it was exactly how she felt right now. She reached for her water bottle and took a swig, trying to stave off a cough.

Cough, cough, ouch.

Curling tighter, she tried to breathe through the pain. From her cracked ribs, to the pounding headache—that no amount of painkiller seemed to ease—she wished she were dead. That wasn't exactly true, she wished Luce was dead and then she could die a happy woman.

"Who did this, Water?" Scarr demanded.

She squinted at him through her half-opened eye, hoping she looked menacing. "Look, I'm going to tell you this one more time. I got hit from behind, the goose egg on the back of my head should be proof enough. After that they kicked the shit out of me."

"Why? Why you?"

"I'm assuming it's my charming personality, when I told them to go fuck-off. Just like I'm about to tell you, Scarr."

She stared at him, know he was running the same profile on her that she would run on anyone she thought might be lying. She didn't look away, blink or even clench her jaw. She didn't want him digging further and she wasn't going to budge. She'd take care of Luce Potter herself, her way, in her time.

"Here you two are. Jesus Christ, Water, you look like hell." Deputy Chapel showed up in a warm-up suit, and running shoes. She wasn't fooling anyone; she didn't exercise, not unless you counted walking to the Starbucks counter in the lobby exercise and she did that at least five times a day. Colby wished the woman a good case of gallstones with all that caffeine. She deserved 'em, the bitch. "Any idea who did this?" She looked at Scarr.

"Nope, and she doesn't know either."

"Seriously, Agent Water? You get the shit kicked out of you and you don't know who did it?" The dubious look didn't make Colby suddenly want to kneel in confession and spill her guts. Chapel needed to save it for someone who was begging to kiss her ass, she was long past that point. "There has to be something you remember about the thugs that did this to you? Perhaps, it's the case you're working on?"

"Yeah, if being in the wrong place, at the wrong time is part of the case, then hmm...yep...I think you hit it right on the head." Colby knew she was being insubordinate, but the way she was feeling right now, she was lucky she didn't get up and slap the shit out of them for badgering her.

"I'll excuse that remark and chalk it up to your condition, but don't push it." Chapel put her hands on her hips. "My advice, start with the Yakuza. You've been putting a lot of pressure on your CI's, they might've slipped and let something loose."

Colby sat up straight and saluted. "Yes, ma'am." The medication was making her loopy and she was sure she'd have a reprimand if she didn't get her ass home and away from all the shit Chapel was pushing around.

She didn't have any CI's. Scarr might, but she didn't and she didn't feel like sitting around and arguing.

"Water?" Chapel snapped her fingers in front of Colby's face. "Hey, earth to Water. Haha," Chapel laughed and elbowed Scarr. "How many times do you get to say that, huh?"

"Haha, like I haven't heard that before." The ringing in Colby's head made her dizzy. Along with the headache, her stomach was starting to revolt from the pain and the fact that she hadn't eaten in almost twenty-four hours. "I'm ready to get out of here," she said, stopping just as she was easing herself off the gurney. "Unless of course you have more questions, or suggestions for me?" Colby dipped her head in acknowledgement of the deputy.

"No, no, I think you've had enough excitement for the day. Scarr, get her home. Then update me if you find anything out."

The ride home was mercifully quiet. The walk from the car to her door, not so much. In Scarr's haste to help her, he squeezed Colby around the middle and practically put her on her knees.

"Fuck."

"Oh shit, sorry, Water."

"Just get me to the door."

"You got keys?"

Scarr reached down and picked up the fake rock and dropped a key in his hand.

"That worked out well."

"Well shit, Water," Scarr said, waving his hand around the flowerbed by the door. "You have one rock in the whole flower bed and where do you think I'm gonna look? Shit."

Her mother had insisted on placing the rock with

her house key there. *Just in case, dear.* She was going to call her mom and thank her for being so right; it was the perfect thing to hide a key. If you were from a foreign country that didn't get infomercials.

"Thanks for the ride." She snatched the key from Scarr and slammed the door in his face. She owed him for the car ride and the squeeze. If she didn't know better she would bet Scarr had done it on purpose. That asshole was always trying to screw with her.

"I'll have the deputy call you tomorrow and check on you." Scarr called before walking away.

Colby flipped him the bird and shuffled to the fridge. She needed a beer and more painkillers. She wondered why they called 'em painkillers—it wasn't like they were killing anything. Hell, she wasn't even numb. A little buzzed, but definitely still in pain. Grabbing two beers, she popped the top on one and gently put one against her swollen eye.

"Fuck, that hurts."

Chapter Thirty-two

Peeling Brooke's cat suit open like a grape, Luce pushed it barely past Brooke's shoulders, trapping her arms behind her even tighter than the restraints had. She'd only unzipped it halfway, hoping to add to Brooke's torture as Luce worked her way around Brooke's overstimulated body. She ran her fingers over taut nipples, and dipped her head to leisurely suck on one and then the other. Standing behind Brooke, she hefted a breast in each hand, pinching the nipples into submission. Luce ran her hands down her tight stomach, feeling it quiver as she slowly and gently glided back and forth over the muscles. She reveled in how they still responded to her touch.

Falling to her knees, Luce rested her head against Brooke's abs. She threw her mask to the floor. Brooke's heady sexual aroma drifted up sending Luce into a frenzy. Suddenly, she wanted to strip her lover naked so she could access all of her. Luce yanked the diagonal zipper the rest of the way to Brooke's left ankle and pushed the leather away. Sitting back on her heels, she surveyed the half-leather, half-naked Brooke standing before her. She was beautiful. She was exquisite the way she stood, her dignity never wavering. Even in a submissive role Brooke had a way of holding herself that let the Dom know she never acquiesced all of her power to them. Tonight Luce was her Dom. She loved that about Brooke.

Luce wet the tip of her tongue, and slid up Brooke's leg to her thigh, stopping at the small strip of hair at her pubic bone. Splitting Brooke's labia with her tongue, Luce dipped between the lips tracing over Brooke's hard clit. Each time she flicked it Brooke jerked and then forced herself further on Luce's tongue, her body begging for more contact.

Reaching around Brooke, she hugged her hips and whispered, "I've missed you, baby."

"I've missed you, too."

She refused to look up, sure she would see Brooke's eyes filled with hurt. Luce healed them the only way she knew how. Flattening her tongue, Luce pushed it against Brooke's lips, then pointed it to spear between the lips as she licked up. The salty taste lingered briefly on Luce's tongue, but only briefly. A taste of Brooke wouldn't do. She had to have all of her. Spreading Brooke's lips wider, she commanded, "Spread your leg, baby. I need to have you, all of you."

Arching under Brooke, she buried herself between Brooke's lips and savored her. She reached up with the tip of her finger and barely entered Brooke. She gently pushed on the opening as she pressed her tongue against Brooke's clit and then sucked it in her mouth, flicking it with her tongue. Brooke's muscles tightened around the tip of her finger and Luce let the start of Brooke's orgasm pull her finger deeper.

"More," Brooke said, as she started to quiver.

Luce obliged the request by inserting another finger. This time she slowly, rhythmically worked in tandem with Brooke's body; sliding out as Brooke moved away and entering deeper as she swayed closer. Without missing a beat Luce stood, her mouth covering Brooke's as she pressed into Brooke deeper. Suddenly Brooke stopped. Her muscles spasmed as Luce's fingers pushed further. Jerking through her orgasm, Brooke let her breath out in spurts as she tried kissing Luce. Tongues dueled for dominance between shallow breaths. Luce pulled Brooke's head and rested it on her shoulder.

"That's it baby, just let it go. Let it all go."

The dance of their bodies kept them melded together. Neither wanted to pull away for fear it would put permanent distance between them, and Luce knew she had to say something. "I'm not letting you go this time. Trust me," she said. Her throat dry, her voice cracked.

Luce pulled Brooke towards the chair. She sat and arranged Brooke on her lap. She wasn't done and that was all the talking she was willing to do for now. Threading her fingers through Brooke's soft hair, she arched her back over the arm of the chair. With her hands still bound, Brooke's breasts pushed up, delicious rosy peaks that called Luce to lick them and suck on them. Luce was tactile, skin on skin, tongue on skin, tongue on pussy. She licked Brooke's skin, the salty taste lingering on her lips and tongue. She felt like a vampire that needed to feed, to be reborn through the nourishment her lover's body provided. So she fed, lapping at Brooke's nipples, up her throat and finally pulling Brooke towards her, she devoured her mouth with kisses. Reaching between Brooke's legs, she found her wetness inviting. Brooke accommodated her just enough so she could slip inside and start her rhythmic play all over again. The second time came quicker than the first. What was it Brooke would tell Luce, *once the pump was primed it was easy to get it flowing again.*

She smiled. She wanted to crawl between her legs and never leave the warm, security of Brooke's love.

"Oh god, oh...fuck...Luce...please."

Chapter Thirty-three

Her forced leave-of-absence didn't thrill Colby, but she had no choice. The fact that she was kidnapped off the street, her gun and badge taken and having the shit beat out of her didn't sit well with Deputy Chapel. She slipped gingerly out of her SUV. After two days she still felt like a ton of bricks had landed on her. A long soak in the hot tub and a nap would right her world, if only in her mind.

Hitting the porch she stopped dead in her tracks. A package sat at the door. Looking around her neighborhood she didn't see anyone who shouldn't be there. Her neighbor was pruning her roses as she always did. *She baby's those things as if they were her kids, who are long grown with children of their own.*

"Morning, Mrs. Zachery. How are you this morning?"

"Colby, how are you dear?" Mrs. Zachery struggled to get to her feet and shuffled over to Colby. "You look like you're healing nicely. I see that menthol rub I sent over is working."

Colby didn't have the heart to tell the older woman she hadn't tried it. The smell had burnt her nose, and made her want to gag, so she tossed it in the garbage.

"It was very thoughtful of you, Mrs. Zachery," she said, patting the hand resting on her arm. Opening the screen door she bent over and noticed there was a return address on the padded manila envelope. *Yoshida Enterprises, fucking arrogant woman,* she grimaced in pain as she reached for it.

"Oh, the delivery man came earlier. He wanted to leave it with me, but I told him to go ahead and leave it on the stoop, that you would be home anytime. I hope that was okay?"

"Of course, Mrs. Zachery. What would I do without you watching out for me?" Colby smiled. She was part of the reason Colby never brought women home. It would be all over the neighborhood. "Well, if you'll excuse me, Mrs. Zachery, the doctors have advised me that I need more bed rest."

"Of course, dear. If you need anything just holler."

"Thank you, Mrs. Zachery."

The day she *hollered* for help from Mrs. Zachery was the day she hung up her badge.

She turned the package over in her hands to study it. No tell-tale signs of a bomb. Pulling the label off, she dropped it on the porch, just in case. The bomb team would find it and connect the dots with a little help. *Doubtful,* but she wouldn't put it past Luce Potter. Gently squeezing the package, she could feel...a gun, at least it felt like a gun.

Fuck, she thought. *What is this bitch up too?*

Colby carefully lowered herself to the couch and placed the package on the coffee table. She stared at it, contemplating her next move. Take the risk and open it, or call it into the agency and have them send out the bomb squad. If it ended up being nothing she would look stupid. More importantly, she didn't know what was in it and *that* could blow-up in her face. *Open or call, open or call.* She strummed her fingers against her thigh chanting the mantra.

Weighing each option, she stood and made her way to her office. Maybe she could avoid disaster by a strategically placing a hole in the package. Grabbing her scissors, she hoped she wasn't making a mistake that could cost her life. What did Luce have up her sleeve? A better question was how did Luce know where she lived? *Shit*, she had underestimated the woman and now she sat facing a *situation*.

As she studied the package she squeezed the tip of the corners. Lightly at first and then she applied a little more pressure. She tried to feel for a wire, a bulge of some type. Inching slowing down the package, she worked her way down the edge. She couldn't feel anything. She took a deep breath and slipped the edge between the blades. Forcing the breath out between pursed lips she snapped the blades closed...nothing happened. Her heart pounded in her ears.

Squeezing the envelope open, she tried to look inside. *Fuck*. She gently shook the contents to the bottom of the package and looked again. Still nothing. Colby turned on the light. She put the envelope under it and looked again. Still nothing.

Knock, knock.

Colby jerked.

"Fuck," she said, shaking out her hands. "Who the hell could that be?"

Looking at the manila envelope, she contemplated letting whoever was knocking go begging. *Damn.*

Knock, knock, knock.

Persistent fucker.

Approaching the door she wished she had put in a peep hole, but several movies where the viewer is shot through the peep hole had changed her decision.

She peered through the curtains. All she could see was someone dressed in black with their back towards her.

"Who is it?" she yelled. Damn, she should have picked up her back-up weapon, but her head wasn't where it should be lately. Maybe it was a good thing she wasn't back at work. She'd felt off-kilter since the beat-down at the warehouse. Not the best time for her, that's for sure.

"Luce Potter."

What? What the fuck does she want? Another shot at finishing the job?

"Leave Potter or I'm calling the cops."

"It looks rather seemly, me standing out here with my big black limo parked in front of your house and talking to you through the door till the police arrive. Besides, what will your people say if they see me standing out here?" There was silence as Colby contemplated what Luce said. "Besides, I'm connected, and unless you're ready to explain what I'm doing darkening your doorstep, I suggest you let me in. I promise I won't hurt you."

If it wasn't for the fact Luce was right, she'd pick up the phone and call her department to get someone down there. Colby tossed the deadbolt and unlocked the door. She opened it enough to see Luce starring back at her. Luce looked like she stepped of the cover a GQ magazine. The androgynous suit and tie made Colby's heart skip a beat. What was she thinking? She hated this woman with a passion. *What's that they say, fine line between love and hate. Oh gees*, she needed to get rid of Luce and fast.

"Are you going to let me in, or are we going to talk through this..." Luce motioned up and down. "this crack."

"What do you want?"

"Ms. Water—"

"Agent Water."

"So they didn't fire you for losing your weapon and badge. Good, I was afraid I'd compromised your employment. Now, are you going to invite me in?"

Colby swung the door open and stood on the threshold, barring Luce's entrance. "Tell your men to get lost. You'll be out in ten minutes."

She didn't miss the look Luce tossed at her for the command. Turning, she said something in Korean to a man who stepped from around the corner, tucking a gun into his holster. Bowing, he walked down to the car got in and left.

"Happy?"

"What do you want?"

"May I?" Luce motioned inside.

Stepping aside, she allowed Luce in and slammed the door behind her. Her blood boiled at the fact she had just let the person in who was responsible for her swollen face, cracked ribs and a few loose teeth. Worse, she had had to call Scarr to pick her up after escaping Luce's goons. Now she was off work for the next two weeks thanks to Luce.

Luce sat on the couch, in front of the manila envelope, clearly making herself at home.

"Please don't make yourself comfortable, you aren't staying long."

"That isn't very hospitable, Agent Colby.'

"Look, I'm not playing hostess to you. Say what you have to say and get out."

Colby sat in a chair closest to access to her bedroom and her gun. If Luce made a move she was sure the rush of adrenaline that was coursing through her would push her past the pain and into the safety of her room and the gun under her pillow.

"You wouldn't happen to have something to drink would you? Perhaps some water?" Luce said, clearing her throat.

"No."

"Really, a beautiful home like this doesn't have indoor plumbing? Shameful?"

"What do you want?"

Colby leaned forward as Luce reached for the envelope.

"I see you haven't opened your package."

"I don't trust you. How do I know you didn't put a bomb or something else in it?"

Luce reached into her jacket and extracted a stiletto, flicked it open and sliced the package wide open, spilling its contents on to the coffee table. Closing the blade with a snap, Luce smiled and looked at Colby.

"Because, if I wanted you dead, you would be. I thought you might want your things back."

Colby looked at her wallet and gun sitting on the table with a folded piece of paper. Luce picked it up and unfolded it. "Agent Water, I thought you might want your service weapon and government ID back. I hope you don't think ill of me, I'd like us to be besties. Perhaps we can even have lunch sometime. Your buddy, Luce."

"It doesn't say that."

"No, it doesn't, but it does say: I'm sure you need these items back. L.," Luce tossed the paper back on the table.

Grabbing the gun by the barrel, she handed it to Colby butt first.

Colby pulled the slide back and checked for ammunition. *Damn, empty.*

"Seriously, you didn't think I would hand you a loaded gun, did you?"

"One could hope." Colby held onto the weapon. If she had to she could hit Luce with it from where she was sitting. At least that was something. There were times when she could kick herself for not being more prepared and right now, her leg didn't reach behind her.

"So, I'm assuming your boss, Deputy Chapel, doesn't know how you got those..." Luce pointed to Colby's face. "...bruises."

"What in the hell makes you think I didn't tell her?"

"Because I didn't get a *friendly* visit from her, or anyone for that matter."

Colby felt like she was playing a game of poker with a master. Show her hand and Luce ran with it. Play her cards closer to her vest and maybe she could get something she could use against the arrogant ass. Trying to look relaxed she, let out a dramatic sigh.

"Well now, isn't that a little—"

"Arrogant."

Colby flashed Luce one of her patented, *I got this*, smiles. "I'm sure I'm not the first to call you that. In fact, I'm betting...you're pretty disappointed when someone doesn't."

"Doesn't what?"

"Call you arrogant. You get a perverse pleasure being *arrogant*. Don't you?"

"Agent Water, I'd love to sit here and play words games with you, but this isn't a pleasure call—not unless you want it to be." Luce stretched herself out on the couch, getting comfortable.

"In your dreams. Now, what the fuck do you want, or did you come by the finish the job you started?" Colby settled back into the smooth velvet chair. She didn't often sit in it, so it wasn't as comfortably broken in as her favorite spot Luce occupied.

"I want to trade."

"Trade?" Colby wasn't in a bartering mood and she doubted Luce had anything she needed.

"Trade what?"

"Information."

"What the hell makes you think you have anything I want? Better yet, what makes you think I want to share what I have?"

The nonchalant Luce sat picking at the seam of her slacks. Colby had seen men who didn't rattle, even when caught red-handed in a crime, but Luce took the cake. Sitting on her couch as if they were friends talking a about the latest movie release. Luce was a cold-hearted bitch responsible for her injuries, and her forced two-week leave. Paybacks were a bitch and Luce would get hers, eventually.

"So, exchange information?"

"You show me yours and I think about it?"

"Trust me," Luce said, clearing her throat. "My information will trump anything you have, but then again ignorance might be bliss in your case. Since I couldn't convince you to tell me who fingered me for the drug action, I figured I might as well take a different tactic." Luce was cool. In fact, Colby was sure ice ran in her veins. This was a woman who used pain as an aphrodisiac.

"I doubt it."

"Someone in your department is dirty."

Colby sat forward, squared her shoulders, and glared at Luce. While she wasn't naïve when it came to the possibility that agents could blur the lines of morality, she didn't like the term *dirty*, so often used it when all an agent did was offer to help. Often times it was the wrong person, they would later find out, but it wasn't as if the department was issuing crystal balls as part of their work equipment.

"If I had a dollar for every time someone accused an agent of being dirty, I could have a nice home in say...the hood." Colby hoped that Luce could make the connection without her having to connect the dots for her. It wasn't often.

Luce made a dramatic point of looking around Colby's house before she commented. "Looks like you live pretty nicely. I don't know why you would want to give all this up to live there, but hey to each his own, I say."

"My point is, it doesn't happen often."

"Yeah, well this has been going on for a while, so if you haven't caught it by now, you aren't going to catch it without a little help." Luce stared at Colby, cold and firm in her resolve that she was right. "All I want is Frank. My second-in-command who betrayed my grandfather. For that, you get a twofer; the Russians and your dirty agent. While you think about it maybe you could make some tea?"

"You've got to be kidding me?"

"You're really a shitty hostess, but I'll give you a chance to redeem yourself. Unless of course you would rather I call one of my guys to hit-up the local coffee house and talk to barista here about delivering a pot of that coffee you really like. It's Columbian right? Milk and four sugars, right?"

Colby flinched internally. She suddenly realized she had been the one being watched, just as much as she had watched Luce. She had underestimated Luce as another thug in nice clothes, but she was much more than that. She was an adversary worthy of more respect than Colby had shown her.

"I think I can rustle up some tea. Darjeeling, green or lemon zest?" Colby struggled to get up.

"Darjeeling would be fine, cream and sugar if you have it."

Colby tossed Luce a look that if it had wings would have stung. A smile was all she received for her trouble.

"Anything else since I'm up?"

"No, that should be good."

Colby set the gun on the coffee table. It wasn't any good to her empty and Luce surely was carrying multiple weapons, so why bother worrying? Besides, hadn't she shown her lack of respect for Colby already? Brandishing a firearm wasn't going to impress the ice princess, as she'd heard Luce called at the department. Now she could confirm the name, if she could just get a leg-up on the Yakuza leader maybe she could crack her case wide open.

※ ※ ※ ※

Luce smiled. She had tossed a grenade right in Colby's lap and the poor agent didn't know what to do about it. She wouldn't apologize for busting open the department, she would do whatever it took to keep her business healthy and strong. If that meant exposing an agent who had been a pain in her ass, then so be it. If she got Frank in the end, that's all that mattered. She would put an end to betrayal that was running rampant in the family, once and for all.

Luce was sure it would take some convincing on her part once she told Colby who was dirty, but if she worked it right she could kill two birds with one stone, the Russians and the DOJ. Luce stood, took off her jacket and tossed it on the couch. The room was neatly organized, almost too Spartan for Luce's tastes. It was clear Colby's designer went by the name IKEA, perhaps it reflected Colby's Nordic background. The blond hair and blue eyes gave Colby that soft look that reminded Luce of the one and only trip she had taken to Sweden. It had turned out to be too damned cold for her, even in the spring, so she shortened the trip and spent the rest of her vacation on an island off the coast of Greece. Now that was nice.

Very few pictures hung on the white walls and those didn't have people, only a dog. Hmm, a pet and no people. Looking around she didn't see the tell-tale signs of a pet. No chew toys, no bed, nothing. She checked her black slacks she didn't see pet hair, another sign of a roaming dog. Personal items were at a minimum and Luce wondered what kind of woman didn't have family pictures, tokens of past lovers, or the usual knick-knacks that usually cluttered even a house like her own. Perhaps Colby had a wall-of-fame somewhere in the house where she enshrined her achievements in life.

"Here ya go. I even found some cookies, assuming you eat." Colby's snarky tone only made Luce smile. Even after getting her ass kicked, she still found it in her to be defiant with Luce. Nice!

"Thank you, that was very thoughtful."

"Not really. I can't vouch for their freshness, so

caveat emptor." Colby prepared her own cup of tea and settled back in her chair.

Luce look at her and quirked an eyebrow.

"Surely, you don't expect me to pour your tea, too?"

A wicked smile broken across Luce's lips before she answered. "I'll send you over Ms. Manner's book, *How to be a Hostess*. Civility should never be replaced by the casual exchange unless of course we're friends, even then there is a certain—"

"Oh fuck me." Colby jumped to her feet and leaned over the coffee table to pour Luce's tea, splashing the serving tray. "Sugar? Creamer?"

"Thank you, that's very kind of you."

Luce watched as Colby's had to control her anger while she prepared the tea.

"Here," Colby said, shoving the tea cup towards Luce. "Cookie."

Luce put up her hand, rejecting the offer of the possibly stale concoction. "So, Colby—do you mind if I call you that?"

Colby rolled her eyes and shook her head. "No, please, continue."

"I'm sure it's unsettling to find out someone you work with closely is on the take, but I'll exchange that name for information on who pointed you in my direction and tried fingering me for the drugs coming into the city, and of course, Frank. The Russians, consider them the booby prize."

Luce could see Colby struggling with a decision. Either way she was screwed. Give Luce the information and she found out someone she worked with as dirty. If she didn't give Luce the information she would just continue to follow her until something broke free. It didn't matter to Luce, one just took more time than the other.

"What about Brooke?"

"What about Brooke? Are you telling me Brooke is your source?"

"No, not even close."

"Then what about Brooke?"

"I want you to leave her alone."

"Brooke is her own woman, she does what she wants."

"Yeah, but she's in love with you."

"And?"

"And I want you to stay away from her. Hanging around you will get her killed. She's already being followed."

"Are you in love with her?" Luce probed. She wanted to know if she had competition and if that competition was Agent Water, she'd handle it her way.

"No."

"You said that a little too fast."

"I can't win with you. If I'd have thought about it you would have read into it. I answer too fast and you read into that. So take my word on this, I care about her. What we had was over a long time ago."

"Hmm."

"So, tell me who's dirty in my operation and maybe I'll share what I have. If it's bullshit though, no deal."

"Okay," Luce said, setting her cup on the table. Resting her elbows on her knees, she studied Colby for a minute before reaching into her jacket and pulling her phone. She touched the face and tossed it at Colby. "A picture is worth a thousand words."

☙☙☙☙☙

Brooke stretched, careful not to accidently hit her bed companion, but she needn't worry, Luce had left earlier. Luce *had* been there hadn't she? Last night wasn't a dream, was it? Grabbing the pillow next to hers, she snuggled it close and buried her nose into the fabric. Traces of Luce still clung to it. The smell of sweat and *Seduction*, Luce's own fragrance, relaxed her instantly, letting her heart purr in contentment. Remembering the night sent a shiver raging through her. What they said about make-up or break-up sex was true, it left you wanting more and she definitely wanted to make up for the last two weeks.

She tried to wrap her mind around what Luce had told her while they were entwined in the room.

"I'm so sorry Brooke. I've been such an ass." *Luce buried her head between Brooke's shoulder blades and let the tip of her tongue trail down between them.* *"There's a reason I had to make that scene at the bar and break-up with you, but now's not the time or place to talk about it. Let me take you home and—"*

"I'm not going home with you." Brooke said.

"Why? I'm trying to explain to you that your life is in danger and—"

Brooke stiffened at the comment.

"I've been in danger before, Luce. Remember?"

Luce had assumed that Brooke couldn't take care of herself one too many times. This was a different Brooke, though. She'd been through hell watching Luce cozy-up to Kat, she'd been through hell watching Luce almost self-destruct the night of the funeral with no explanation, and now she was just supposed to accept that what Luce did was in Brooke's own best interest? Brooke decided what was in Brooke's best interest now, not Luce. She had lost that privilege weeks ago, and Brooke wasn't so sure she was ready to allow Luce to reassert it. Not after the way Luce had treated her. Sex with Luce was one thing, but coupledom? That was something else.

"Frank's been sending me, and anyone associated with me, death threats. I couldn't bear to live with myself if anything happened to you. God, Brooke don't you understand how hard this has been on me? I have the feds breathing down my neck over some bullshit drug connection—"

"Wait, so that's what Colby was talking about. Fuck me." Brooke pulled the sheet tighter around herself, closing herself off from Luce.

"Hmm, I'm surrounded by betrayal and lies. Frank, my father, my grandfather and now my girlfriend and a fed," Luce said, covering her eyes with her arm. Brooke could hear the ache in Luce's voice, but it wasn't her fault. Jumping to conclusions wasn't asking questions.

"Colby's not my girlfriend. We haven't seen each other in years. You should have asked me. No. You should have trusted me, Luce."

"This woman shows up at my office, telling me she's with some bullshit organization," Luce said. She pulled the top sheet off the bed, wrapped herself in it and sat on the chest at the end of the bed, her back towards Brooke. Burying her face in her hands, she continued, "She had fed written all over her. From her Dr. Martens to the slight bulge under her left shoulder. Gees you would think they would be smarter about how they dress." Luce took a deep breath.

If Luce was waiting for Brooke to say something, she had better keep talking because Brooke wasn't going to let her off the hook, death threats or not. Sitting in the center of the bed she waited. She wasn't ready to offer comfort just yet and if she knew Luce, she didn't need it. The independent, self-exiled, leader of one of the biggest crime organizations didn't cry on anyone's shoulder and that's what's got her into trouble with Brooke. A partnership was all Brooke wanted in a relationship, but looking back now, it was on Luce's terms and not hers. Well, thing would have to change if Luce even thought she would come back to her.

"So, I figured out she's a fed. I let her do her spiel, she sees a pen on my desk that I have especially for rats, and I give it to her. Stupid bitch doesn't know it's a listening device and I get to hear almost everything she's got going down." Luce turned towards Brooke. "Even her conversation with you."

"Then you heard me tell her that I didn't want anything to do with her, right?"

"I heard you say that what was between you and I was over."

"What did you expect me to say after she tossed those pictures of you and that little *dancer*—and I use the word loosely—in front of my face?"

"I'm sorry, Brooke. It wasn't what it looked like. I'm starting up these clubs so I can tap into what's happening at the top levels of business. She's just an employee." Luce crawled to the center of the bed, losing her sheet along the way. "Besides, I don't know who to trust anymore. I have Frank sending me *love* notes, the Russians trying to hone in on my businesses, my grandfather dies without telling me he's married, and a fed who just happens to know my girlfriend in the biblical sense, who's trying to put me in prison for drugs that I don't sell. I'm not asking for a pity party here, Brooke. I just want you to understand that I'll do whatever it takes to keep you safe and my ass out of jail."

"Why can't you take them to lunch?"

"Huh?"

"The businessmen, why can you just take them to lunch like other *normal* business people? I'm sure you can charm them into giving up their secrets. I hear you can be very persuasive."

Brooke let Luce pin her to the bed. The weight of her body felt good on Brooke. She liked when Luce rubbed her body against hers. She felt a sense of security and safety when she was covered by her Yakuza lover.

"The cut on your arm, has it healed?" Brooke grabbed Luce's arm and turned it over. A fresh tattoo covered the healing scars. "That couldn't have been safe, a tattoo over a cut."

"I'm tough, besides I needed to cover it. It was a reminder of something I lost control over and I'd rather have something that I'd like to look at instead."

Brooke ran her finger over the fresh ink of the tattooed Koi fish. The artistry was amazing. The colors were more abstract that the usual orange and gold normally reserved for traditional Koi tattoos. Luce had use a lavender instead, Brooke's favorite color, with spots of brown to add to the realism. Luce often told Brooke that she reminded her of the beautiful Koi fish in her pond. Only coming to the surface for the right person, retreating when a stranger approached. They'd spent many afternoons sitting by the pond talking about their future, family and what may lie ahead. Now that future was in doubt. If it was only about sex, then they were good, but it was about so much more than that, at least for Brooke.

Chapter Thirty-four

Colby caught the phone and turned it so she could see the photo. *Fuck!*

"I don't believe you," Colby said, looking back up at Luce.

Luce only shrugged then nodded at the phone. "Swipe to the next picture."

Colby hesitated, did she really want to confirm Luce's accusations? On the other hand, did she want to ignore what could possibly be the most credible lead on a dirty agent? She wasn't sure, but she'd gone too far to turn back now, unfortunately. Swiping the face of the phone she looked at each photo, hoping there wouldn't be another one, but it went on for at least ten more photos.

"I have video and audio on there, if you want to see it for yourself. I can see you're surprised, but I did warn you."

Luce's smug attitude pissed Colby off. She sat there acting like this was something that happened to her all the time.

"Where did you get these?" Colby felt her chest tighten. She had to push the breath from her lungs. Her headache was back with a vengeance and her mind raced trying to think about how she was going to prove Luce Potter wrong.

"Look, I'm not going to hand over proof of a dirty agent so you can climb the ladder. I'm just showing you who's dirty. Call it a good faith gesture. I want something in exchange."

"What?"

"I want you to help me get Frank."

"Why would I do that?"

"Because you care about Brooke and I care about Brooke."

Colby twitched as Luce reached back into her coat.

"Calm down, Agent Water," Luce said, pulling out another envelope. "I'm just getting this." She tossed the envelop towards Colby.

"I don't take bribes."

"I didn't suspect you did."

Colby reached for the envelope, opening it slowly and peering inside. "What are these?" she said, pouring the notes into her hand.

"Threats from Frank. I've been getting them almost every day. You'll notice he mentions Brooke in at least two of them."

Colby pulled the pieces of paper apart, reading each one then tossing it on the table. Frank was stupid or just didn't give a shit about the paper trail he was leaving. Probably both, but it was likely he was baiting Luce, if Colby were a guessing woman, which she wasn't.

"That's pretty ballsy if you asked me. He does know you'll kill him when you find him, right?"

"Well, thank you Captain Obvious, now what's your next conclusion?"

"Look, what do you want from me? I have no idea where Frank is, and I have no idea what you think I can do."

"You said that you had information we were

dealing drugs. Something about your informant delivering drugs to a Yakuza. I'm telling you that we're not involved in the drug trade, so that only means one thing–Frank is setting me up. I can think of a dozen reasons why, but even he isn't that stupid. So, I figure someone else is pulling his strings and setting me up. I think we both know who that is." Luce gathered up the notes and put them back into the envelope. "I think it's your dirty agent, but I don't have your deductive reasoning skills."

"Again, what do you want from me?"

"I want Frank."

"I already told you I can't deliver Frank."

"No, but your friend there can," Luce said, referring to the photos. "Look, think about it. I don't need an answer right now, but things are going to get dicey for you at some point. When that time comes, are you ready to make the hard decisions? Because if you're not, I am. I can help you when that time comes."

"Why should I trust you?"

"Because I didn't kill you."

"Oh, well that's a stellar reference."

"I could have, trust me. Well," Luce said, standing. "I need to get going. Think about what I said."

Key's in the door made both women turn.

"Hey babe, I thought I would stop by on the way to the club."

Colby froze when she saw Cheryl. Luce knew her as Cher, the bartender in her new club, but now the cat was out of the bag. *Fuck.*

"Well, this is awkward," Luce said, looking over at Colby.

No one said anything, each woman looking back and forth at the other two. Colby's insight into Luce's gentlemen's club was over, but it didn't seem to matter now. She had a bombshell of a night and this was just more shrapnel as far as she was concerned.

"Oh, this isn't good is it?" Cheryl glanced at Colby and then Luce. "I guess I don't need to show up for work tonight, huh?"

Chapter Thirty-five

Hello, Ms. Erickson," the low rumble came from across the room.

Brooke had just pushed the end of the belt through the buckle when she heard the male voice. Frozen, the hair on the back of her neck stood, but she didn't look up. She knew that voice. She hadn't heard it in a year, but she knew the voice. How she wished she could retreat back into the bathroom and lock the door. Her mind raced. Where was that gun Luce gave me? Where was Lynn? The questions pinged out of control like hail when it hit the car.

"I don't think you have to worry about Lynn. I took care of that little bitch." Brooke's head snapped up and looked at Frank sitting in her reading chair. The shadow hid his face, but the gun with a silencer he was pointing at her was well within her view. "She should never have been moved up the ranks like she was, guess the Oyabun has a thing for all women. Now, doesn't she?"

Brooke opened her mouth to speak, but nothing came out. She stared at the gun and then into the dark, trying to get a glimpse of Frank's face, and then back at the gun. Frank wouldn't have any problems kicking in the bathroom door, so that only left one option. Run! In a panic, she darted for the open bedroom door. It was closest to her, so it was her only shot.

She slammed the door behind her, hearing Frank

cuss as he hit the closed door.

Ping, ping, ping. Splintering wood sounded behind her as he fired shots through the door. Brooke ran down the hall. A sharp pain on her left side made her flinch. She spotted Lynn lying on the marble floor in a pool of her own blood. All she could focus on was the dark red stain contrasting with the stark white of the marble. Lynn's face was turned away so Brooke didn't know if she was alive or dead. *Oh god,* she thought. Lynn's gun was still in her shoulder holster. *She's dead,* Brooke told herself. *She's dead.*

As she sprinted for the kitchen, she heard the door slam against the wall. Don't look back. Brooke bolted to the left and weaved her way into the kitchen. She grabbed a knife out of the block on the island and waited behind the pantry door. Afraid he'd hear her labored breathing, she held her breath. She slowly let it out through her nose and mouth before taking another. She held it again and then slowly let it out. Brooke concentrated on the noises—or lack of noise in the house. Surely, she'd hear Frank lumbering down the hall. She took another slow shallow breath. Her side ached from the sprint, or maybe anxiety.

Lynn. *Oh god what will I tell Luce?* She thought she heard a step. She froze. The pain on her side sent a shot through her. Brooke reached down and squeezed it the way she did as a kid. Pinch the pinch, she'd tell herself. Her fingers felt warm and sticky. She looked down at her hand and saw blood. *Oh Christ.* A door handle rattled down the hall and then a door slammed. Frank was making his way towards her. She had to think fast. Before she could move, footsteps echoed in the kitchen.

Brooke squatted against the wall, trying not to

fall. The smell of blood—her blood—was making her nauseous. She gripped the knife with both hands at her chest and held the point towards the corner of the wall. Brooke watched the floor. The tip of Frank's polished loafer just made the corner. She thrust as hard as she could, burying the knife into his thigh.

"Argh!" Frank grabbed Brooke by the hair and pulled her up. "You fucking little bitch." The painful grimace contorted his features as he held her face-to-face. "You're going to pay for that, you fucking little bitch."

He jerked Brooke to her feet. She kicked wildly, struggling against his grip. Brooke kicked the knife and Frank screamed in agony. He released his grip just enough. She stumbled to her feet and ran for the door. Frank blocked her exit, so she sprinted for the island to separate them.

"I don't know where you think you're going." Even hurt, Frank was menacing.

"What do you want, Frank?"

Frank aimed the gun at Brooke and waited a moment before he answered. "My orders are to bring you in, but I'd just as soon kill you." He took his belt off with his left hand and cinched it around his thigh, but he never took his eyes off Brooke. Pulling it tight, he grimaced and grunted.

"Why don't you just go out the way you came in?" Brooke said. She eased towards the knife block. If she was going down, she was going down fighting. *God, where was Luce?* "If you leave now, Luce won't find you. I'll give you time to get the fuck out of town before I call the police."

"Wow, you'd do that for me, Ms. Erickson?"

"Of course, Frank. Let me go and I'll wait. I can't

guarantee that Luce won't come looking for you, but you'll at least have a head start." She watched Frank working the belt tighter around his massive thigh. She'd been lucky to get the drop on him. He was huge, over six foot and easily two hundred fifty pounds of pure muscle, even at his advanced age. His meaty hands had easily pulled her off her feet, even with a knife sticking out of his thigh.

"You must think I'm crazy as fuck. You're not going anywhere. I've got my orders and you're coming with me, alive or dead. It's completely up to you." Frank pulled tighter on the belt, tucking the end under the strap and tying it off again. "Either way...you're... bait," he said.

The sucking sound as he pulled the knife out of his leg almost made Brooke heave. Frank's focus on his leg gave Brooke the second she needed. She pulled another knife from the block. Frank looked up at the sound of metal against wood. He smiled and re-aimed the gun at Brooke.

"Nice try, but I don't think so. Put it down or I'll blow your brains out." He gestured with the gun towards the door. "Let's go." He waited.

When Brooke didn't move he screamed and pulled the hammer back for effect. "Let's go you bitch. Now...drop the knife...now."

Brooke raised her hands and the knife clattered to the floor. Out of the corner of her eye, she caught sight of her blood-coated hand and swayed a little at the sight. Frank's own blood-coated hand pulled at her shoulder and shoved her towards the front of the house. He pushed her along with the muzzle of the gun.

Brooke pressed the back of her hand against her lips trying to stifle a scream. *Oh shit, oh shit, oh shit.*

Looking down at Lynn as she passed, panic gripped her. Her heart felt as if it would beat out of her chest. The blood rushed in her ears, making it hard to focus on anything but running. If he had killed Lynn that easily, and she was a Yakuza, what would he do to her? The muzzle of the gun pushed her forward again.

"Keep walking or you'll end up just like her. Move it," he said, reaching for the front door.

How had Lynn been caught by surprise? She'd trained in Tae Kwon Do and she had extensive firearms training, just like Luce. She was no slouch when it came to her work ethic, just like Luce. So, how could Frank have taken her by surprise? It didn't matter now. She lay in a pool of her own blood all by herself. Now Brooke wasn't so sure how Luce would fair against Frank. She looked back at Lynn and couldn't stop the tears from falling, her lip quivering as she sucked in a breath.

"What's the matter, sweetheart? Are you scared?" Frank's voice was low and menacing in her ear. "The boss has plans for you. Don't worry, you're worth more to him alive right now."

A long black sedan waited in her driveway. A man stood by holding the backdoor. Frank shoved her towards the door. He mumbled something to the man who was obviously the driver before climbing in behind her. He practically sat on her as he slid in. Brooke moved against the door, instinctively putting her hand on the door handle.

"Uh, uh, uh. You'll eat a bullet before you get halfway out, so don't even try it." Frank waved the gun in her face.

Her shoulders slumped forward in defeat. There was no way out, so it was best to save her energy and wait for a better opportunity. She had a pretty good idea who was behind her abduction. Proof waited for her at the end of this journey, but she wasn't sure she would get answers.

Frank yelled to the driver. "Hey, give me your phone." He reached forward, waiting for the cell phone. "Come on, I don't have all day."

He set the phone on his good leg and tapped at the screen activating the operating system. He raised the phone and snapped Brooke's picture, and then another, before instructing her to look at him. She stared down at the floor and resisted his order. That earned her a smack on the head with the silencer of the gun.

"I said, look at me."

Snap, the sound of the camera app signaled the picture had been taken. Then another, and another. Frank tapped the screen again and placed a call.

"I got her, but I had to kill her bodyguard. Yeah, no big loss, she was a bitch anyway. If she'd have kept her mouth shut she'd be hurt but not dead." He shot Brooke a look as he said it and she took Frank's explanation as a warning.

"I'm going to need some first aid when I get there and I think she's hit, too." Frank raised Brooke's arm. He pulled her hand away and spotted the blood oozing down her blouse. "Yeah, she's hit, too. Yeah, I snapped a few, want me to send them to her?" A pause tore through the car. Suddenly, Brooke felt lightheaded and faint. Leaning against the window, she closed her eyes and waited.

"Yep, I got her number, no worries. I'll send them right now. You want me to say anything?"

"Okay, you're the boss. See you in a few?"

Frank elbowed Brooke. "You still alive?"

"Fuck you," Brooke said. She had nothing to lose. She'd already been shot, and it was looking like she might just die today. Brooke thought about all the things she had yet to do in her life. Get married, have kids, win a Pulitzer, kick Luce's ass. She smiled at the last thought. Oh was Luce going to hear about this for a very long time. Shit, she would come back and haunt her if she had too, just to get her revenge. What if she died? She hadn't told Luce she'd forgiven her earlier when they made love. She hadn't told Luce she loved her. Hell, she hadn't said anything. She was too focused on loving Luce, trying to make up for the last two weeks they'd been apart. Now she was going to die and Luce would never know Brooke had forgiven her.

Chapter Thirty-six

No one picked up at Brooke's house. Luce dialed her office at the Financial Times. She felt bad now that she'd left Brooke in such a hurry, but she wanted to catch Colby before she ratted Luce out, assuming she was wrong about Colby. Their meeting had been more than she was sure Colby could digest. Luce had just informed her of a rat within her own department and if the look on Colby's face could be trusted, she was a little more than stunned. Luce knew what she did to rats, but this was a government agency, and so there was probably policy she had to follow. A bullet was all the policy she needed to handle a sell-out.

"Ms. Wentworth, can you dial Ms. Erickson's office please? Transfer the call when you have her on the line."

"Yes, Ms. Potter."

Luce tossed her long wool coat on the sofa and paced the floor. She was nervous with anticipation. She wasn't sure why, but she was anxious to talk to Brooke. Luce wanted to explain why she had broken up with her in such a nasty and public way. Brooke seemed to understand the brief explanation last night, but sex had clouded everything. Luce needed Brooke to understand the danger she was still in, but she wouldn't let Brooke out of her sight now. Her bodyguards would be with her twenty-four hours a day. It was only a matter of time before she found Frank and killed the bastard. His death would be slow. Torture wasn't out of the question, he'd earned it betraying her and her grandfather. *Seppuku* was too good for Frank. He didn't deserve the honor of committing suicide. Luce wanted to kill him. She wanted to watch him die a slow, painful death.

"Ms. Potter, I'm sorry Ms. Erickson's assistant said she hasn't arrived yet. Would you like me to try back later?"

Luce looked down at her watch. Brooke was never late to work.

"Can you call her home, please and put her through when you get her on the line?"

Maybe she was still sleeping. They had played hard last night, so she couldn't blame Brooke. If she'd had her way she'd still be wrapped around her, snuggling or...Luce needed to focus on work. Thinking about how sexy Brooke looked in her leather cat suit didn't help.

"I'm sorry, Ms. Potter. No one is answering at Ms. Erickson's home. Would you like me to try her cell phone?"

"No, please call Lynn. I'm sure they've stopped for coffee or something." Luce could feel her gut tighten. Something wasn't right. If anything happened, she'd curse the time she'd spent at Agent Water's house this morning when she should have been wrapped around Brooke rekindling their relationship.

She pulled out her phone and dialed Sammy. Things were falling apart around her and she wanted answers. The men who'd let Colby slip through their fingers were gone, she'd taken care of them without hesitation.

"Sammy. I can't get in touch Brooke or Lynn.

When was the last time you talked to Lynn?"

"Boss?"

"Lynn, have you talked to Lynn today?"

"No, she's at Brooke's house. I told her to stay outside and keep an eye on Brooke from there. You want me to call her?" Sammy didn't sound worried, maybe that was a good sign.

"Ms. Potter, Lynn isn't answering her phone."

"Thank you Ms. Wentworth. You left a message that I wanted to talk to her didn't you?"

"No, boss, but I'll call her and find out what's going on." Sammy said.

"Hold on Sammy. I'm not talking to you." Luce said, frustrated that she wasn't getting anywhere.

"Oh gotcha."

"Yes, Ms. Potter."

"Thank you, Ms. Wentworth. Sammy?"

"Yes, Oyabun."

"I want you to meet me at Brooke's house, now."

"Yes, Oyabun. I'll keep trying Lynn's phone. If I get a hold of her, I'll call you."

"You do that. I'll see you in a few."

Luce felt sick to her stomach. Something was wrong. It was too coincidental that neither Brooke nor Lynn answered her phone. She grabbed her pistol from the top drawer and pulled back the slide to ensure a round was chambered. Luce shoved the gun into her shoulder holster and snatched her jacket off the back of the sofa. As she stormed from the office, she barked some orders to Ms. Wentworth to hold her calls and reschedule her appointments. Her mind raced with all the possibilities. Brooke could be at work – in a meeting, she could be in the shower, she could be sleeping the sound sleep of a lover, or she could be driving down the highway rocking out with the top down. There was probably a logical answer. When she saw Brooke she would give her a piece of her mind, but only after she wrapped her arms around her and told her how much she loved her, how she could never live without her.

She exhaled sharply, trying to think of last night, but every time she did her gut told her something was wrong. Hitting the phone button on her steering wheel she waited for the operator.

"Hello, Ms. Potter how can I help you?"

"Can you dial John Chambers at the Financial Times magazine please?"

"Of course."

"Hello. John Chambers, here, how can I help you?"

"Mr. Chambers, this is Luce Potter. I'm looking for Brooke, have you seen her this morning?"

"Ms. Potter? I thought you two were broken-up?"

"Mr. Chambers, I don't have time to explain. I'm worried about Brooke. Please tell me she's at work and in a meeting or something."

"Can you hold for a moment?"

"Sure."

She'd already called Brooke's assistant and knew she hadn't made it to her office, but it never hurt to double check. Today wasn't her day, as she weaved in and out of traffic. Nervously she drummed her fingers against the steering wheel. *Positive, just think positive. Come on John, come on.*

"Ms. Potter?"

"Yes."

"She hasn't shown up for her nine o'clock appointment. What's going on?"

"I'm not sure. I'm on my way over to her house right now. I'll have her call you when I see her. I'm sure she's probably over slept or something. Thank you for checking Mr. Chambers."

"I think I should call the police." He sounded frantic.

"I think we might be over-reacting, but if she isn't there I'll call the police. I would hate have them show up at Brooke's house and find her in the shower or something. Think how embarrassed she would be."

"I suppose you're right. Call me when you get there. Better yet, tell Brooke to call me."

"I will. Thank you, Mr. Chambers."

The drive to Brooke's house took forever. The traffic wasn't cooperating and she was more than a little agitated. Two near misses didn't make her slow-down, in fact she sped through the city as fast as she could.

The ring of her phone startled her. She practically ripped the pocket of her jacket as she jerked it out.

"Yeah."

"Oyabun…"

"Sammy."

"Oyabun…I'm…" Sammy paused again.

"Sammy spit it out, Jesus Christ."

"It's Lynn…she's…she's dead."

"What? Where?"

"I'm at Brooke's house, she's dead."

"Where is Brooke?"

"I don't know."

"What do you mean you don't know? Knock on the door and go in. If she's hurt, she may not be able to answer. Now get your ass in there and find her." Sammy's silence scared her. "What aren't you telling me, Sammy?"

"I am inside."

Chapter Thirty-seven

God baby, you look like hell warmed over," Cheryl said, reaching for Colby's dripping body.

"Yeah? Well I feel like hell," she said, leaning over Cheryl.

"So, what now?"

"You mean right now, now?" Colby tried to smile, but her split lip ached and pulled against the stitches. "Ow." She reached up and touched her lip. "Remind me to beat that bitch next time I see her."

"Who? Luce Potter? She did this to you?"

Colby stiffened. She hadn't meant to say that aloud.

"Naw, Potter didn't do this, but she pisses me off, coming here to my house. Now she knows you're a fed, too." Colby pulled off the lie easily enough, but she needed to watch what she said around people, especially people she slept with.

"Fuck her. Now where were we?" Cheryl pulled at the towel wrapped around Colby's waist. The warm skin-on-skin contact felt good. "Does this hurt?'

Her warm tongue flicked Colby's nipple.

"Hmm, do it again and let me see. I wasn't focusing," she said, straddling Cheryl's legs and pulling her closer.

"How about this?" Cheryl ran her hand up

the inside of Colby's thigh stroking the taut muscle just at the apex of her legs. "Or maybe, this?" The gentle pressure of Cheryl's fingers pressing her clit in a circular motion was starting to make her grind against the strong fingers. She'd found the only spot on Colby's body that didn't ache, from pain at least. How could she think about sex at a time like this? Easy, it was Colby's way of compartmentalizing her life. She did it all the time. Sex was like taking a Valium; it had its place and right now was the place for sex. There was very little that could make Colby turn down sex and her aches and pains weren't enough to stop her from enjoying what Cheryl was offering. Besides she'd earned a little recovery.

"Geez, Colby it doesn't take much to get you wet does it?"

Cheryl's slick fingers pushed past her tightened muscles. Her mind blanked on everything else bothering her as Colby focused on the sensation of being spread open further. Cheryl added another finger, laying waste to anything left of her mind. Sex was like a balm to any wound Colby carried around. It soothed her when nothing else did. It buoyed her when life threw her a curve ball, and today Luce Potter had thrown her a curve. Trying to push the thoughts aside, she focused on the way Cheryl worked her body. Like the crashing waves in a storm, Colby's body arched in the pounding orgasm forcing its way through her. She didn't know what felt better or worse; the jerking of rapturous pleasure, or her aching muscles that forcing her to relinquish control.

Twisting, she fell on the bed, pulling Cheryl gently down with her. Blackness engulfed her as she thought about the betrayal she felt. Thing were starting to make sense to her now. There was only one problem. She didn't have shit as far as proof was concerned, so knowing wouldn't do her any good. Setting a trap to catch a fellow agent wasn't easy. It took time and energy, both of which she had short supplies of at the moment. Yet, if she didn't do something it could compromise the case she was working on. If she wasn't careful, it could bite her in the ass later. A dilemma. Do nothing and it was a wound that festered and eventually poisoned everything she did, or do something and she could have it backfire in her face. She'd have to give some serious thought on how to bring this shit into the sunlight, so everyone could see it, but without getting any on her. Another dilemma. Sometimes life sucked.

"Hey, earth to Water." Cheryl giggled.

"Funny."

"Where did you go just now?"

"Nowhere, just wondering how I got so lucky to have such a hot girlfriend."

"Girlfriend, wait a minute." Cheryl eased up on her elbows to look at Colby.

Why had she said that? Colby wasn't ready to settle down. Hell, she barely shopped on a regular basis, her refrigerator with the empty pizza box still in it was proof of that.

"Sorry. I think I had a momentary loss of memory due to a traumatic experience. Who are you by the way? My name is Colby." She laughed and pushed her hand out to shake.

"I thought so." Cheryl flung herself back on the bed. "You know you aren't getting any younger, Water."

"No, no I'm not."

"Hmm, and you'd think you'd want to start

settling down in your advanced years. You know, have someone to come home to, a home cooked meal, a warm bed."

"You cook?" Colby flinched as Cheryl faked an elbow to the ribs. "I guess I didn't know you could cook. All we seem to do is—"

"Fuck."

"I call it making love, but if you insist." Colby rolled over on top of Cheryl and pinned her down. "I like fucking, too."

"Aren't you tired of the playboy life, Colby? You got your ass kicked out there the other day. Didn't it make you think about life, about *things*?"

Staring into Cheryl's eyes, she didn't want to admit that all she had done lately was think about *things*. Her future with the agency, her life or lack of one—hell she'd even thought about whether she wanted kids, but that took a wife and well...Colby wasn't sure she was wife material. To have a wife meant you had to be a wife and Colby didn't know how to do that. She knew how to make women happy, just not daily or beyond the physical.

She brushed her finger against Cheryl's lips before she replaced it with her own. The soft, pliable kiss made her tingle. Cheryl pushed her shoulders back and Colby tried to maintain contact.

"Off," Cheryl said, under her kiss.

"What?"

"What happened out there, Colby?"

Colby rolled off Cheryl again and huffed.

"Don't huff on me. Something's wrong. I can feel it."

Scrubbing her fingers through her hair, Colby searched the ceiling for answers, but none were forthcoming. She'd have to wing it.

"You know when you have to do something you don't want to, but you know you have too?"

"It's called being an adult, Colby. You should try it sometime." Cheryl wrapped the blanket around her and curled against Colby's shoulder.

"Again, funny. I'm being serious here." Colby pulled Cheryl tighter as if through osmosis she'd pass on her load to her. However, it was all Colby's to carry this time and she knew it.

"Is this your way of breaking up with me?"

"No. Geez. I'd just send you a text if I wanted to break up, besides I like you." That was as close to saying *I love you,* as Colby was willing to get.

"Hmm, thanks. I think."

Before Colby could say anything else her house phone rang. It never rang, ever. In fact, she couldn't remember where it was.

"What the fuck?"

Searching it out, she finally found it under a pile of clothes on a chair in the corner of her room. Pulling the cord, she liberated it from underneath everything and dropping the receiver. The voice coming from the phone sounded familiar, so familiar it made her blood boil.

"What the fuck do you want, Potter?"

"I called your cell phone but no one answered."

"How did you get this number? It's unlisted."

Every agent had an unlisted number. It was standard procedure. Now, she wished she had gotten rid of her landline, if for nothing else than to avoid another confrontation with Luce Potter.

"I'm busy, what do you want?"

"It's Brooke. She's missing."

Colby felt a chill finger its way through her body. She heard the fear in Luce's voice, something she never thought she would have the pleasure of hearing, but this wasn't the way she wanted to experience it.

"How do you know she's missing?"

"'Cause, I'm standing over the dead body of the woman who was supposed to be protecting her."

"Where are you?"

"Brooke's house."

"I'll be right over. Don't touch anything. Did you call the police?"

"Hell no, I don't want them involved."

"Then why did you call me?"

"Because you know who did this and you're going to help me get her back. That's why. Now get your ass over here, or would you like me to call Agent Scarr instead?"

The hair on the back of Colby's neck stood up. She didn't like being ordered around by a civilian and especially not by Luce Potter.

"I'll be there in half an hour."

"Make it twenty and use your red and blues," Luce ordered.

"You don't order me around, Potter."

"Are we seriously going to argue right now? Brooke's missing and you're going to—"

Colby slammed the phone down on to the cradle and cursed. "Fuck."

Chapter Thirty-eight

Luce stared down at the bloody shoe print. The size and imprint gave away its owner, at least as far as Luce was concerned. She wasn't an expert, but you didn't need to be to know it was a man's foot. That was obvious. The tread was wide and long, at least a size thirteen, but she was guessing. The only person she knew who wore something that big was Frank. The petite print beside it was clearly Brooke's high heels. She followed the trail towards the kitchen and then noticed they ran out of tracks, the blood finally wearing off.

"You go that way. Brooke's bedroom is off to the left. Check it out but don't touch anything." Luce pulled her gun and nodded towards the kitchen. "I'll follow these and see where they lead."

She wasn't anticipating trouble, but better prepared than dead. Cupping her gun, she kept it close to her body and walked into the kitchen. Blood dotted the floor around the island, and the pantry. Walking further into the spacious kitchen her nostrils flared as the coppery smell of blood assaulted her senses. She noticed a blood smear on the knife block, a bloody handprint on the counter to her right and a pool of blood on the floor by the handprint. Scanning the room quickly she tiptoed around the spots as best she could. Craning her neck around the corner she saw another smear of blood halfway down the wall. Another small pool of blood was on the floor.

Luce's head swam with the possibilities. There was no way all of this blood was Frank's, he was huge and Brooke was petite. The law of averages were in Frank's favor. Anxiety streaked through her as she circled around the island. She needed to find Brooke. With this much blood loss she didn't have much time.

"Oyabun," Sammy said from the door.

"Stop." Luce held up her hand as if it would physically keep Sammy from entering the kitchen.

"Agent Water is here, Oyabun."

"Get a blanket and cover, Lynn. Call the mortician to come and pickup the body. I don't want anyone touching her. I'll call her family."

"Yes, Oyabun."

Luce heard voices in the hallway, and then Colby replaced Sammy in the doorway.

"What the fuck happened here? Where's Brooke?"

"Frank has her."

"How do you know that?"

"Because she isn't here, dead." Luce made a complete circle finishing her inspection of the kitchen.

"I need to call this in," Colby said, pulling her phone from her jacket. "There's a dead body out there and…" she paused looking at the handprint on the counter and then the pool of blood on the floor. "all this blood. Fuck. Do you think it's Brooke's?"

"Who else could it be? Put the phone down." Luce pointed her gun at Colby.

"Are you fucking out of your mind?"

"Maybe, but if we call the police they're going to take their sweet-ass time getting to the bottom of this. They don't know where Frank is, but we do."

"We, who?" Colby pointed to herself and then

to Luce. "You mean you and me? I don't know where Frank is."

"No, but your rat does."

"How?"

"Because your rat is in bed with the Russians and Frank works for the Russians, now. They want me dead, so we flush them out before they can flush me out."

"What do you have up your sleeve, Potter?"

"Call your rat and have 'em meet us at the warehouse. Tell them you've got me and the drugs in the same place and you need them to come down and help you out."

Luce hoped Colby would buy into her plan. She didn't know of any other way to flush out the Russians and Frank. Besides, she was doing Colby a favor by setting up the rat in her organization. If Colby played her cards right, she could get something out of all of this double agent shit.

"I don't think so, Potter. I don't trust you. Besides, that's what we have law enforcement for. They do the heavy lifting." Colby holstered her weapon, her phone still in her hand.

"Are you willing to bet Brooke's life on a couple of local shields getting her back? I'm not. So," Luce paused. Sammy signaled to her. "I guess I'll do this on my own."

She slapped Colby on the shoulder as she passed. "Way to be a team player, too bad it's for such a dirty team at the moment."

Luce watched as Lynn's body was loaded into a non-descript white van. Two men were already busy sanitizing Brooke's house, getting rid of any evidence of a murder and struggle. Two more walked past Colby.

She froze as she watched them make quick work of the bloody kitchen.

"What the fuck are you doing? This is a crime scene." Colby grabbed Luce's arm and spun her around.

"Not anymore. Now if you're not going to help me get Brooke back, get the fuck off." She wrenched her arm from Colby's grip.

Luce's phone rang. *Fuck.* She was too late to get the jump on Frank.

"Frank, what the fuck did you do with Brooke?"

"Luce Potter, good morning. How are you today?" Petrov's voice boomed through the phone.

"What the fuck do you want?"

"Well, I think it's what you want that's important. Da?"

"Where's Brooke?"

"She's, how you say, spunky for such a petite little thing, you know?"

Luce's jaw clenched as she thought about all the things she wanted to say to the Russian bastard but couldn't because she didn't want to risk Brooke's safety.

"What do you want from me? Brooke has nothing to do with you and me. Let her go and I meet you one-on-one."

"Oh, you're so macho, or maybe I mean butch. I like that though. You get right to the point. So let me get to the point. I want *you*. We'll trade Brooke for you. That's fair right?"

"Where and when?"

"I'll call you later with more details. I have some business I have to take care of."

"Put Brooke on the phone, I want to make sure she's okay."

"She's fine."

"Put her on the phone or no deal. There's too much blood here for her to be okay."

"She has a scratch, that it all."

"Put her on the phone you prick, or I'll kill you the next time I see you."

"You don't have the cards to call the game, Luce."

"What?"

"I call shots, not you."

"Put her on the phone you asshole."

Click, the phone went dead. Punching dial she tried to dial back Frank's phone but it went to voice mail. "Fucking prick."

Sammy, Colby and two of the cleaners where standing around Luce, waiting. Luce raised her hand to throw the phone, but Colby caught her arm.

"That's the only link to Brooke, so don't do anything stupid."

Luce dropped her head. Colby was right, if she lost the phone it would take time to re-establish a connection with the Russian asshole. He held all the cards and Luce didn't have any to play now.

Luce nodded her head towards the door and Sammy and the cleaners disappeared. She tucked the phone inside her jacket for safe keeping and grabbed Colby's jacket, pulling her close.

"Listen to me…very…carefully. I want Brooke back. I'm not going to play catch-up with Petrov. He is one step ahead of me, but we're going to change that. Do you understand me?" Luce shook Colby. "If anything happens to Brooke, I'll kill you if you don't help me. Now, I gave you proof of the dirty agent. That agent was meeting with Petrov. They were sharing more than a cup of coffee, they were doing business.

So, call your rat to the warehouse, so I can find out where Petrov is, do you understand me?"

Luce released Colby with a push.

"If you care at all for Brooke, you'll help me and in turn help yourself. Because we both know that when someone's dirty in an organization it poisons the rest of the good work others do. Do you get my drift?"

Hell, Luce knew part of Colby still loved Brooke, if she were honest with herself. If something happened to Brooke, she knew Colby wouldn't rest until everyone connected with her disappearance was dead, that include her. Colby had to know the DOJ needed an enema, but Luce suspected Colby was still unsure if her info was on the up-and-up, but Brooke's life was at stake.

"I'll meet you at the warehouse. I want to set-up some cameras and get this shit on tape. If I'm going to ruin my career, I might as well have some video of it for posterity. I'll call and set the meeting from the warehouse."

"Fine by me, but if you're thinking of double crossing me, I won't be alone. So don't be stupid."

"I wouldn't think of it."

"Good." Looking down at her watch, Luce said, "I'll meet you in an hour. That should give you enough time to get your surveillance shit together and set-up before you make the call."

"See you in an hour," Colby said, looking down at the pristine white marble.

Chapter Thirty-nine

Colby pulled up to the side of the warehouse, parking between two buildings to hide her agency SUV. She had driven by the location several times to make sure she wasn't followed, and then doubling back to make sure Luce didn't have more help than she needed. She'd only spotted one car at the warehouse. Colby wasn't sure if it was a good sign or not. She figured there were probably four people at the most inside. But then again, it was Luce Potter she was working with. She couldn't believe she was about to join alliances with a major crime boss to expose a dirty agent and hopefully to get Brooke back alive. Taking a deep breath, she pulled the Velcro of her vest and grabbed her jacket. She hadn't been this nervous in a while. It wasn't every day that you fingered a dirty agent and if she was right, this one wasn't going down without a fight.

"You okay," Cheryl asked, patting Colby's arm.

"Yeah." She pulled her ponytail through the back of her baseball cap. "I don't know what's going to happen in there, but I want you to be careful. If all of this goes south I want you to get your ass out of there. You got me?"

Cheryl kissed Colby, pulling her closer as she deepened the kiss. "I trust you."

"Thanks, but I'm just pulling this out of my ass right now."

"Get out," Cheryl said to the passenger they had picked up on the way over.

Colby slid out of the SUV, grabbed her gear out of the back, and walked towards the warehouse. Before she got past the open door, she heard Luce call to her.

"What the fuck?"

The sound of a gun cocking echoed in the dank space. Colby dropped her duffle and raised her hands. Cheryl did the same.

"Why did you bring them?" Luce said, pointing her gun at Cheryl and the woman in handcuffs standing next to her.

"If I'm right, I brought a little insurance for the job." Colby carried her duffle to the table, tossing it down.

"Stay right there," Luce told the two women and moved closer to Colby. "What the fuck are you doing?"

"Look, I'm putting my career on the line right now. I need someone to witness what's about to go down."

"And Kat? Why did you bring a dancer from the club here?"

"She Petrov's daughter."

❧ ❧ ❧ ❧

Brooke's head ached. She felt as if someone was beating a bass drum inside her head. She tried to open her eyes but the light made it worse. Her tongue was swollen from where she had bitten it when Frank slapped her. Brooke's mouth felt like a wad of cotton had been shoved in it. This feeling was worse than her best hangover, only she normally had a hell of a story to tell after an all-night drunk. Trying to open her mouth, she stopped halfway when her jaw popped. It was probably broken. She noticed her shirt was gone, but her bra was still on as she reached down and felt her side. A bandage of some sort covered the gunshot wound. Warmth seeped through. She was still bleeding.

"Aw, you are awake, Ms. Erickson. How do you feel?" Petrov's voice made her head ache more. Keeping her eyes closed, she groaned as she tried to get up. "Stay. I don't think you should be moving. You might hurt yourself."

A firm hand held her down.

"Luce's is going to kill you, you know that don't you?"

"Funny you should say that. I just talked to her. She's worried about you, but I told her not to worry," he said, laughing after. "You American women are so macho. Give me a good Russian woman any day. Well maybe not Russian, perhaps Ukrainian, or maybe French, now those are women. I had this one French—"

"Shoot me."

"Excuse me?"

"Either shut-up or shoot me," Brooke said, resting her forearm across her eyes. She was starting to feel faint from the loss of blood. Death was only a matter of time if she didn't get some help, soon.

"Wow, I like you, Ms. Erickson. You're very brave to talk to me like that."

"I'm almost dead so I don't think I have anything to loose, do you?"

"Well no, but still." Petrov whistled to someone. "Water?"

"Got any morphine?"

"Hmm, that bad, huh?"

He sounded sympathetic, like the way a rattler

stops rattling giving a person the impression they aren't dangerous anymore. He just wasn't rattling, yet.

Brooke felt her head raised and a bottle pressed against her lips. She took all she could before turning her head away, coughing.

"Slowly, Ms. Erickson, slowly." Petrov raised the bottle to her lips again.

Her brain felt like it was resting in a fog bank. She had a hard time focusing on anything. The last memory she had was looking out the window of the sedan as they pulled away from her house with Frank sitting next to her.

"Did I kill Frank?"

The deep belly laugh drilled through her. Now, she wished she'd kept her mouth shut for the sake of her head. Rubbing her temples, she tried to unwire her jaw, but only felt the stabbing pain shoot through making her headache worse.

"No, Frank is not dead. He will walk with a limp, but I think it adds character. What do you think?"

Why was Petrov being so nice to her? Wasn't he the one who practically had her killed? Now he wanted to play nice. The arrogance of the criminal element never ceased to amaze her.

"Why am I here?"

"I'm going fishing," Petrov said, picking at the dirt under his finger nails.

"Fishing?"

"Hmm, and you're the bait. I'm fishing for Potter fish. Ever heard of them?"

Chapter Forty

"What do you mean she's Petrov's daughter?" Luce couldn't hide the surprise this time.

"It's a long story, but suffice it to say that one day I went for coffee. Maybe you remember that day?" Colby stared through Luce, looking around the warehouse she thought she would die in. "I saw her get into a big black sedan with a guy and play a little tonsil hockey just before she went into Yoshida Enterprises to see you. But I can't be sure because I was whacked from behind." Colby finished unpacking her gear. She glanced over at Cheryl who was just out of earshot, her gun pointed at Kat.

"Well, this changes things doesn't it?"

"I'd say it puts things in our favor. If he loves his daughter, he'll trade her for Brooke."

"She was a plant in my club. Fuck, how could I not see that?" Luce suddenly realized the lengths Petrov was willing to go to get to her. Planting his daughter in her club would put her life at risk if Luce found out. She'd fallen for the pretty face, hook-line-and-sinker. Her blind rage with her grandfather's betrayal had kept her from focusing on things around her and now Brooke was paying for her mistakes. She couldn't believe how stupid she'd been.

"What about Frank?" Colby wondered if Luce would let revenge rule her head, or love rule her heart. The answer came quick.

"Fuck Frank. I want Brooke back unharmed. I can get that bastard Frank later."

"Okay," Colby said, unloading bundles of white powder.

"Holy shit, you brought real drugs? I'm impressed, you do want to take down your dirty agent." Luce hefted one of the bundles.

"It's a prop. We use these when we want to look like we're carrying the real stuff. Besides, if things go sideways, and they always could, I don't want to get busted for stealing from the property room."

"Gotcha."

"So this is how I figure we'll do this." Luce whistled to her crew who came out of the woodwork.

"Gees, I didn't know you had this many people here."

Colby saw ten guys walking towards her, all of them looked like they could play for a professional football team. She was sure each of them was packing and one wrong move could send anyone of them into a tizzy. Today wasn't the day to state the obvious and ask for gun permits, or ID, but what she wouldn't do to get them on her radar for future reference. She was always thinking about her job, always.

She jerked her head towards Cheryl. Colby suddenly felt underpowered with only Cheryl with her, but she was there to observe and keep an eye on Kat. Cheryl walked over dragging the gagged and handcuffed woman.

"I'm feeling a little understaffed at the moment, Potter."

"I'd say that's an understatement." Luce laughed, but her eyes were focused on Kat.

Luce walked over to Kat and threaded her hands

through the thick red hair. She pulled her close so only Kat could hear what she said. Colby's instinct was to stop Luce, but getting in her way was tantamount to stepping in front of a speeding car. She'd be lucky to walk away with only a few bruises and she already had those, courtesy of Luce.

Cheryl looked from Luce to Colby. Colby shrugged her shoulders and raised her hands. *Speeding car.*

"All right let's get this show on the road." Colby said.

꙰꙰꙰꙰

Luce knew she had to put herself in Colby's hands. She hoped that the need to expose the dirty agent was a more powerful emotion than getting revenge on her. She'd given her men detailed instructions on what to do if things went south. They'd all agreed except Sammy.

"I'm not going to shoot you, Oyabun. Neither will any of these men," Sammy said, gesturing around the room. "We'll get you out of here before that happens and if that agent over there even thinks about touching you, I'll kill her myself."

"If things work out the way I think they will, you won't have to worry about that." Luce tried to calm Sammy's fears, but she had to admit even she was worried things might not go as planned. Colby was going to call the agent in charge, who Luce suspected would play right into their hands. Then Luce would go after Petrov and get Brooke back. She knew that catching the dirty agent was priority number one for Colby. Luce would have to hope and pray Colby would live up to her end of things.

"Keep Kat in the back and don't come out until

I give you the sign. My hand will be behind my back. Watch for two fingers, that's the sign to move in. An open hand means shoot 'em all. If something looks weird, go with your gut on this one."

"Are you sure you trust her?" Sammy tossed his head towards Colby and Cheryl.

"Yeah, I'm going with my gut on this," Luce lied. She didn't trust anyone, least of all a federal agent.

"Okay, you're the boss."

Luce smacked him on the back. "Thanks, I knew I liked you for some reason." Luce rarely joked but she wanted to lighten the mood, if possible. Men wound this tight made mistakes and she was trading favor-for-favor with Colby right now.

"Okay, you ready?" Colby walked over to Luce.

"Yep, you ready?"

"I'll make the call and get this train moving." Colby didn't answer Luce's question. The stress on her face said everything Luce needed to know.

Colby pulled her cell phone and dialed. The tension in the room was starting to hit and a pin dropping would sound like a gunshot right now. Luce didn't have to wonder what the betrayal felt like to Colby; she knew it first-hand. She only hoped Colby could handle what was about to come her way.

Luce listened intently to the conversation for signs of any information leaks, just in case Colby was really going to turn on Luce.

"Deputy Chapel, Agent Water here. You were right, Potter is involved with the cartel."

"Excellent, Agent Water. How did you pin it on her?"

"I've got her, the drugs and the money all in a warehouse. I'm getting ready to call in for the team to come in and tag and bag everything."

"You've killed her?"

"Took her by surprise. She was meeting with her lieutenant, Sammy something-or-other, and I got the drop on both of them."

Luce knew the story was pretty far-fetched, but she was counting on Deputy Chapel's, greed to get the better of her.

"Is she dead?"

"No. Wounded, but not dead. Her lieutenant is, though. Okay, I'll get the team in here so they can document everything."

"No wait. I mean, I'll call the team. Damn, Water, you did it. You brought down one of the worst crime families in the city. Great job!"

"I hate to admit when you're right, you're right, Deputy Chapel." Colby knew enough buttering-up and she wouldn't be worried about all the holes in her story, not yet at least. "So, then I should wait until you get here to call the team?"

"I'll call 'em. Besides I want to come down and see this Luce Potter for myself. How much money and drugs are we talking about here, Agent Water?"

"Well, let's just say enough money to fund a small militia and enough drugs to well-fund another small country for at least a year."

"Okay send me your twenty of the warehouse and I'll be down with a team in ten minutes."

"You got it Deputy, see you in ten."

Colby closed her phone and shook her head. She knew there was no way she could assemble a team in ten minutes. Her story was so thin that Chapel wasn't even putting two-and-two together. She was blinded by setting Luce up and whatever else she had in mind for the crime leader.

God she hated that it was proving out Luce was right about her dirty agent. The pictures were bad enough. The grainy video with bad sound wouldn't prove good enough quality in a court of law, but now there was little doubt about Chapel's alliances. Sadly, it was the top agent in her division, but nevertheless, Deputy Chapel was proving she was dirty. Colby had suspected something was up when Chapel told her to get off the Russians and focus on Potter. How deep was she with the Russians? Who knew? Today she was about to find out the depths of Chapel's betrayal.

"She's on her way." Colby stepped closer to Cheryl, refusing to give Luce the pleasure or the opportunity to say, *I told you so.* "Get her in the back with the rest of Luce's men. When you see the signal, let Luce's men take the lead. Don't come out until I tell you to, okay?"

"Are you sure about this, Colby? This could cost you your career if you're wrong."

"I'm not wrong. I wish I was but I'm not. I saw proof earlier on Potter's phone."

"She could be setting you up. Have you thought about that?"

"Yeah, I thought about that, there's just one problem. They have Brooke Erickson. Kidnapped her from her house and killed one of Luce's Yakuza."

"Did you call it in?"

"No time. Look, I don't have time to tell you all the details, so you either trust me on this, or walk. We'll just call what I have with Potter an unfriendly alliance, for now."

"Okay, I hope you know what you're doing."

"Me too, trust me, me too."

Chapter Forty-one

Luce was getting impatient. She didn't need to explain herself and Cheryl just needed to be a good soldier and follow Colby's lead. Get with the program, dammit. Besides, she was the one getting ready to be tied up a like a Christmas goose and put her life in Colby's hands, so to speak.

Walking over to Kat, she grabbed her arm and pulled her aside.

"You're lucky Agent Water found out who you were before I did. I can assure you it wouldn't have gone as well for you."

Kat glared at Luce over her gag. *If looks could kill, fuck 'em, they couldn't,* she squeezed Kat's arm tighter. She knew Colby and Cheryl were watching her closely. She didn't care, she hadn't gotten this far by being influenced by others. She answered to no one now that her grandfather was dead. Looking at Kat and at the agents, it was clear – the webs of betrayal were the same for good as they were for evil. Honor seemed to be a dying concept, but one she wasn't ready to part with quite yet.

"You better hope you're daddy's little girl, cause he has my girlfriend and I want her back. If Brooke dies, you die right in front of his eyes and then I'll have the satisfaction of killing him when I'm done. So, you better hope daddy wants his little girl back in one piece."

"Fuck you," Luce heard muffled through the gag. "He'll kill you."

"You better hope not, because my men have orders to lay waste to whatever is left standing in this warehouse, and trust me, they follow orders."

Luce pushed Kat towards Cheryl and ordered, "Get this little whore's ass out of here."

Luce walked over to Colby and looked at the drugs and money on the table. There wasn't a lot of cash or drugs, but the way it was disguised, it gave to illusion of quite a haul. Luce was counting on Chapel's greed and her ties to Petrov to do her in.

"I know you still have doubts about Chapel being dirty, but the photos, the video, and now the fact that she wants to come down her and handle the drugs and money should seal the deal."

"I know. Look, Chapel and I aren't best friends, but the thought that she's dirty..." Colby looked off into the dark warehouse. "Well, let's just say things are starting to make sense now."

"Good. I just want get Brooke back. I'll take that over getting to Frank right now. So, we need to find out where Petrov is and that means getting her to talk."

"I know how to do my job, Potter."

Luce knew Colby was pissed. She didn't make the problem, but she knew how to fix a Judas in the ranks.

"This situation might have to be handled differently. I don't think the normal line of questioning is going to work here. Let me state the obvious. She's going down for a federal crime and she has nothing to lose."

"Are you proposing a beat-down? If so, I'm not going for that, she's still a federal agent and I need to bring her in. Regardless of what you think, I still have honor and respect for my agency."

"I can respect that, but just don't misplace that loyalty. This is a fluid situation with no script. The unknown is what will put us all in danger. So be ready for anything."

Luce wanted to tell Colby that she shouldn't be surprised if at the end of all of this Chapel went out in a blaze of glory, but she didn't have the heart to bust her bubble. She knew it was a real possibility she would be the one taking her out if they didn't get information on Petrov's location.

"Oyabun, she's here. They just called from the gate."

"Okay everyone, lets do this. Sammy, if anything happens, you know what to do."

"Oyabun—"

"Don't argue."

"Yes, Oyabun."

Putting her hands out towards Colby, she directed. "Loose. I want to be able slip out of them."

"If you want this to look realistic put your hands behind your back. I would never allow a criminal the advantage of hands in front. Cheryl, tie her gag."

"You're getting some perverse pleasure from this, aren't you?"

"Some." Colby snapped the cuffs on. "But probably not in the same way you are. You like this sorta thing, remember?" Colby whispered in Luce's ear.

If Colby was trying to intimidate Luce, she had another thing coming. Luce smiled before the rag was shoved in her mouth and tied off. She pushed her tongue against it to prevent it from being too tight. Luce felt like she was choking as the anxiety of being in someone else hands took control.

"Sit." Colby pushed Luce down on the chair.

Luce looped her arms over the back so she could give the signals to Sammy and get quick access to the gun at her back. It had taken some convincing with Colby, but she wasn't going to sit here with cuffs on, gagged and not have options. Her heart raced now. She was vulnerable and in a weak position. Her life depended on the very agent who she had just beat the shit out of days earlier. Her fight or flight response was in full effect and it was all she could do to sit. *Brooke, Brooke, Brooke, I need to save Brooke,* she chanted in her head.

"Places everyone," Colby said, as people receded into the darkness. "You'll need to keep her quiet." Colby kissed Cheryl on the cheek. "If she gets out of line, smack her."

"You got it." Cheryl pulled the struggling woman. "Knock it off. Let's go."

Luce looked around the warehouse. Everyone was gone. Her anxiety kicked up another notch as she heard a car door slam, then another and then another. *What the fuck.*

❧❧❧❧

Three doors shutting. Something was up. Fuck if Luce wasn't right about this being a fluid situation, Colby thought. She glanced over at Luce. A momentary hint of panic crossed her face and then the stoic Luce was firmly in place. Luce shrugged her shoulders, a signal she'd heard it, too. Colby stood behind Luce, and moved her gun to her waistband. She wasn't going to be taken by surprise, not this time.

"Agent Water?" Deputy Chapel shielded her eyes, looking into the dark warehouse.

"Over hear ma'am." Colby gripped Luce's shoulder, more to anchor herself than as a show of dominance. "Are you alone?"

"No, I brought someone to help with Potter."

Colby couldn't believe her eyes. Petrov followed Chapel in, along with a tied up and gagged Brooke. Luce saw Brooke at the same time and tried to say something through her gag. Colby pushed down on Luce to hold her still. This was her operation now and she had to think fast.

"I don't understand Deputy Chapel?"

"Of course you don't, Agent Water. That's why you're such a great agent to work with. You just do what you're told and you *just* do your job. You're more interested in bedding all the hot little agents than you are in being more thorough. That's what I was counting on. You and Scarr are agency *men* and agency men— or in this case, women— just survive in the agency. You don't want more, you don't want to be deputy, you don't want to be chief. You're happy working in the field, getting the shit kicked out of you and having lots of sex. Well, there's more to life than the agency and sex, Agent Water."

"Really, Deputy? So betraying your country is—"

"Agent Water, I'm planning for my future outside of the agency. My piddly pension won't even get me a condo in Boca Raton, but what I have now, I can live anywhere."

Colby's couldn't believe what she was hearing. Luce had been right, loyalty came with a price and the agency obviously didn't pay enough for that kind of loyalty.

"Ladies, please," Petrov's voice boomed throughout the empty warehouse. His gun was aimed at Brooke. "Can we compare employment compensation later? I'd like to finish my business with Potter and get the fuck out of here. Yes, Luce. I have Brooke." Petrov reached over and landed a kiss on Brooke's face and she jerked her head away.

Chapter Forty-two

Brooke couldn't hide her shock as her gaze met Luce's. Luce wouldn't be of any help to her now. Her hope of being rescued evaporated with each passing minute. She was suddenly lightheaded and her knees buckled putting her in a heap on the floor.

"Get up."

Petrov jerked her arm up, but she couldn't move. She'd lost too much blood. She felt tears start to fall. Brooke knew this would be the last time she saw Luce. With a hard swallow she staggered to her feet, but her knees started to give out again.

"Get the fuck up, Potter," Petrov yelled at Luce.

Brooke looked up at Luce as she stood. The wink was undeniable, but couldn't Luce see the shape she was in? Surely, she knew Brooke was dying. Sitting on the chair all she could see was a dark tunnel. In the center of that tunnel, Luce's back was to her. Was that a gun shoved in her waistband? *A glimmer of hope.* If Brooke had her wits about her she knew she would've seen the situation for what it was, but she could barely stay conscious. Luce moved backwards, next to her. Resting her head against Luce's hip, she tried to feel bolstered by the touch, and yet all she wanted to do was close her eyes and let death take her. Brooke closed her eyes, barely hearing the voices around her.

"So let's take a look at what we have here, Agent Water." Deputy Chapel moved towards the open duffels.

"Feel free, Deputy." Colby spread her hands wide.

≈≈≈≈

Luce wanted to reach out and touch Brooke, even if it was just her hair, to reassure herself that Brooke was really there. She had thought Brooke dead and now she sat resting her head against her thigh. Something wasn't right, though. She had fainted and her pale skin told Luce that there was more than met the eye with Brooke's condition.

Petrov showing up with Chapel had changed the plans. She could only hope that Colby knew that as well. Petrov's smile sickened Luce. She wanted to reach over and wipe it off his face, but she needed to be patient right now more than she needed revenge. Her only thought was to get Brooke out of the warehouse alive. Frank would wait, but not for long. Waiting for a sign from Colby might prove to be a wasted effort as Luce noticed Petrov creep closer to Brooke.

"Get the fuck away from her," Luce said.

"Well Potter, I don't think you are in a position to tell me what to do. You see…" Petrov smirked. "You are going to jail, and I am going to be taking over your businesses."

"How do you figure?"

"Well, just look around you. I don't see your people anywhere, do you? And you are in handcuffs."

"What about Agent Water? Do you plan on killing her, too?"

Petrov shrugged his shoulders and sneered. "Minor technicality, but not my problem. That's why

I pay Chapel lots of money, to handle my federal friends."

Luce wasn't sure if Colby heard Petrov, but she if she had, she didn't flinch at the implication that she was expendable. She slipped a cuff off her wrist and let it dangle. Just as she was reaching for her gun, Chapel's voiced boomed through the warehouse.

"What the fuck is going on here?" Chapel thumbed through a stack of bills then tossed it down and picked up another. "These are just props, stuff we use at the agency. What the fuck is going on here?"

Chapel pulled her gun, followed by the crashing of the table as Chapel tossed it over. Colby pulled a gun. Luce drew her gun. Too late—Petrov pulled Brooke off the chair and in front of him, his gun to her head.

"Uh, uh, Potter. Put it down." Petrov pushed the barrel against Brooke's temple, forcing her head over.

"I wouldn't do that if I were you," Luce said calmly. "You aren't holding all the cards you think you are."

"I live rent free inside your head and you don't like that do you? You wake up and think about me, you spin your wheels trying to think about how you're going to get me and that just, how you say – burns you." Petrov shook his head and laughed. "I see you are still arrogant as ever."

"Some things never change, do they? You think the world revolves around you. Now let go of her and maybe I'll let you go back to living in your own little world, for now."

"I don't think you understand, Potter. I have your girlfriend, you have nothing. Put your gun down before I shoot Brooke."

Luce gave the signal and waited. She wanted to

tell Petrov to screw-off, but the look on his face would suffice. A door creaked open behind her as she kept her eyes on Petrov and Chapel. Her men flooded the warehouse followed by Cheryl dragging Kat out of the office. His face froze for a brief moment telling her everything she needed to know. He knew Kat.

"Let Brooke go and maybe I'll let Kat live." Luce kept her gun on Petrov. "While we're talking about giving up...we were talking about giving up were we not? Where's Frank?"

"What the fuck is going on here, Agent Water?"

"Actually, Deputy Chapel, I was just about to ask you the same thing."

"You're going to be put away for a very long time Agent Water if you don't get a handle on your investigation."

What the hell was Chapel talking about, Luce wondered. Did Chapel actually think she was walking away free after all of this mess? Balls, Luce had to give her that, she had big brass ones.

"Well, it looks like we have a Russian standoff, Potter. I have Brooke and you still have nothing." Petrov didn't look at Kat, he purposely avoided it. "So, I'll tell you what. I'll walk out of here with Brooke and drop her off somewhere. She'll call you to let you know she's safe and we're even." Petrov took a step back and then another stopping when he had to hold Brooke's dead weight up.

"We'll never be even. I'll tell *you* what, you let her go and I'll think about letting Kat live." Luce walked over to Cheryl and pulled Kat towards her. "Let her go, now." Luce directed Cheryl. She looked at Colby and raised her eyebrows in question, waiting.

"Let her go, Cheryl."

"But..."

"We have our own little problem." Colby kept her gun aimed at Deputy Chapel. "Did you get everything on video?"

"Everything."

"What the hell is going on here?" Deputy Chapel looked the worse for wear now. She'd been caught red-handed and there wasn't any way out but off to jail. "You two are insubordinate and are facing a heavy reprimand if you don't put your guns away and take control of this situation."

Luce shook her head at the statement. A bully and bull-shitter all the way to the end. Things seem to slow down around her as conversations started to buzz between Chapel and the agents, Petrov and her.

"Everyone shut up," she yelled.

Luce's heart raced. Brooke was sweating, pale and almost unconscious. Her plan would need to happen fast. Luce looked over at Sammy for a split-second and that was all it would take to spin things into overdrive.

Brooke sagged closer to the floor.

The lights went out and shots echoed through the warehouse. The flash of guns made the scene surreal, like a silent movie. Luce pushed Kat to the floor, crouched and aimed in Petrov's direction. He let Brooke fall in a heap. His bulky frame stumbled to the partially opened door. She fired at his shadow as another flash illuminated the room and then he was gone. Luce fell to the floor as more shots ricocheted off the cement floor and the steel supports.

Finally silence.

Luce crawled over to Brooke. "Baby, are you okay? Brooke?" Short shallow breaths were Brooke's only answer. "Hold on baby. We're going to get you help. Sammy, the lights."

The hum of sodium lights was the only sound as they started to light up the empty space. Colby was the only person still standing. Luce's men had taken cover the instant things went south. Stepping out of the darkness Sammy made his way over to Luce and Brooke.

"I've got a car waiting outside, Oyabun. We can get to her to the hospital faster than waiting for an ambulance."

"Did you send someone after Petrov?"

"Yes, but I think he got away before we could get a line on him. I think he was shot."

"Fuck, don't let him get away. Grab her," Luce said, pointing at Kat, who still laid on the floor covering her head. "Agent Water, you okay?"

Luce looked at Cheryl, clutching her side, blood oozing out between her fingers. Deputy Chapel sat on the floor, cupping her ears with a shocked look on her face.

"Get the fuck up. You shot Cheryl you fucking bitch." Colby jerked on Chapel's arm yanking her off the floor.

"I was aiming at you, Agent Water."

"Get an ambulance here."

"You sure you want to do that? I mean, we're still here."

"What you're suddenly scared of a few feds snooping around?" Colby's anger laced her voice. Cuffing Chapel, she turned her attention to Cheryl. "How bad is it?"

"Just a flesh wound. Thank god she's not a better shot." Cheryl showed Colby the bullet hole.

"You just missed a murder charge you scum-sucking bitch."

The sound of a slap brought everyone's attention front and center. The quick red-mark on Chapel's face the only indication of the action.

"Brooke. Hold on, baby. Sammy, the car. I wish I could sit here and watch you put Chapel through her paces..." Luce said, picking up Brooke's limp body.

"Get out of here. I've got this. Take her with you," Colby pointed to Kat, who was trying to pull herself out of a Yakuza's grip.

"You sure?"

"She'll just fuck everything up."

"Thanks."

"Don't thank me. We'll talk later and be ready to explain how you knew Chapel was dirty. I'm thinking you're a witness now. So be ready to testify when I need you."

"We'll talk," Luce said, shuffling quickly to the door.

Chapter Forty-three

Luce rested her head on the edge of the bed, gripping Brooke's hand. Brooke had made it through surgery, but now she was in critical condition. She'd lost a lot of blood and the wound had started to fester, infected because Petrov didn't get her the necessary medical treatment. Luce felt her temper starting to get the best of her again. She'd almost lost the most important thing in her life. Thankfully, she'd been given a second, probably a third chance at a life she knew she desperately wanted with Brooke. She had only two goals in life now, Brooke and Frank. One she knew would take some convincing to stay, and the other she wanted dead.

Once Brooke had been stabilized in the hospital, she'd met Sammy at her offices with Kat in tow. The shooting seemed to put the fear of god in to Kat and she spilled her guts about her father's operations. Unfortunately, Petrov not only got away, but he had taken everything important to him. Kat clearly wasn't one of those things important to Petrov. Kat now had a whole new perspective about her father. Blood obviously didn't matter to Petrov. He used his family as he used people. When they were no longer advantageous to have around he dumped them. Luckily for Kat, Luce was in a forgiving mood—to a point. She'd explained how Kat's *new* life would work. She didn't have options, not yet, and Luce made it crystal-clear. Kat stayed put, in town, until Luce was ready to cut her loose. She still wanted Frank, and Kat was the only link she had right now to Petrov, and Petrov was the link to Frank. Frank would die for shooting Brooke.

"I want you to put out the word that there's a bounty on Petrov's head," Luce said.

Sammy's look of surprise was priceless. His conservative ways kept him sidelined to being a good soldier, but not so heavy in the decision making skills. Luce wondered how long he would last as her first. She'd worry about it later, right now she needed to focus on getting Petrov and Frank. She wasn't about to spend the next year looking over her shoulder.

"But, Oyabun that will start a war."

"Petrov started the war when he shot Brooke and killed Lynn." Luce slumped back in her chair. "A million dollars to the person who brings Petrov in alive or dead. The same for Frank, but he's to be brought in alive. If he's killed no one gets paid, so make sure you highlight that point: dead no money, alive he's worth a million dollars."

"Yes, Oyabun. What about Kat?"

"I have a feeling the feds are going to be bugging her place, too. They want Petrov as much as we do, so let's make sure we get him first. Let her go. Bug her place, hack her email and phone, do whatever you have to, just keep track of her. I want to know where she's going, who she's meeting and when. We might be in bed with the feds now, but I don't trust them and they don't trust us."

"What a mess."

"Yep, what a mess. Go now. Check back in with me later. I'm sure I'll have some more business that needs to be handled."

Now more than ever she was on a mission to kill the bastard. Frank wouldn't be able to hide. She'd made arrangements to bring Frank's family to the U.S. under the guise of helping them out of the poverty they lived in. It was all a plan to draw Frank out and she had plenty of time to *wait* him out.

Sammy had come by with a change of clothes and kept her updated on business. He felt responsible for Brooke's shooting and Lynn's death. Nothing Luce said made any difference. He had thrown himself into finding Frank and had made some headway. While the trail on Petrov was cooling quick, Frank's leg wound turned out to be serious, courtesy of Brooke. Luce smiled as she thought about Brooke taking a swing at Frank. He didn't know what a hell-cat she was. Now he had a lasting reminder to carry for the rest of his short life.

"Hey," a hoarse whisper stirred Luce.

Sitting up, Luce smiled at a half-awake Brooke. She was the most beautiful site for sore eyes. Luce grabbed Brooke's hand tighter and pulled it gently to her face. Rubbing her cheek against her open palm, she placed a kiss on it and then leaned in for a kiss. A sheet met her lips.

"Hey, what gives?" Luce leaned her forehead against Brooke's.

"Dragon breath."

"Oh sorry," Luce said, covering her mouth.

"No, me silly."

Luce grinned and then bent down again for another kiss. She pulled the sheet away and lowered her lips to Brooke's. She whispered, "I don't care."

Warm, soft lips met hers as she pulled Brooke's hand against her chest, pressing it against her heart. "I love you."

"I'm sorry."

"For what?"

"For putting your life in danger."

"You didn't do anything, Brooke. I'm sorry I wasn't there to take care of you. I promise you this, I'll never leave your side ever again."

"Don't make a promise you might not be able to keep."

Luce felt her chest clench at the comment. She deserved that, hell she deserved whatever payment Brooke wanted to exact from her. As long as Brooke allowed her to stay in her life, she would do whatever it took to earn that position.

"I promise, I'm not going to let you go, ever again. I'm here for as long as you'll have me."

"I think we have a lot to work out, don't you?"

"Yeah, and I'm the one who should be apologizing. I wanted to protect you and clearly I didn't do a good job."

"You can't be responsible for others actions, only your own."

Luce nodded in agreement. She had a lot to atone for and it would take her a lifetime to make it up to Brooke. A lifetime she would gladly commit to.

"Did you get Petrov? I don't know what happened to Frank, Luce. After we got to Petrov's he was gone and I didn't see him again."

"We didn't get him or Frank. Turns out, he must've had a plan to exit the states as soon as I was dead. I think he expected Chapel to walk, and he would melt into the background."

"He wants you dead. I don't think he's going to stop until that happens."

"I know, but I have a few cards left to play. Kat's his daughter and we have her."

"You mean you've kidnapped her?"

"No, but she's smart enough to know her dad sold her out. It's a long story, but she's here for now."

"Really?"

"Don't worry, she's not my type. I only have one type and she's sitting right here."

"Hmm."

"I love you, I want to spend the rest of my life proving how much I love you, so give me your best shot. I'm not going anywhere."

"I love you too, Kaida."

Luce smiled, leaning into Brooke's fragile hand caressing her cheek. Her gaze locked with Luce's and softened. Time would tell how things worked out and Luce was sure Brooke wouldn't forgive as easy as she hoped.

࿐࿐࿐

"Hey, Potter. You awake?"

Luce popped her head up. She was surprised to see Colby in her office drag, her badge on her belt and her ID tag hanging from the lapel of jacket.

"Agent Water, how are you?" Luce stood and extended her hand. "It's good to see you."

"How's she doing?" Colby shook Luce's hand and smiled briefly before looking at Brooke. "She looks—"

"Alive, she looks alive and I'm grateful that you let us get her to the hospital when I knew you could have stopped me."

"I didn't do it for you. I did it for her."

"I know. I'm still grateful." Luce pointed to the

door. "I assume this isn't a social call."

"Actually, I did come to check in on her. But, since you're here we might as well talk."

Luce jerked her head towards the door. "We can talk outside. I don't want Brooke to hear our conversation."

"What's her prognosis?"

"She needs time, but she'll recover."

"And you?"

"Me?"

"Petrov got away and that means Frank got away."

"Well you know that old adage – you can run, but you can't hide? I have a little wager out in the community, I think it'll help find Frank. Besides, Frank betrayed Sammy a few years ago, and it cost Sammy his pinkie. Sammy was willing to let that slide, chalking it up to the Yakuza experience, but he was close to Lynn. When Frank killed Lynn he killed part of Sammy, too. By the way, how did you explain things to your superiors?"

Colby didn't look at Luce, she was obviously struggling with what she'd done. Looking out the window, she cleared her throat and relayed the story she'd concocted to explain Chapel's betrayal of the agency.

"I told them that I had evidence of Chapel being dirty. So, I followed a lead from an informant and caught Petrov and Chapel together in the warehouse, exchanging money for drugs."

"So, I guess I'm the informant?"

"Yep."

"And Cheryl?"

"She's on board. I told her about Chapel before

we met at the warehouse. I had to tell her. The pictures, the video, it all made sense. The way she threw me off the leads linking the Russians and the drug cartel. The little snitch in jail, tied it up in a nice package when he told me Chapel had made a deal with him. I guess I didn't want to believe what was right in front of me."

"Sometimes we don't want to believe that those we trust are only human and sometimes we have to lie to more than just ourselves. Trust me, I know."

"Well, I don't like lying, least of all to protect you." She looked evenly at Luce. "I guess those are the lies that bind you and me together now, Potter."

"I guess so," Luce said. She slapped Colby on the back. "I guess so."

About the Author

Isabella lives in California with her wife and three sons. She teaches college, and speaks at high schools and universities on current issues facing the LGBT community. She enjoys traveling with her wife, riding her motorcycle, and spending time with her family. She's also the owner of Sapphire Books Publishing.

She is a member of Gold Crown Literary Society, Romance Writers of America. She has written several short stories, and writing as Jett Abbott she is now working on the follow-up to *Scarlet Masqurade - Scarlet Assassin.*

You can follow her on Facebook at

www.facebook.com/isabella.author

or at the Sapphire Books website

www.sapphirebooks.com

Other Isabella titles available at Sapphire Books

Award winning novel - Always Faithful - By Isabella ISBN - 978-0-9828608-0-9

Major Nichol "Nic" Caldwell is the only survivor of her helicopter crash in Iraq. She is left alone to wonder why she and she alone. Survivor's guilt has nothing on the young Major as she is forced to deal with the scars, both physical and mental, left from her ordeal overseas. Before the accident, she couldn't think of doing anything else in her life.

Claire Monroe is your average military wife, with a loving husband and a little girl. She is used to the time apart from her husband. In fact, it was one of the reasons she married him. Then, one day, her life is turned upside down when she gets a visit from the Marine Corps.

Can these two women come to terms with the past and finally find happiness, or will their shared sense of honor keep them apart?

GCLS Nominated - Scarlet Masquerade - By Jett Abbott ISBN - 978-0-9828608-1-6

What do you say to the woman you thought died over a century ago? Will time heal all wounds or does it just allow them to fester and grow? A.J. Locke has lived over two centuries and works like a demon, both figuratively and literally. As the owner of a successful pharmaceutical company that specializes in blood research, she has changed the way she can live her life. Wanting for nothing, she has smartly compartmentalized her life so that when she needs to, she can pick up and start all over again, which happens every twenty years or so.

Clarissa Graham is a university professor who has lived an obscure life teaching English literature. She has made it a point to stay off the radar and never become involved with anything that resembles her past life. She keeps her personal life separate from her professional one, and in doing so she is able to keep her secrets to herself. Suddenly, her life is turned upside down when someone tries to kill her. She finds herself in the middle of an assassination plot with no idea who wants her dead.

Broken Shield - By Isabella - ISBN - 978-0-9828608-2-3

Tyler Jackson, former paramedic now firefighter, has seen her share of death up close. The death of her wife caused Tyler to rethink her career choices, but the death of her mother two weeks later cemented her return to the ranks of firefighter. Her path of self-destruction and womanizing is just a front to hide the heartbreak and devastation she lives with every day. Tyler's given up on finding love and having the family she's always wanted. When tragedy strikes her life for a second time she finds something she thought she lost.

Ashley Henderson loves her job. Ignoring her mother's advice, she opts for a career in law enforcement. But, Ashley hides a secret that soon turns her life upside down. Shame, guilt and fear keep Ashley from venturing forward and finding the love she so desperately craves. Her life comes crashing down around her in one swift moment forcing her to come clean about her secrets and her life.

Can two women thrust together by one traumatic event survive and find love together, or will their past force them apart?

American Yakuza - By Isabella - ISBN - 978-0-9828608-3-0

Luce Potter straddles three cultures as she strives to live with the ideals of family, honor, and duty. When her grandfather passes the family business to her, Luce finds out that power, responsibility and justice come with a price. Is it a price she's willing to die for?

Brooke Erickson lives the fast-paced life of an investigative journalist living on the edge until it all comes crashing down around her one night in Europe. Stateside, Brooke learns to deal with a new reality when she goes to work at a financial magazine and finds out things aren't always as they seem.

Can two women find enough common ground for love or will their two different worlds and cultures keep them apart?

Executive Disclosure - By Isabella - ISBN - 978-0-9828608-3-0

When a life is threatened, it takes a special breed of person to step in front of a bullet. Chad Morgan's job has put her life on the line more times that she can count. Getting close to the client is expected; getting too close could be deadly for Chad. Reagan Reynolds wants the top job at Reynolds Holdings and knows how to play the game like "the boys". She's not above using her beauty and body as currency to get what she wants. Shocked to find out someone wants her dead, Reagan isn't thrilled at the prospect of needing protection as she tries to convince the board she's the right woman for a man's job. How far will a killer go to get what they want? Secrets and deception twist the rules of the game as a killer closes in. How far will Chad go to protect her beautiful, but challenging client?

CPSIA information can be obtained at www.ICGtesting.com
Printed in the USA
LVOW08s1417180913

352971LV00001B/43/P